LOSING MOBY DICK AND OTHER STORIES

Other Books by Ian Gouge

Novels and Novellas

On Parliament Hill - Coverstory books, 2021
A Pattern of Sorts - Coverstory books, 2020
The Opposite of Remembering - Coverstory books, 2020
At Maunston Quay - Coverstory books, 2019
An Infinity of Mirrors - Coverstory books, 2018 (2nd ed.)
The Big Frog Theory - Coverstory books, 2018 (2nd ed.)
Losing Moby Dick and Other Stories - Coverstory books, 2017

Short Stories

Degrees of Separation - Coverstory books, 2018
Secrets & Wisdom - Paperback, 2017

Poetry

The Homelessness of a Child - Coverstory books, 2021
The Myths of Native Trees - Coverstory books, 2020
First-time Visions of Earth from Space - Coverstory books, 2019
After the Rehearsals - Coverstory books, 2018
Punctuations from History - Coverstory books, 2018
Human Archaeology - Paperback, 2017
Collected Poems (1979-2016) - KDP, 2017

Anthologies

New Contexts: 1 - Coverstory books, 2021
Triple Measures - Ian Gouge, K.M.Miller, Tom Furniss, Coverstory books, 2020
Oak Tree Alchemy - Coverstory books, 2019
Play for Three Hands - Tom Furniss, Ian Gouge, K.M.Miller, pamphlet 1981

Ian Gouge

Losing Moby Dick
and Other Stories

First published in paperback format, 2017;
published by Coverstory books (this
edition 2021)

ISBN 978-1-9997840-2-7

Cover credit: cover based on a photograph
published as a National Geographic 'Photo
of the Day', 6th October, 2014. It was
taken by Shane Gross off the coast of Sri
Lanka. Used with the kind permission of
Mr, Gross.
www.grossphotographic.photoshelter.com

Contents

LOSING MOBY DICK

ONE

It wasn't such a big thing, not in the grand scheme of things. It wasn't as if he had been looking for it in the first place. Quite the opposite in fact; he had been looking for something else (though, having been knocked sideways, what that had been he was now unable to recollect). His eyes had scanned the shelves with the kind of automatic glancing that arose from familiarity. How often for example, do we cease truly looking at something because we have seen it so often that we are certain we know what it looks like? The parade of shops in the High Street; the church at the end of the road; the neighbour's dog; our own faces in the mirror. After a time - and after a very short time! - we stop examining, searching, defining; we take things for-granted, assuming they will be there, in their place, and will always be the same. Perhaps that's why it comes as such a shock on the day when, for once, we do actually look at our faces in the bathroom mirror and then suddenly realise that we have grown old, or grey, or that we have jowls where taut skin used to be.

And so it was that standing before the bookshelves in the back room, searching for something for which the motivation was now lost, his eyes had made their way through the alphabet beyond 'L' to be suddenly brought up short by a book that should have been there but was not. Had he, for some inexplicable reason, suddenly started looking again instead of scanning? Had he - unconsciously of course - actually been looking hard all the time? Or was it inexplicable? Whichever of these, the simple fact of the matter was that his old, orange-spined, Penguin paperback copy of 'Moby Dick' was absent. It should have been one side or the other of 'Billy Budd, Sailor', his only other Melville; but nestling against 'Billy Budd, Sailor' were just interlopers: two books, Malory and Milne. And 'Moby Dick' was thick; too big to miss. As he asked himself the obvious questions to which he knew the answers - "were these all his books?", "were they all in alphabetical order?"; "yes" to both - he moved the sole Melville to check that 'Moby Dick' had not fallen behind the others (even though the shallow depth of the shelves themselves made this impossible).

He stood back, two paces, and tried to take in the whole expanse of books, as if the missing volume might leap out at him somehow. And then - now really looking - he went back to 'A' and slowly, painstakingly, and with a growing sense of confusion and loss, actually read each spine one-by-one. Alphabetically the authors responded to him, all the way up to 'Billy Budd, Sailor' - no, he had not missed it - and beyond. And then Wyndham, Young, Zola - and after Zola there was just the wall. Where was it? And - more profoundly - what had he done with it, and why couldn't he remember? He hadn't even liked 'Moby Dick', so it wasn't as if there were an emotional attachment to the story. He had read it under duress (there was an essay that had to be submitted), and he had found it long and boring - a little like his essay, which had scored poorly. The novel had not been all drama; it had not been Gregory Peck and Richard Basehart. It had been dry (so unlike the sea!); a dull polemic on industrialisation in America. Or at least, that was how he recalled it now, sitting back in his desk chair like a boxer in his corner winded after a tough third round. But for all that, the book had been his. He had written his name in it; there would have been his pencil marks and annotations in the margins, folds he had made in some of the corners; the spine would have been imperfect, creased the way that large paperback books' spines crease because you have to force them open to get at the words right on the inside. That had been the attachment. It had been - as with all his books, good and bad - a bond created by their interaction; generated by the fact that he had read them, and that they had given him something (though some more than others, clearly). In a way they had given each other a sliver of identity.

'Moby Dick' - for all its faults - had made a small contribution to making him what he was; the totality of him.

So where had it gone? This was the question he inevitably asked himself next. There were few options. Had he given it away? Not possible. He never gave any of his books away - not in the sense of one giving a friend something to keep accompanied by the words "You should read this. And, keep it; I don't need it back". Very occasionally there had been trips to Oxfam to dispose of clothes that had ceased to fit or had become too unfashionable for even he to wear. Yes, once or twice books had accompanied them, but these tended to be either non-fiction or works of so little merit that he had chastised himself for acquiring them in the first place. Whatever he thought of 'Moby Dick' it was not a book without merit. On that basis alone - never mind the memory and trauma of that essay - the Melville would never have found its way into the charity sack. Perhaps it had been stolen? Was it possible that one of his friends had, without his knowing, so taken a shine to the prospect of engrossing themselves in a semi-dramatic tale about a man with a beard fighting a big fish, that they had removed it from his shelves? He trusted his friends - at least in the sense that he was pretty sure none of them had ever been thieves - but maybe this had happened, and they had intended to return the book once they were finished with it… It was possible, but as he considered the prospect, he simply couldn't think of anyone he knew who might be remotely tempted to undertake such an enterprise!

So had he lost it? Was it possible that, during one of his many house moves from both student days and beyond, it might have been misplaced? Might there have been some kind of accident where it had been left behind, or not pulled out from the bottom of a box? He knew he was meticulous about packing and unpacking, so the 'left in a box' theory simply didn't stack up. And when he unpacked and rearranged his books on new shelves it was something like greeting old friends; those who failed to show up from roll-call would soon be noticed.

All this rumination took a matter of a few moments as he sat staring at the shelves. He was about to attempt a metaphorical shrug of the shoulders and rise to go make himself some coffee, when two final possibilities hit him hard. The first was the prospect that he hadn't lost a single book in the process of a house move, but perhaps a whole box of books! And the second was that he had, at some point long forgotten and for reasons unknown and unimaginable, just thrown the thing away. He was suddenly back in the ring for round four and feeling worse than ever!

The prospect of misplacing a large cardboard box replete with 'Moby Dick' and perhaps twenty or thirty other books suddenly filled him with can only be described as panic. He stood up. What else had he missed? What else was not there that should have been? Instinctively he went back to 'A' again and started re-reading the spines. This time he tried to cross-reference the titles against a catalogue that simply did not exist. He tried to recall other mental images of his book shelves and compare what he saw now with those imagined snapshots. Simultaneously, when he came across an author he tried to recall all their books he knew he owned, as well as trying to conjure what should have been either before or after them in alphabetic sequence. It was an impossible task, whichever way he came at it. How could he look at things that were in front of him in plain sight and then see beyond them to things that were simply not there? No, it was more than that: there were books that weren't there, of course, but then that was correct as they should not have been. He knew, when it came to Dickens for example, that he would not find 'The Mystery of Edwin Drood'. It was a book that he had never owned, nor possessed any desire to own; so, on this basis, its absence was entirely legitimate. (If he had found it, what a can of worms that would have opened!)

Finding absence was perhaps the ultimate tautology, yet this was his immediate and inevitably fruitless quest. The exercise - of going even more slowly from 'A' to 'Z' - triggered all sorts of tangential memories for him, a little like the 'Moby Dick' essay. Many of these reflections were not surprisingly from his time at university; the period where perhaps three quarters of his books had been acquired. With these titles came not only more recollections of essays - 'Northanger Abbey', 'Victory', even 'Beowulf' - but also images of people and events. Recalling the day when he spent the whole morning in the second hand bookshop in town with Chris and ended up buying Homer, Chaucer and something from most of the Romantic poets, was a fond memory closely linked with the books themselves, so of no great surprise; but sudden reflections on a day trip to Winchester or cinema visit came from left-field. How had reading the spines of books made those connections?!

Having long-since passed 'L', he found himself looking back at 'J' and his two copies of 'Ulysses'. Why had a bought a second copy? And why were his eyes now darting upwards in seemingly random fashion across his entire estate? Presumably there was a part of him that didn't trust what he had seen, that needed spontaneous verification - as if a quick darting glance might just have taken something by surprise, either a book he had missed or misplaced. Surely it was not possible to find an 'M' in any other location than between 'L' and 'N'? But what chance did he really have of finding what he was looking for (or not finding it, depending on your perspective) if he was suddenly unable to trust his own eyes?!

He gave up and sat down, hit hard by an old memory and an uneasy feeling. As a child he had struggled a little with dyslexia. In those dark days before he had begun to develop mechanisms to compensate for his disability, individual letters used to play hide-and-seek with him, page-by-page, line-by-line. He used to say what he had seen, often to the vast amusement of other children when the words he uttered were simply not there. Perhaps inevitably he had been unable to cope for while, and at that point his only strategy for dealing with his foe was to run away and never face it. So he gave up any kind of voluntary reading, confining himself to the most minimum activity needed to get by. This approach caused 'issues', and was never going to be a viable longer-term solution. Then an inspirational young English teacher - Miss Vine - had introduced him to Thomas Hardy, and had taken the trouble to make Jack her 'project' for the year. He had been twelve. Miss Vine, ably assisted by Michael Henchard - and then later Tess and others - led him from the darkness, helped him to develop coping strategies; indeed, forced him to do so as, for whatever reason, he had fallen in love and the only way to consummate that love was to be able to read. It had been slow, painful and frustrating; but after three terms of Miss Vine, letters and words were less pronounced in their deceiving page-bound gymnastics, and he began to catch-up. The fact that he eventually read English at university obviously meant that he did more than just hold his own, of course - but this present dilemma, and the sudden influx of that memory, served up a sharp reminder that perhaps, even after all this time, nothing was certain.

Indeed, the only thing that appeared to be certain right now was that 'Moby Dick' was missing.

❉

Looking out of the train window watching nameless hamlets and villages speed by, he could not help but feel a small degree of folly in his present course of action. There was a certain logic in the impulse that had seen him, the next morning, eschew the plans he had already made for the day and head, via the number twenty-four bus, into town and the railway station. It was rare that he did things on impulse or without planning, and he comforted himself with the reasoning that this present adventure did not actually succumb to either challenge; he had thought about the idea for at least twelve or fifteen hours (even if he had been asleep for most of those!), and he knew the trains ran regularly enough not to warrant booking ahead.

The cost of the ticket surprised him somewhat, but given this was the only way he could make it out and back in a day, he had little option. When 'Moby Dick' failed to materialise - on either the bookshelves themselves or throughout the finger-tip search of the rest of his apartment - then a return to the second-hand bookshop of his student days became the only viable option. He knew, of course, that he could simply seek out a new copy of the Melville in his local Smith's or, more reliably, via Amazon, but this would simply not do. He didn't want something pristine. He knew he would not find the exact book (his misplaced book!) materialised there on the shelves of Twerton's - that particular volume was presumably gone forever - but it was the only place he might find its best approximation: it would be old; it would come from a location with which he had massively strong connections; and it would allow him to invest, in a surrogate kind of way, at least some of his history into the replacement copy. For a short while between Burton and Derby he also allowed himself to fantasise that he had indeed bought the lost copy of 'Moby Dick' from Twerton's in the first place, even though he knew for certain that it had been sourced, unblemished, from the Waterstones on campus.

During his meagre preparations, he had taken the trouble to confirm that Twerton's was still in business; the last thing he needed now was to lose a bookshop as well as a book! The internet confirmed that the bookstore was still trading, though its somehow appropriate last century website gave little else away. When he had known it - in its 'hay day' one might have assumed - it had occupied a tall, narrow and deep building in a short terrace just off the High Street. A bookshop was an inadequate name for what was, in reality, a 'bookhouse'. Joined by a narrow and somewhat creaking wooden staircase, rooms fed off each landing on the six floors of the building; each floor, and then each room within each floor, had a specific focus or subject area. He had spent most of his time on the second and third floors (novels) and fifth floor (poetry and literary criticism), though this had not stopped him, at one time or another, visiting every room on every floor. It had been an Aladdin's cave. Better than that, an Aladdin's cave where the jewels were cheap enough for him to be able to afford them.

Stepping out from the station was a little like going back in time. He had not been to his university town for a number of years now and the mix of the familiar and the new - usually in the concrete form of buildings or roads - was only to be expected. His route towards the High Street remained unchanged of course, apart from the addition of a couple of extra pedestrian crossings and one subway underpass that had not been there ten years ago. The fabric of the place - the clock tower on the town hall, the art deco style cinema building (now a bingo hall!), the fire station - all succeeded in replanting him there. Yet it was a replanting that felt a little uncomfortable, as if his age had come and gone, and the inanimate relationships he had once held there were lost forever.

At least Twerton's appeared the same. Indeed, as he walked up to it he was forced to wonder if the building had even seen a coat of paint in the last decade. Though the entire terrace was looking down at heel - compared to the High Street itself, which had seen a major facelift at some point - Twerton's stood out, superficially at least, as the most neglected. Feeling a surprising sense of excitement and anticipation, he walked up the three well-worn stone steps to the entrance door.

The shop had always possessed that unique, old bookshop smell in spades: the aroma of tired leather, fading paper; it was almost as if the store itself was going brown and curling at the edges. It had been a smell that had delighted him and, stepping into the 'front room', he was pleased to be greeted by that particular old friend. His optimism increased.

The old, dark wood counter had been replaced by something a little more stylish, and he could see that the prehistoric till he remembered had been supplanted by a more modern equivalent, including card reader. Behind this new desk, a youngish person sat, working hard at her mobile phone. She glanced up at him and then carried on. Sometimes old Twerton himself would man the front desk, though he was probably long gone now, either retired or dead. He stood looking at those same old bowed shelves that had enchanted him many years previously. The catalogue had clearly changed and they had moved sections around - there were books here he would have expected to find on the top floor - but essentially the place appeared to be in a time warp.

"Can I help you?"

The young lady behind the counter had given up on her phone and was staring at him impassively.

"It has been years since I was last here," he said, then added, "Sorry."

"Yeah, we get that sometimes. Do you need help?"

He smiled, aiming to look totally comfortable and at home.

"I think I'm fine," he said. "I'll just start on the fifth floor and work my way down."

"Fifth floor?!" she said, in surprise. "There's no fifth floor. Haven't used it for as long as I've been here. Years, probably. We only go up to the second."

"Really?" This was disappointing. He felt his optimism begin to fade. "I'm looking for novels. Paperbacks."

"Right. Second floor; room at the front."

"Just one room?"

"Sorry." Assuming her help-giving was over, she returned to her phone.

Well at least the stairs still creaked. In places it used to feel as if they were just about to give way - and he was reassured to get that same feeling again.

The window of the second floor front room looked out onto the street, as did all the front rooms windows (except on the fourth floor, where the window had been bricked up for some reason in the distant past). He recalled that there used to be a hard chair in front of this particular window, which had been a boon after three floors of browsing with still three to go. Although here too the shelves themselves appeared to still be the ancients from his earlier days, they appeared slightly less dense than he remembered them. Perhaps that was just a sign of the times with people eschewing the printed word in favour of the electronically delivered. Either way, it was a sad state of affairs.

He started immediately inside the door expecting to find 'A' and then working his way from there - that was the way old Mr Twerton used to like things. However, he found Joyce and not Austen, so had to trace his way around the room backwards to find the 'A's. Of course, Joyce was much closer to Melville, and he could have taken perhaps a step or two to his right and found himself where he needed to be, but he had long since decided that if he was going to do this he was going to do it properly, and that meant trying to recreate something for his past along the way - an acceptable by-product or bonus, if you will, from his excursion. Yet even when he found the 'A's he was not that satisfied. Their ordering was approximate at best, with a few rogue titles from elsewhere in the alphabet popping up unexpectedly; finding 'The Midwitch Cuckoos' between 'Northanger Abbey' and 'Emma' was vaguely surreal.

Undaunted, he continued on until, a few minutes later, he found himself back at the door and back with Joyce.

Going methodically row by row became more of a challenge as he neared the end of his quest. Knowing that the Melvilles (if there were any) would be on the shelf directly beneath the one has was currently examining generated a real strain on him, forcing him to concentrate twice as hard to prevent the lazy short-cutting of his eyes towards their quarry. But he was there soon enough, and the first thing he saw was a copy of 'Billy Budd, Sailor' in the same Penguin livery as his own. Then, immediately alongside the first, were another two of the same. And then…

Nothing. No 'Moby Dick'. Not in the Penguin edition, nor in any other edition - neither paperback nor hardback (they were mixed together). 'Billy Budd, Sailor' then 'The Woman Upstairs' by Claire Messud. He couldn't believe it. How could there not be a copy of 'Moby Dick'? How was it possible that all owners of it actually wanted to keep their copies of the damn thing? He thought of the Wyndham sitting between the Austens; perhaps somewhere on the shelves a copy of 'Moby Dick' might have been similarly misplaced. He would have to go back to the beginning and check every shelf - very carefully.

❋

When he appeared in the ground floor front room about an hour later, the girl was still sitting behind the desk. She had heard the creaking of the stairs under his footfall and was already turned towards him as he walked into the room.

"It's you," she said, unable to conceal the surprise in her voice, "I thought you'd left ages ago! Any luck?"

He paused and showed her his empty hands.

"Ah," she said, her tone softening, "I guess you must have been looking for something specific? That's usually the way with people who are here an age but leave buying nothing."

"Yes," he said, feeling an age older than when he had entered the shop, "'Moby Dick'. I was looking for a copy of 'Moby Dick'."

"And we don't have one?"

"Not that I could see. And believe me, I looked!"

There was another of Twerton's random chairs near her desk, set aside in a small alcove between bookcases. He went over to it and sat down, sighing slightly as his thighs complained about the repetitive up-and-down they had been subjected to over the past hour or so.

"Can I get you a coffee?" the girl suddenly said, rising. "I was going to get myself one, and - well - you look like you could do with something."

His surprise made him reappraise her instantly.

"That would be great. White without, please. And thanks."

"Just keep an eye on the shop for me?"

He watched her disappear through the back of the store, leaving him alone with the books. She was unusually tall, he noted, quite slim but with a slightly uneven way of moving - perhaps owing to her sitting for a long time behind the till. She had short-cropped, bright red hair - close enough to a natural colour for him not to know if it were dyed or not - and crystal clear hazel eyes that seemed almost too perfect. He was still fairly sure that his initial impression was correct and that she was probably a student, earning a little something to help pay off her debts, but she was probably slightly older than the norm by a couple of years. Vague memories of old friends came back to him and he found himself trying to fit her into the frame of one of those.

After a few minutes she came back with two mugs of coffee.

"While I was waiting for the kettle to boil I checked a couple of boxes of stuff back there to see if I could see your book. You know, the things we haven't got round to pricing or putting out yet." She handed him his coffee. "But no luck, I'm afraid."

"Thanks for looking." The cup was warm in his hands.

"We've got a couple of rooms out the back. I know they keep some stock in there, but don't know what exactly. Not my realm really. I don't get to go back there much. But we could look - I mean, if it's really important to you." She resumed her seat.

"I don't want to cause you any trouble." He thought about trying to tell her why he was there, but decided on the abridged version. "I had an old copy and seemed to have lost it, that's all. It's left a bit of a hole in my - collection. That's all."

He had hesitated over the word 'collection'. It didn't sound right, but it was all he could offer on the spur of the moment.

"And you don't want to get a new one?"

The fact that she had phrased her question this way impressed him. Most people would have said "why don't you get a new one?", and that would have been to misunderstand his situation completely.

For a few minutes they chatted in a staccato kind of way, then another customer came in - a young woman - who was obviously a regular given her greeting of "Hi Jen!" to the girl behind the counter. She disappeared upstairs only to reappear a few minutes later carrying a single volume. Jen checked the price, took her money, then the shopper was gone.

"Another student?" he asked.

Jen looked over to the sofa.

"Yes, of course," she said, "who else comes in here?"

"Really?"

"Really! Pru's studying History with something; I forget what. We were holding a book for her; that's how she was so quick."

He drained the last of his coffee.

"And you? Studying History also?"

She shook her head.

"No, not History. I just know her through a friend."

Sensing she did not want to elaborate, he stood up and offered her the empty cup. It was somehow symbolic of his day. Having travelled optimistically, hoping that he would not only be able to plug the physical gap left by 'Moby Dick' but also to reconnect with his lost past, he felt defeated on both fronts. Most decisively he had been unable to find the book, and in a more abstract sense, his past had eluded him too. Yes, Twerton's was still there and trading, and yes, the stairs still squeaked, the smell was the same, but it had changed too: fewer floors, less books, less discipline in the organisation. And there were soft chairs in place of hard! Yes, they had been welcome to him, but in the Twerton's he knew - well, there would have been no place for sofas in that version.

He liked Jen; she had been kind to him - the coffee had been just what he needed. But when he tried to fit her into the old familiar Twerton's world that he knew, that past experience, she seemed to firmly belong to the here and now. Or at least, not to his world. Checking his watch he felt older and sadly wiser. Somewhere a door was closing softly. It had crept up on him unexpectedly, and he had no idea how he could possibly prevent it from closing.

He checked his watch. The next train would be in about forty minutes. The long journey home.

"Well..." he said, smiling at her.

"Look, we could still check that back room. You never know what you might find."

"Thanks," he said, and he offered her his hand. "You've been very kind. Good luck with your exams."

It was a limp farewell, but enough for her to blush slightly. At least that was something. Turning, he opened the door and stepped down onto the street.

❀

So, what do you want? A short story? If so, then you can leave it right there; just close the book, and move on. Imagine our man, sad and disappointed, sitting alone on the train, going home without 'Moby Dick', going home to the space in his bookcase and the space in his life.

Or not.

Think about it now. Before your eyes wander down the page and then turn over.

Made your mind up?

Are you sure? Really?

❀

He checked his watch. The next train would be in about forty minutes. The long journey home.

"Well…" he said, smiling at her.

"Look, we could still check that back room. You never know what you might find."

"Thanks," he said, and she offered him her hand…

TWO

She led him towards the passage at the back of the room from which the stairs went upwards. Ahead of them was the second ground floor room. He hadn't been in there today, but from what he could see through the doorway it appeared to be stocked with large, over-sized books: Art, Geography, those kinds of things.

"What about the shop?" he asked, forcing Jen to pause. She looked back at him.

"Don't worry; Mrs Mason will look after things."

And then, as if right on cue, a small, older woman appeared from the back room carrying two huge volumes on the Impressionists and shuffled past them as they squeezed against the wall to let her through.

"Don't mind me, Dear," she said, seemingly to no-one in particular, and with a slightly annoyed tone in her west country burr, "I was only sorting, that's all."

He couldn't work out from what she said and the way she said it whether 'sorting' was the least or most important job on the planet. He watched her disappear into the front room, presumably to take up station behind the counter. Somewhere above him he thought he heard the stairs creak.

"It's through here."

Jen's voice brought him back. Ahead of them on the left was a plain, dark door inset in the wall just before the first flight of stairs. He hadn't noticed it before when he had walked past to go up in search of his book; he had obviously been so intent on his quest - and perhaps also deflected by a quick glance into that back room - to see it. She put her left hand on the doorknob.

"What do I call you?" she asked, pausing, "I mean, you know my name from Pru, so I'm at a disadvantage - and if I spot something on the shelves and want to call you over, what should I say?"

"My friends call me Jack," he said. "It's not my proper name, but a kind of nickname that I've grown up with - or into. Or out of. Long story."

"Hello Jack," she said. Having still been holding his hand, she now proceeded to shake it formally and then release it. He looked down. It had been the most natural gesture and feeling, her taking his hand; so much so that he had instantly forgotten she had grasped it. But now it was suddenly not there, he felt as if he had lost something else.

He looked up; she was smiling.

"Hello Jen " he said, closing the loop, at which she opened the door.

If he was expecting the door to reveal a stock room of some persuasion, then he was to be surprised. Immediately ahead of them was a small almost wardrobe-sized space, large enough for one person, off which, to the right, a set of stairs descended. Although Jack had never thought about there being a basement in the building, there was no reason why there shouldn't have been one. The fact that the ground floor stood proud of the pavement - those three steps up - was perhaps one indication of a lower level. Also, it occurred to him that, as far as he could tell, all the rooms in the building (at least when he had known it) were given over to the display of books for sale, and if that were the case, then where was the non-display stock kept?

"It's a bit of a squeeze on the way down, and the steps are quite steep; there's a right angle turn about three quarters of the way down, so be careful. Just follow me."

Jen flicked a switch inside the door frame and a bare bulb sprang grudgingly into life over their heads, casting a weak yellow light on the stair well. She led him downwards, making sure that he held both handrails.

The stairs were steep and the ceiling quite low.

"Must be a bit tricky bringing books up," he offered.

"There's a dumb waiter in the back room," she said over her shoulder, "we use that most of the time. It's tucked away behind the door in there, so most people don't even realise it's there."

For some reason he counted the stairs. There were thirteen of them. Ahead of him, Jen flicked another switch once she had reached the bottom, and once again a pool of yellowish light was generated. Turning to the right, she disappeared from his view momentarily, but was waiting for him at the head of a corridor that sat at right angles to the bottom step. Two more weak spots of light illuminated it further along. Jack could see at least two doors on either side, but they were difficult to make out definitively.

Mentally he retraced his steps from the front room.

"This corridor must go out under the pavement," he suggested, "not under the building. Is that right?"

"Not this immediate part, but towards the end of it. I think the last two rooms are for certain as there are those glass pavement slabs in the ceiling that lets in some light. You can see people's feet sometimes when they walk by."

She walked forwards a little and opened the first door on the right.

"We'll try here first. This is where they keep the things that are ready to go upstairs - though I have to say, I don't think you'll find what you are looking for in here."

In contrast to the corridor outside, the light in this first room turned out to be surprisingly bright. Jack blinked involuntarily to allow his eyes to adjust. On three sides there were temporary shelving units; each shelf seemed to have a label, and most of these shelves were about half-full. The other wall paid host to a large, dark brown table; far larger than most average tables. Arranged here were several piles of books plus, at the front, two notepads with accompanying pencils. Under the desk were two boxes. From what Jack could see, these were opened and also contained books.

"This is where they sort and price the books after they've come in," Jen explained. "From the boxes, they go onto the table where they're sorted into categories of some kind. Then they're priced, and finally moved to the shelves to await shifting upstairs. They tend to move a dozen or so at a time in special little trays - like those over there. I've never seen them re-home ones or twos."

"I see," said Jack, noting the small pile of shallow trays stacked in the corner. "Very organised."

"You'd think. Anyway, any novels are on the two shelves in the far corner, the middle two. There might be some in a pile somewhere on the table."

"And the boxes?"

She shook her head.

"I'm not supposed to go into the boxes. Actually, I'm not even supposed to let the customers down here at all."

"Well, let's have a quick look," he said, encouragingly, "I'm sure we can be out of here in no time."

Jack moved over to the shelves in question and began to search. The books were not yet in any kind of sequence, so he had to check them individually, though given there were at most forty or fifty there, it was not something that was going to take him much time. Within a couple of minutes, he turned back to Jen who had been writing something in one of the notepads on the table. She closed it and replace it as soon as he spoke.

"No luck, I'm afraid. Mostly not my cup of tea, to be honest."

"A bit too 'cheap and trashy'?" she suggested.

"I wouldn't go that far."

"It's what Mr Twerton says."

"Twerton?! Is he still alive?" Jack couldn't hide his surprise.

"Yes, of course." She seemed a little shocked that he might think otherwise. "I mean, he doesn't work in the shop much any more, but he's still around. We can always feel him about the place. Anyway, he says that's what's killing it the shop; why we only need three floors now instead of six. Because people's tastes have changed; because they've found other ways to spend their time. Technology and such." She pulled her phone from her pocket as if to illustrate. "So it's a bit sad really."

"I know what he means," Jack concurred, "and I think he's probably right."

She led him out to the corridor.

"Of course, it's not something that I've seen personally. I've only stories for how it used to be - from when people like you come in. Or from some of the old timers, like Mrs Mason."

"The lady from the back room? With the Impressionist books? She seemed a bit grumpy."

Jen laughed.

"Don't mind her. She remembers the old days; has been here donkey's years. She talks about it sometimes. I know she misses it and is a little bitter. Thinks the world's going to the dogs and all that. But her heart's in the right place."

Jack tried to recall from that brief glimpse of her whether he had seen her there before, but failed.

"I'll keep that in mind," he said, smiling.

She paused before the second door.

"That's one of the reasons I wasn't that optimistic of you finding what you were looking for in that first room: too much modern trash in the novel department. You might have a little bit more luck in this next room."

"What's in there then, if this one was where the stock is kept."

"Well, not a lot of people know this, but we also do repairs here. You know, books that have lost a few pages, or where the spine has gone. Stuff like that. It's harder with paperbacks of course, which is why most of the ones in here will be hardback - but you never know."

"I never realised."

"See. Anyway, I'm guessing that you still won't find your lost 'Moby Dick' in here, but who knows?"

"Certainly worth a look," said Jack, edging forwards. Whether he was successful or not, this was turning out to be an interesting day at least.

"Before we go in, I need to warn you about Adam."

"Adam?"

"The bookbinder, or book-mender - whatever he's called. Like Mrs Mason, he's been here a long while too; maybe even longer. He hates what people have done with books - both physically and in terms of content - probably more than anyone else on the planet. Has known Mr Twerton since Noah was a lad, and isn't afraid to share some of his stories with you given half the chance."

"Sounds an interesting character," said Jack.

"He is that," Jen agreed. "And he's losing his sight a little bit, so don't be surprised if he confuses you with someone else, or comes up really close to get a good look at you." She paused. "And look, if you don't mind, I think you should hold my hand again" - she offered it to him - "it's just that if he sees that we're friends, he's more likely to be reasonable. Is that ok?"

Jack smiled and took her hand for the second time.

"We don't want Adam being unreasonable, do we?" he said with a smile.

Opening the door, Jen revealed a room similar in size to the first, again with shelving, this time against just two walls, the one adjacent to the door on the right and against the far side. The light from the ceiling was dimmer in here, but there was a brighter glow coming from behind the door. She led him in towards the centre of the room, turned and paused.

Behind the door and along the left-hand wall was an arrangement of tables and benches with two spotlights placed to cast bright shafts of light over particular areas of the table. It was these that were providing the glow. Spread across the table were a range of tools, small sets of drawers, and materials, each seemingly in its appropriate place. Again there were two notebooks. On the nearest edge of the benches, a small pile of books in a very poor state of repair; on the furthest side, a similarly small pile of books looking pristine. A few had made it to the shelves. In the midst of all this, sitting right in the corner where the benches joined, Jack could make out the hunched back of a man. He was largely balding, but with wisps of long grey hair straggling down to his shoulders.

"Hello, Adam; it's Jen. How are you today?"

He shuffled a little, and murmured something unintelligible.

"I've brought a friend whose looking for a book."

Adam froze momentarily, then slowly placed the book he was working on down on the table. He turned slightly and looked over his shoulder. Jen raised the hand that was holding Jack's as if in demonstration, then moved forward to pick up one of the notebooks.

"You'll be fine now," she whispered to him as she released his hand.

As Adam stared at him, Jack tried to establish his age. He was at least seventy. Although his face was worn and a little gnarled, he could see there was still a surprising quality about his skin, and his eyes were lively, if not fiery.

"Friend, eh?" Adam's voice was a little thin and harsh, like a slightly discordant note from a cinema organ. "Come looking for books, eh?" He stood up - not without difficulty - and came closer to Jack. "Well let me tell you, laddie, you've come to the right place! Oh, we're got books all right. Lots of books. Not as many as we used to have mind - but you know why that is don't you?"

Jack, assuming the question was rhetorical, said nothing.

"I've explained to Jack, Adam," said Jen, jumping in. "He doesn't like the new way either. Used to come here years ago, didn't you Jack? When there were all six floors, Adam."

The older man took one step nearer. He was about a foot shorter than Jack, and was tilting his neck both backwards and sideways to look at his face.

"Hmmm. Not that long ago I'd say."

"This used to be my favourite place," Jack offered with some honestly. "I used to spend hours in here - mainly on the second, third and fifth floors."

"Literature student, eh? And a bit of philosophy? When was that; let me see. About six years ago?"

Jack smiled.

"Something like that," he said.

"You're still a baby!" Adam declared, then turned back to his benches.

Jack moved forwards. The pile of books to Jack's left were entirely hardback. It was evident that most of them had detached covers, with one book in particular also appearing to have been torn into at least three sections.

"See what people do to their books these days?" Adam rasped. "No respect. No love."

"And you mend them, Adam?"

"I give them their souls back."

Jen passed him a volume from the other side of the table. It was a hardback copy of 'Hard Times', skilfully bound in a dark green leather, with gold tooling and lettering. Jack opened it and checked the date on the frontispiece; it was nearly a hundred and twenty years old.

"It's beautiful work," he said.

"You should have seen it when they brought it to me," Adam said, "I thought I'd lost him. Ripped and torn and broken. Lost; almost completely lost. Took me days to get him back. Hours to get the lettering right."

"It's perfect."

Adam looked round at him, his stare forcing Jack to hand the Dickens back to Jen.

"Perfect, young man? Perfect? I'll tell you what's perfect. Perfect is not having to work on these pour souls at all. Perfect is them being looked after, cherished; never breaking - or being broken. That's what perfect is."

"I didn't mean…"

"I know, I know," said Adam in a mix of frustration and resignation. "And thank you for the compliment. The fact that you're down here at all means something. Jen doesn't let just anyone down here, so that's all right…"

He allowed his sentence to trail away. Jack glanced at Jen who had replaced both the Dickens and the notepad she had written in, and who was smiling at him encouragingly.

"So what are you looking for," said Adam suddenly.

"Me?"

"You're looking for something, Jen said. Something's lost, is that right?"

"Yes, yes," said Jack, tuning in. "I've lost a copy of 'Moby Dick'. It was only second-hand - I may even have originally bought it here…" He allowed the white lie to fade away.

"But it means something to you," Adam intervened. "It's left a hole in your collection and you want to have it filled. That's it, isn't it? Without it, well, it feels like you've lost part of yourself?"

Jack felt the analysis was accurate if a little over-stated - but he wasn't going to disagree.

"That's pretty much it, yes."

"Hardback; which edition?"

"Actually," and here Jack's voice was involuntarily apologetic, "paperback."

"Ha!" Adam almost spat out his disapproval. "Heaven help us! I see very few paperbacks, young man, and do you know why? Because when they've gone, they've gone. They weren't designed to last. Throw away, just like our sad world today." He shook his head. "Oh sometimes I get a few in worth the trouble - older ones; one-offs; originals. They take time too. I have to use glue only. And the paper's often of poor quality." He sighed and shook his head again. "But there it is."

Jen, who had been standing back throughout almost the entire exchange, moved forwards now.

"Have you seen a copy, Adam? Of 'Moby Dick'?"

"No, I haven't. And if I do - especially if its that thick Penguin one - then I'll probably just throw it in the bin! Oh, you can look on the shelves there, but you won't find it, I know that much."

There was a finality in his last phrase that was accompanied by him bending his head to his work again. Jack turned and glanced over to the shelves. He could see instantly that there were only two paperbacks there, and neither of them the size or colour of the book he was seeking.

Jen took his hand and led him back to the door.

"Thank you, Adam," she said as she opened it.

"Wow! Some guy!" said Jack, this when they were back outside in the corridor and the door to Adam's room had been closed.

"I tried to explain," she offered, "but you can see how it was hard to. He's a little bit special." Jack laughed lightly. "By the way, that last bit about paperbacks; he says that, but doesn't mean it."

"Sounds like he meant it."

"Did you see his waste bin, on the floor by the desk?" she asked.

"No, can't say I did."

"Empty. Completely empty. Adam never throws anything away. There is never a lost cause for him."

Jack looked down towards the section of the corridor that extended out under the pavement.

"Is that it?"

"It?"

"Well, we've seen your store room and your Restorer; I assume that's all you can do for me. I either have to accept that I've lost the book and that you don't have a second-hand one here, or buy a replacement new one."

She looked at him with a soft smile playing on her lips. Although she was younger than he, Jack sensed a degree of maturity and wisdom about her that belied her age. Perhaps it was the effect of working with characters like Adam; maybe something rubbed off on her.

"That's up to you really," she said. She nodded back towards the stairs. "You're free to leave Jack, of course. As you say, then it's on to Amazon to buy your replacement and to give up that piece of your history."

"You make it sound a little melodramatic!" He laughed. "It's only a book!"

"Is it?" She paused deliberately. "If it were 'only a book', then why did you jump on a train at such short notice and come all the way down here?"

"But you don't know where I've come from," he protested.

"'Next train in about forty minutes'," she quoted, "'the long journey home'."

Jack couldn't remember if that's what he had said, but he laughed as if she had caught him in a trap.

"Look, you're right Jen. Yes, actually it is only a book but it's what it represents that's somehow important. It doesn't just leave a hole in my bookcase, but it means there are some things I can't remember now. It was a kind of trigger. I want to be able to recall what I thought about it, what I wrote in the margins, where I bought it, who I was with, what conversations it led to... Oh, I know I won't get most of that stuff back because I'll never find the original - my original - but that's not the point somehow. And maybe we lose all those kinds of things over time anyway..." There was a pause she chose not to fill. "I know that's all rubbish. Maybe I should just go."

He didn't move. He wasn't sure if going was the right thing to do. It was the easiest, perhaps; it would mean that he knew what the score was. He checked his watch. That next train would have gone by the time he got to the station; perhaps he would have the opportunity to check out other bookshops in town before the one after that.

But there were two more rooms down here.

"It's not rubbish," she said, "of course it isn't. Once, I went to Belgium - to Bruges actually - with my family for a holiday. We found a little restaurant down a small side street and I had the most wonderful dinner. I remember the starter: a fantastic lobster bisque. After the meal, I asked my Dad if I could keep the receipt; it had all the dishes we'd eaten itemised on it. I wanted that receipt to be my memory of the dinner. But it got lost. Now all I can remember is the lobster bisque. It's not the same, but I know what you mean."

Jack smiled. He suddenly wanted to say something to her, but was unsure, hesitant. He felt uncomfortable, and a little warm.

"Come on," she said, a little bounce back in her voice, "why don't we try the next room anyway? What else have you got to lose?"

"So what's in there anyway?' he asked. "We've seen finished books and books being repaired, so I'm assuming it must be something different."

"What comes next?"

"Next?"

"In the sequence," she said, "if you were working backwards, that is. New book, second-hand book; before the second-hand book, books being repaired - made finished, if you like. What's next in that backward sequence?"

Jack wasn't sure if this was a game he wanted to play. He looked at his watch again.

"I'm not sure..." he said - meaning he was not sure about staying, rather than what was in the next room.

"Come on, Jack. Just try; for me."

He shrugged his shoulders. Suddenly it felt a little like a game, and not something designed to help him out. He didn't like the notion of him being some kind of pawn. Just then he was pretty sure that Jen wasn't doing this for his benefit; Adam certainly wasn't.

"I don't know. Before books get broken? People read them I guess - but you aren't going to read books for people are you? Defeats the object somewhat."

Jen laughed at the idea.

"That's quite funny," she agreed. "Logical, perhaps, but funny."

"OK, so it's not that. Before they're read then. They're new; have to be. Maybe that's what's next in the sequence."

She smiled and began walking away from him.

"But you just sell books here, right? I mean, that's what Twerton's is." He was being forced to walk after her if he wanted an answer. "I mean, whoever heard of a second-hand bookseller actually making new books?! It wouldn't make sense."

"Maybe not," she said, pausing before the next door.

Jack heard the sounds of footsteps overhead and looked up just in time to see the sole of a shoe land against a glass paving brick and then push off again.

When he looked back, she had opened the third door. He saw her back disappearing through the doorway. With two steps he was on the threshold, and there he was forced to pause. The room was much larger than the previous two. Much, much larger. It was vast. He could see just one bookcase this time, fixed to the wall just inside the door. A few volumes were resting there, but for the moment he paid them little attention. Around the rest of the room - hugging the walls, but with a few work-stations elsewhere - numerous benches and trestles, many of them home to machines of various sizes, one or two of which were enormous.

Jack could tell many of the machines were running, and yet the noise was surprisingly low; more a hum with a backing beat of clicking and tapping than anything else. It was pleasantly cool given the activity in-train, helped to some extent he was sure by the fact that the lighting was subdued; only in three or four places were the spotlights over the desk truly bright. In amongst the machines, Jack could see two figures moving around. Jen, who lad located another pair of notebooks on the desk nearest the door, had picked one of them up and was walking over to the nearest of the two men.

The bench nearest Jack - and from which Jen had taken the notebook - was stacked with boxes of what appeared to be raw materials. There were reams and reams of paper. He could see from the package labels that they varied in grade and finish. Close by, was a computer screen. Excluding the till upstairs, this was the first such device he had seen in the shop and its presence surprised him somewhat.

"Yes, I know," said a voice suddenly close by. Jack looked up to find the first of the two men approaching him. He offered Jack his hand. "Who would have thought it, monitors in Twerton's! Hi Jack; my name's Luke."

Dressed immaculately in the trousers and waistcoat of what was clearly a three-piece suit, white shirt, and bright red bow-tie, Luke appeared to be a little older than Jack. Not only was he perfectly presented, his smile was even, the tone of his voice even; he gave the impression of being a perfectly measured specimen.

"You're a bit surprised I'm not like Adam, I guess!" He laughed. "Adam hates it in here. Thinks we're committing some kind of crime; that we're not being true to our roots somehow."

"What are you doing?" Jack scanned the room. The other man was now walking towards them. Jen had moved away to check another monitor on one of the tables on the far side of the room.

"Doing?" echoed Luke.

"Doing!" said the other man now joining them. He laughed. "We're making books, of course!"

"This is Matt," said Luke.

Matt looked a little like a hippy out of the seventies; as far from Luke as Jack could imagine without making the transition all the way to Adam. They seemed about the same age. There was a vague smell of patchouli in Matt's presence - although Jack acknowledged that he could just be imagining this because of his dyed t-shirt, linen trousers and sandals. They too shook hands.

"But how? I mean why?" Jack was flabbergasted. "Twerton's sells books; and second-hand ones at that. It can't make them.

"Obviously we can," said Matt, smiling. He turned away from them and walked over to a nearby work-station.

"Yes," Luke picked up, "obviously we can. We have been for many years actually - though in the early days nothing as sophisticated as this of course."

"But isn't that illegal, or something? What about copyright? Or the publishers?"

"We have agreements with most publishers; they don't mind. And we've one or two imprints of our own."

Jack scanned the room again. The look of incredulity on his face must have been all too evident.

"I know," said Luke, resting an arm briefly on his shoulder, "so many questions..."

"Yes. Like 'why?' And 'how?' But mainly 'why?'"

"Let's start with the easy one, the 'how'," said Luke, leaning forwards a little. Jen had now walked across to join them. "We start here, with paper - surprisingly. Then we have a succession of machines where the paper gets printed on, trimmed, glued, bound, etcetera. It's a fairly standard process. The finished volumes come out just over there, and then the final two machines 'age' the books."

Jack looked to where Luke was pointing.

"Age them?"

"As you say, Jack, we sell used books here, so we can't put brand new books on our shelves can we? So those two machines 'age' them; make them look as if they aren't new. The first one sort of distresses the volume; you know, ages the paper a little, throws in the odd crease or fold. We can make something look so bad it could go straight to Adam!" He laughed at his own joke. "That last machine - well, that's a new one. And it's really clever. It allows us to 'mark up' the book, to invest some personality into it; make it look as if someone really has read it. I'd like to show you that one, but I'm afraid it's off limits."

Jack looked around the room. He could only see very small piles of books in their various stages of completion.

"But how many do you produce? I mean, a commercial printer would have a run of hundreds or thousands. You're not going to do that here; that would be crazy. You'd suddenly have a shop full of the same thing!"

"You're right, of course. So we don't have big print runs. In fact, our runs can be as small as just one volume. That's what's so wonderful about our little sausage machine here: we can have one copy of 'Emma', followed by one copy of 'Romeo and Juliet'… It's a miracle really."

For a few moments they walked slowly round the room, close enough for Jack to see what was going on, but not so close that he could really see the intricacies of the process.

"But that means you must have the text for hundreds of books stored somewhere?"

"Thousands Jack, thousands," Luke confirmed. "Which is why we need the computers. Couldn't have anything on this scale - in terms of diversity, of course - without modern technology. I know it seems a bit counter-intuitive in a place like Twerton's, but I guess it's all down to necessity and invention and all that. And the foresight and commitment of Mr Twerton himself to provide this kind of a service. Can you imagine how difficult it would have been many years ago?"

They had arrived where Matt was working. He had an incomplete copy of 'Pride and Prejudice' in his hands. Its edges were rough and the cover was, as yet, unfinished, but it looked to all the world like a surrogate copy of the Penguin classics edition. He passed it to Jack.

"Have you done the 'why?' part yet?" he asked Luke.

"Just the 'how?' - which I think we're good with."

Matt held out his hand to take the Jane Austen back from Jack.

"And you'd like to know why we do all this, Jack?"

Jack nodded.

"Let's sit," said Matt, directing them to four upright chairs that were nearby. He quickly arranged them in a rough circle before they sat down.

"In a way the why is also easy," Matt began. "If you wanted to, you could say that we were simply filling a gap in the market. Let's say someone comes into Twerton's looking for a specific book - like 'Moby Dick' perhaps. But it's an old edition they're after, one that may have been out of print for a number of years. Unless they're really, really lucky, their search is almost certain to end in disappointment. This little process of ours allows us to fulfil that need. It means that they can go away happy -"

"Even though you've conned them?" Jack suggested.

"Let's come back to that," said Matt. "So it allows them to go away happy; they have found what they wanted. They tell people how great Twerton's is. People ring us up and ask us if we've got an old copy of this or that; we tell them 'yes', and by the time they come in to collect, we've made it, aged it, and its ready and waiting for them. In many ways a simple but brilliant commercial model."

"Maybe," said Jack, "but I'm not sure I actually buy that - not as the real reason. And what about the fraudulent part. You're not actually selling them the old edition they are looking for, are you?"

"No, strictly speaking we're not," Matt concurred, "but is that the most important thing? Really? Surely the fact that our customers go away happy and satisfied - isn't that the most important thing?" Before Jack could answer, Matt rushed on. "Let's say you had rung a couple of days ago about your copy of 'Moby Dick'. We could have made one for you. When you had collected it, would you have thought - even for a split second - I wonder if this is really old and original, or would you have gone away contented?"

The answer was obvious, so Jack refrained from replying.

"But it's not just that," said Luke, taking up the story. "We aren't just here to provide some kind of mail order service for books. There are things that we won't reproduce, for example. Things that we don't believe in."

"Jack and I have already covered 'modern trash' with Adam," Jen offered.

"Exactly. So if someone wanted a copy of - I don't know, let's be extreme - 'Fifty Shades of Grey', we simply wouldn't produce it. Never. Twerton's has some values that we're trying to uphold here; they are important to us. Sometimes - and here's the second reason for what we're doing - we will reproduce important, brilliant, classic books and ensure they are always on our shelves as our way of encouraging our browsers (and we still have many!) to actually leave with something worthwhile. So, you will never, ever find Twerton's without copies of Dickens, or Jane Austen, or Shakespeare, Milton, Wordsworth... Need I go on?"

"But not Melville," Jack suggested, smiling.

"Touché!" said Luke. "We're simply trying to ensure that there's a balance maintained somehow; that important things - ideals, sensibilities, beliefs, values - are not lost. And that great stories are not lost either. And maybe we should run off a couple of copies of 'Moby Dick'; it is a great story, after all."

"You might think that's some kind of interference on our part," suggested Matt, "and you might be right; market forces, and all that. But Mr Twerton feels - we all feel - morally obliged somehow to give people a little helping hand along the way. Does that make sense?"

Jack, whose head was swimming a little with the incredulity of it all, nodded.

"Yes, I can see where you're coming from. And it is noble, I guess; small scale, but it does have a purpose which you would imagine can only be good."

"I defy anyone to suggest anything negative about it," said Matt, suddenly serious. "We take what we do as seriously as Adam does his restoration work. The goals are pretty similar - and I bet you never, for one moment, questioned what he was doing."

"I'll give you that," Jack agreed.

Against the background humming and clicking, there was a short lull in the conversation. Jack got the sense that Matt and Luke were finished with their explanations, and now they - along with Jen - were waiting. It was gap that he had to fill.

"But," he said, slowly - and three pairs of eyes focussed on him, "there's something else, isn't there? I mean, I just get the sense there's more that's going on here. Even if I buy what you're doing - and to a certain extent I think I do, by the way - I just get the feeling that there's something more; something about the 'why?'; something that you're not telling me. Yet."

"What makes you say that?" It was Jen who spoke.

"I don't know. Because I bet you don't show just anyone who can't find what they're looking for what goes on down here. Because I haven't found what I'm after. Because there's another door in that corridor outside, and I get the feeling that means that there's something else; another 'next'."

"'Next'?" Luke asked.

"Yes," said Jack, also serious now, "another next in the sequence. Going backwards. You know, Jen, like you asked in the other room: before the used book, before the restored book, before the made book... What comes before the book is made?

Does it get written? Is that what's through the door? Though I don't see how even you could make that happen."

Matt rose.

"Over to you Jen," he said as he held his hand out to Jack. "Nice meeting you, Jack. I think our part is over."

Jack rose to shake his hand, and Luke's too who had almost simultaneously also risen.

"We'd better get back to work, Jack. Take care."

Jack watched the two of them walk back to their machines, Matt's hand resting on Luke's shoulder for a brief moment.

"They're great, those two." Jen was still sitting, and suggested with a wave of her arm Jack rejoin her, "like chalk and cheese of course, but really clever, really nice guys."

"And good at what they do?" Jack suggested.

"Just like Adam," she agreed.

"Just like you," he suggested.

Now it was Jack's turn to leave the pause, knowing that Jen would be obliged to fill it. She seemed relaxed, unhurried and unstressed. Her gaze was, as ever, even and unfaltering.

"You're not wrong, Jack; of course there's another door which means, of course, that there's something through it. And what's through there is partly answered by your question - my question, even! - of 'what's next?' But it's not about the books. We've finished with those."

"I'm confused. If I was confused before, then now…"

"Sorry. The thing that comes before the books are the people; not the people who wrote them, but the people who are reading them. It's not about the experience of the writer - at least not for us - it's about the experience of the reader. When you read a book you don't actually overlay the author's world on to your own; what you actually do is to transpose your experience of the world, your life, onto the book. The book is a lens through which to see and interpret your world - not the other way around. That may not be a common view, of course."

"Example?"

"Let's say you read 'Romeo and Juliet'. Great story, of course; wonderfully written. When you read it, you read the story - Shakespeare's story - and you can dissect it and analyse it, you can watch it be performed, write essays about it. All that good stuff. And of course it never leaves you. You may remember it forever, word by word if you like! But how you read it, what you see in it, how you remember it, what it does to you afterwards - because books are powerful things and they can change your life! - all of that isn't about the book; it's about you. It has to be. That's why what I think about 'Romeo and Juliet' will be different in some way to what you think; what I take from it or learn from it will be different. If it wasn't like that, then there'd be no disagreement; everyone would like the same things, and think the same things. The book doesn't change - ever - so the only variable is the person reading it."

"I don't see how I can argue with that," Jack agreed, "though I've never quite thought about it that way."

"Which is why some modern books frustrate us, frustrate Mr Twerton; because the fact that people can take so much from them says more about the people than it does about the books. Do you see?"

He wasn't exactly sure on that point, but the big question hadn't left him yet.

"So that last door? What's through there then, if it isn't related to the books?"

She smiled that perfect smile of hers.

"When people come here looking for things, as you have come looking for 'Moby Dick', sometimes - most of the time probably - that's exactly what they come for; they've lost a book - and it's always a lost book. They believe book's the thing. The reason they're here. There's nothing more to it than that. But just occasionally, people are actually looking for something else. They might think they're after a book, but what they're really looking for is a part of themselves they've lost. If you think about the example of 'Romeo and Juliet'. If someone has just lost the text, they can replace it - from anywhere. The core part of their experience will be the same. But if someone has lost more than that... The text won't help them."

"I still don't quite get it..."

"Your 'Moby Dick'. You could get another copy from Waterstones or Smiths'. The same words; no issue. But you chose to come here, why? Because you have invested in that book - in your experience with Twerton's too! - something about your life. The book - that particular, tired, faded, creased, annotated volume - means more to you than the simple text because of your relationship with it, how you bought it, what you were thinking when you read it, how you lived your life before and since... It's very complex, Jack; a huge matrix of interactions and inter-relations - but it isn't about the book, it's about you. The book contains part of you; it must, it really must. Most of the time people are just looking for a book. But sometimes they're actually looking for part of themselves that has got lost."

"And those are the people that come down here?"

"Just very occasionally, yes."

"And then what's through that last door..."

"Is you, Jack. In some way, shape, or form, it's you. I don't know how or what or any of that; I can't possibly. But what's through there is - maybe - what you're really looking for."

"If it's not just a book."

"If it's not just a book; correct. And we can't know that. Not even you can know that until you step through the door."

"If I want to," he suggested.

She rose.

"If you want to. And I can't help you with that."

Jack stood. On some impulse that was unusual for him, he took her hand and kissed the back of it.

"Thanks," he said, not entirely sure what he was thanking her for.

She blushed slightly.

"After you," she said.

The corridor was still struggling with the wash of yellow light from overhead. Jen joined him, following his gaze across to the final door slightly further along. Again there were footsteps from the pavement above them.

"Maybe it is more than a book I've lost," Jack suggested, as it he were drawing a logical conclusion that were justifying his choice - even though he knew he had no such choice: having been through three of the doors, how could he possibly not try the final one? "But I guess there's only one way to really find out?" Jen gave his arm a squeeze. "Am I right in thinking that you don't come in with me?"

She nodded.

"I'm sorry, yes. I can't really - this isn't about the book any more. My job's sort of over - though I'm pretty sure you'll get some kind of help in there. I mean, this is Twerton's, isn't it? When have you known us not to be helpful to someone!"

It was a rhetorical question of course, and Jack just laughed.

As he put his hand on the doorknob, he felt her hand on his shoulder.

"I'll wait here," she said.

He turned and smiled at her.

"Thanks," he said, then opened the door and stepped forwards.

THREE

He was leaning on the wall just outside the tutorial room. From inside, voices; one was the telltale burr of Mike's West Coast accent. Most people assumed he was American but, as he was sometimes only too pleased to assert, he was simply an Englishman who had spent far too much time teaching abroad. He had his hand on Tim's shoulder and was walking with him towards the door. His habit of being over-tactile was another bequest from San Francisco. Tim rolled his eyes secretly at Jack as he passed him, then Jack was next to feel the warmth of Mike's large hand.

"Are we good, Mr Jackson?" It was impossible not to like the tone. Actually it was pretty impossible not to like the whole package. "You were pretty quiet in there today."

"Was I? Sorry."

"Not your thing, I'm assuming, our Mr Melville?"

Jack felt the weight of the book in his hand. He looked down; he needed to transfer it back into his rucksack along with his notebook; he had written precious little during the tutorial.

"I guess. I know its supposed to be a great story and all that - and that its 'significant', whatever that means - but, well, its also just a bit dull."

Mike laughed.

"Hardly an original critique, Jack, but I know what you mean! Look, just try your best with the essay, OK. It won't be make-or-break by any stretch; just give it your best shot."

He eased himself from beneath the hand.

"Sure thing, Mike; I'll give it my best shot."

He was three steps away, unzipping his rucksack to replace his books on-the-move, when the voice rolled back over him.

"And Jack," he paused and looked back over his shoulder, Mike's face slightly more serious now, "if you need to talk to someone about that other matter at any time" - there was a slight nod of the head upwards at this point - "you know where I am Buddy, OK?"

"Of course. Thanks."

Jack looked back down the corridor and saw the reason for Mike's little gesture with his head. Lucy - 'that other matter' - was walking towards him.

In addition to being the tutor for 'American Literature' (fittingly, everyone thought!), Mike was also Jack's Personal Tutor, which meant that they met one-to-one around every four weeks or so to discuss Jack's progress, both in terms of his degree but also at the university overall. It was an important part of a First Year's induction into the university system, as some found it harder than others. Nothing was off limits during those conversations, their value and benefit being driven by the kind of relationship established between Student and Tutor. Jack had been immediately comfortable with Mike, which was how he knew about Lucy Watkiss.

She had reached him now and took 'Moby Dick' from his hands as he continued to struggle with his bag.

"What's this?" she said, mock enquiry in her voice. She flicked through the pages. "Oh, it's a thick one!"

"Give it back, Luce."

"Wait," she said, producing a pen from somewhere as if by magic, then, spinning Jack round, leant the book against his back. He felt a slight additional pressure, then she had spun him back and placed the book in his hand.

"Having fun?" she asked, her hand brushing his, and then not waiting for an answer, "I'm late for the Old Trout. We're doing something saucy with Chaucer! See you later, maybe?"

And then she was off. Jack watched her walk down the corridor. She was wearing the pale blue, super-tight jeans that he could only marvel at, and a slightly too-loose jumper that, when she leant forward, showed too much of her bra underneath. Her long hair, on the red side of auburn, waved back as she walked. A first year English Literature and German student, she was one of the stunners of that year's intake; everyone said so, even Mike.

Jack was smitten. They had met in a pub near his halls of residence during the first month, although of course he had seen her around the department occasionally by then (though she denied having noticed him). She had been lively, friendly and vivacious. She had laughed at his jokes, and he had been caught off balance by how tactile she was. He had, in the common parlance, reached 'second base' very quickly, but that was where he was stuck. He had been perhaps over-keen to make it further, and Lucy had been pitching a controlled game since then to keep him exactly where he was.

"I suspect the bases might be loaded," he confessed to Mike around a month previously, "and I don't mean a guy on each base; I mean, I might not be the only one on second…"

Mike had laughed gently. It was not a harsh but a sympathetic gesture, and that was the way Jack heard it.

"It may be that she is taking full advantage of the university eco-system," Mike suggested, and left it at that.

Jack knew he should probably just walk off the ballpark, but it was a difficult thing to bring himself to do, especially as it was a game he desperately wanted to be playing in.

He flicked through 'Moby Dick', looking for Lucy's message. He found it second time through, in the blank space at the end of a chapter: a small smiley face with two kisses for eyes. It was something of a trademark of hers. Another one to add to his collection. As he put the book away in his rucksack, shouldered it, and then began to walk towards the exit, Jack wondered what to do next. He had still not quite come to terms with the flexibility university life offered in respect of managing your time. A large part of him had liked the structure and certainty of a day of lessons, one after the other, and the knowledge that your dose of learning was prescribed and carefully medicated. On days like today - one hour with Mike and then nothing - getting the balance right between studying and not was an art he had not yet perfected. A number of his friends had embraced the freedom with open arms, and spent huge chunks of their time playing sports or drinking. Neither of these were Jack's forte.

As he made his way outside and towards the Library building - having decided that he might as well try and make start on the Melville essay, in spite of his current distraction - he couldn't help but feel, suddenly and profoundly, that he had lost something. Jack knew, of course, that in the few weeks he had been at university he had discovered much (Lucy notwithstanding!), and that he had managed to broaden his experience and horizons considerably; he had met a new range of varied and interesting people - like Mike, for example - and on the whole the adventure was turning out to be an extremely positive one. But in discovering more about himself and finding things, he knew he had lost something too, and right at that moment, Lucy's little doodle somewhere in his copy of 'Moby Dick' seemed to represent both lost and found better than anything else he could think of.

One place he didn't feel lost was the library - though it was certainly big enough for someone to someone to disappear in and never be seen again. It was an old, red-brick building, designed before simplicity and sleek lines had become fashionable, and when compartmentalising rather than open-plan was acceptable.

Jack loved the way this generated a whole range of choices in terms of study areas. There were large open spaces of course, and these tended to be found immediately off the large central staircase; but there were also smaller niches of various sizes, often tucked away and found unexpectedly as you turned a corner or followed a trail of bookshelves. His own preferred spot, a little way from the main Literature area, would have held perhaps sixteen people when fully occupied, though it rarely was. The shelves that defined it were home to something of a mix of criticism, philosophy and history that seemed to sit uncomfortably with the mainstream, and they had therefore been gathered together in this overflow area. It was this, Jack was sure, that contributed in part to it being one of the quieter locations in the library. The trek to retrieve and then return books from the core Literature shelves was longer than he would have liked - especially when he had a few to carry - but the benefit of being away from the potential distractions of people coming and going, hushed conversations, direct interruptions and the like was a price worth the paying.

Each niche within the Library - large or small - developed its own set of regulars; patterns of people sitting in particular locations, at specific desks, that appeared after the fog of the initial week or two of the first term like cultures in a petri dish. Sooner or later, you got to know where people sat. One of the other advantages of this location for Jack was that it was nowhere near Lucy, who - when she bothered to use the Library at all - almost invariably sat with her German friends on the floor above.

Maggie was one of the few regulars in Jack's study cave. Like him, she was also a First Year Literature student. Occasionally they would be joined by Paul, who, whenever he appeared there, was invariably signalling that he was up against a tight deadline - or worse, late! - and needed to leave his rugby training behind for a while to actually get some work done. On this basis, Paul's visits, though irregular, tending to comprise of long stints of desperate hours. The other regulars were taking different subjects or from different years and where nodding acquaintance was all that was needed.

Jack liked Maggie. In being slightly too short, and slightly rounder, with a pugnacious but kind face, she was almost the antithesis of Lucy. With Maggie, what you saw was what you got; there never appeared to be anything other than honesty about her. If something was good, she told you; if it stank, she told you that too. When Jack turned into their little area now and headed for his regular desk - 'Moby Dick' in tow - he was pleased to see her there, head down, surrounded by individual sheets of A4 as if she had been caught in a paper snow storm. Unlike Jack, Maggie was not that tidy or structured.

He started work on his essay, following his usual pattern of dissecting the question to pull out the core components or themes he would need to address, then, with these in mind, to define a structure within which he could tackle them. This then gave him his framework. Critical works - and even the text itself! - would then be recruited to fill in the blanks and add weight to the argument that Jack wished to put forward. This was where he found 'Moby Dick' hard. With most assignments he knew what he wanted to say - or what he was expected to say - but the Melville was like a secret code to him, something he was unable to crack, a door that refused to open; its subtleties eluded him, and he never got past the pastiche Hollywood image of Gregory Peck, hair flying wildly as he was tossed on the seas in the whaling boat.

"Struggling, huh?"

Maggie's intervention a little while after he had started was welcome. Jack looked down at the atypical scattered notes he had made; these were a million miles away from his usual tidy beginnings, and so obviously so that Maggie saw it clearly too.

"How about a coffee, Ishmael?"

"Have you read this thing yet?"

"Yep, of course."

"And?"

"And what?"

Jack stood up, not sure exactly what the question was he wanted to ask.

"Do you get it?" he said, vaguely.

"I like it," Maggie said as they started to walk towards the main stairs from where they would go down two flights to the coffee bar in the basement. "It's not 'easy', of course. I mean, it's not like most normal novels in many ways; all that history stuff, you know? It's a bit like two different books interwoven. Know what I mean?"

Jack did.

"But I can't seem to join them up in a way that works for me," he said. "And I actually don't think I like either of them very much."

"Prefer the film, huh?"

"Why do you ask that?"

"Because that's what all the guys say!" And Maggie laughed.

A few minutes later they were sitting silently over coffee, the background chatter typical of a university refectory, though toned down a little here as the coffee bar was smaller and - Jack liked to think - subject to a little more respect as they were still within the confines of the library.

Maggie touched his arm and pointed behind him.

"Isn't that Lucy?"

Jack looked over his shoulder. Lucy was sitting at a table in the far corner with four people none of whom he recognised.

"Must be with her German chums," he offered. "She's not often in here - must be serious!"

Despite that attempt at levity, it was a flat response.

"Right," said Maggie, not missing the tone. "Still besotted, huh?"

Jack picked up his coffee, smiling weakly.

"I don't know," he said, taking a sip. "Maybe; maybe not."

"Not is better," said Maggie, definitively.

"Why?"

"I think you can do better, that's all. She's not right for you, Jack. None of my business of course," she said with a short laugh, "but for what it's worth…"

"I did ask…" Jack smiled.

There was a short pause, before Maggie filled it.

"Fancy stretching your legs to the bookshop before we go back to the grind? Fresh air and all that."

"Sure; why not. And maybe I'll find something to help with 'Moby Dick'."

"Like an abridged version with all the boring bits cut out?"

"Now that would be a slim volume!"

They both rose.

"I just need to pay a visit," said Jack, "see you in there."

He watched Maggie walk away, glanced over to where Lucy was sitting, then made his way to the male toilets in the lobby outside.

Walking through the door, Jack found himself back in the corridor at Twerton's. Jen was waiting for him.

"Whoa!" he said, suddenly rooted to the spot.

"That was quick," she said.

"What? What was quick?"

"You," she smiled. "You've only been gone a couple of minutes."

"Minutes! What? I don't understand."

Jen pointed behind him to where two stools had now appeared.

"Let's sit down," she suggested. "I got these out in case we needed them. Come on, Jack."

Jack turned, took the three steps necessary and planted himself on one of them.

"What just happened?"

"You tell me," Jen said, joining him. "I've no idea what goes on in there, Jack. All I see is you going in and then coming out again. Honestly."

"Really?"

"Really!"

Jack looked back to the door that had now closed behind him.

"I was back at university. Crazy! I mean, I was actually in a tutorial; then left and went to the library, met a friend, had coffee… everything."

"And how did it feel, Jack?"

"Feel?"

"Yes. Real? Weird? You know…"

He paused before answering.

"Real. I mean, it was like I remembered it; just like it happened - except it was happening again. But somehow it was a bit different; almost like I was re-living a memory, you know? On rewind. Doing it all - for real - as if it was the first time all over again, but somehow a part of me knowing it wasn't. Is that how it's supposed to be? Is that what's supposed to happen?"

Her smiled had not left her face since he re-emerged, and remained there now.

"That's your room, Jack. Whatever happens in there is down to you. There's nothing planned or set-up. Don't forget, that room's all about what comes before the book, remember?" She paused, and when he did not answer offered: "Was any of it to do with 'Moby Dick'?"

"The tutorial," Jack nodded, "and the work in the Library. And part of my conversation with Maggie."

"Maggie?"

"A friend. We had coffee. It was all about 'Moby Dick'." He remembered Lucy. "Most of it anyway."

"Well then," said Jen, "isn't that what you'd expect? If the room is about what comes before the book, then isn't it logical that the book will trigger your memories of it, give it context?"

"I guess so," he agreed, "but I'm still struggling. I mean, I go through a door and re-live part of my life and the trigger is a bloody book?"

"Of course! If the possibility is that you've lost more than just a book, doesn't it make sense that you go back and try and find what that was - if the link between whatever it might be that's missing is the book? I know it's hard," she could see him struggling, "but did you learn anything, or see anything that was new for you? Was there anything there that you'd forgotten somehow, or your memory had misplaced?"

He considered for a moment.

"New? I guess so." He was speaking slowly now. "I had a kind of girlfriend. Lucy. I could see how I was wasting my time; beginning to see what a fool I was being."

"And you didn't see that then?"

Jack laughed.

"I was an idiot then; I couldn't see anything!"

"What else?"

"My friend, Maggie. I don't think I ever really recognised what a good friend she was; what her qualities were."

She put her hand on his arm.

"Isn't that a good thing Jack? Aren't there positive things that you can take that will help you now?"

"But how does it help me? Can I go back in there any change things; make things better? Can I go and dump Lucy faster than I actually did - though she probably dumped me, in reality! - or tell Maggie how great she was?"

There was an appeal in Jack's eyes that Jen could not answer, and the smile left her face.

"If it's in the past Jack, how can you change it? The room gives you a chance to see things again, if that's what you choose to do. The only fixed point is you coming into Twerton's looking for your book. You will leave - either with or without a copy of 'Moby Dick'; that's the one option we have got! - but that's it. What you do when you leave, what happens in the future, all that's down to you of course. What you might learn in here, in that room, can make your future better - or worse, I suppose. But the past is the past. You can't go back and dump Lucy or marry Maggie because it didn't happen. That would change everything! Do you see?"

Jack didn't think he did see. He had just looked into some kind of mirror and back at himself, living his life; re-experiencing himself living his life. He didn't know if this was a blessing or a curse. Part of him wished he had never gone into the room; that he had taken the offer to simply leave Twerton's when he had the chance. But, as Jen said, that was now the past. He hadn't left the bookshop; he had gone down into the basement; he had chosen to go through the door. All he could affect was what happened next.

"Let's say that tomorrow, or next week, or next month you meet another incarnation of Maggie. Just as a for instance." Jen's voice had a kind of coaxing lyrical quality to it when she spoke quietly, as she did now. "Let's say you become friends; maybe you get to see in her what you now know you saw in your old friend from university. Would what you have learned today make any difference to you? I mean, would you do anything differently - guessing what you might have done yesterday, if you see where I'm going."

There was a short silence as Jack untangled the hypothesis.

"I suppose I might be inclined to be more appreciative; to be a little more ready to recognise this new Maggie's qualities." He paused. "Is that what you mean?"

"It is. And how do you think your new Maggie would feel about that? How would you feel about that?"

"Okay, I get that. We'd both feel good about it wouldn't we? Inevitably."

"So doesn't that show something?"

"About what?" Jack asked. "About going into the room?"

"About the value to be had from the opportunity to review, if you like. To be given the chance - the remarkable chance! - to go back and learn a lesson. To learn how to do things better almost. That's quite something."

"But," Jack was feeling a little calmer now, and able to enter the debate in a more level-headed way, "if the idea is that I have lost something in addition to my book - and I can't remember when that notion came up, to be honest - then learning something new doesn't quite fit the bill does it?"

Jen smiled again.

"Correct. But only if you assume that what you learned - about appreciating friends, being honest with them, all that - only if you assume that this was new to you. Deep down, don't you know that's the right way to be with people you have an affinity for or care for? Haven't you always known that? If so, then it isn't new is it? That would be something you lost along the way."

Jack wanted to argue, but could not. He knew Jen was right; he knew that telling Maggie that she was great and that he appreciated her qualities was the right thing to do. He knew it now - even without being shown - and probably, in his heart-of-hearts, knew it then too. And now he regretted bitterly, and with a sudden pain, that he had not told her when he had the chance.

"So is that it?"

"'It'?"

"My lesson, if you like. What came before the book? The thing I lost?"

Jen stood up.

"What do you think, Jack? Is there just one thing that was missing? Just one attribute that 'Moby Dick' provides a link for or context to? If so, then 'yes'; that's 'it'." She paused before continuing. "But if there's more… and only you can know that. Don't ask me how you are supposed to know. Maybe you try and look inside yourself somehow; look for things that leave you unsatisfied or unhappy; where you have let yourself down - or let others down. Look for things where you have been unhappy with the outcome, or your part in it. Maybe look for imperfections. Ask those questions."

"How can a lost book provide a context for all those things?"

"You'd be surprised, I suspect. Maybe it won't work for every one of those things - but would you have imagined you might learn (or re-learn) the lesson you just did based on losing it?"

It sounded fanciful. But then so did a bookshop printing and then ageing books in its basement so that they could sell them as second-hand on their store shelves. And a bookshop with a somewhat remarkable assistant (as Jack was now seeing her) and a room at the end of a corridor where magic happened.

He had an idea.

"What about everyone else?"

"What do you mean?" she asked.

"The others who have come down here, and been through that door. What about them? Do they make one trip through the door? Or two? Or three?"

"Some don't make any!" She said it as if his decision to do so was a mark in his favour. "Some just leave straight away - even after they've seen Adam. Most people, Jack, never get down to the basement at all."

"So how do you choose?"

"Who comes down here?" The smile faded. "I can't say; I'm not sure I know. But don't assume that you're somehow special, Jack. We've all lost things along the way. Maybe we should all get the chance you've been given."

There was an empty moment Jack declined to fill.

"Look, you could go in once, twice, a hundred times. It wouldn't take long. You'll still get home today, if that's what you're worried about."

"It's not that," he said, slightly disappointed that the tone had become suddenly prosaic. "It's not that at all. I don't know, I'm just trying to get a sense of... scale, I suppose. I just want to know what to do."

"You could just leave." This after she had allowed the briefest of lapses in the conversation. "Just stand up and walk down the corridor, up the stairs and out the shop. End of. Or not. If you feel that there is more to be gained, re-learned - however you want to phrase it - then go through the door again. If it will make you better, somehow."

"Will you come with me?" It was a question he had been wanting to ask for the last few minutes.

"How can I? This is about you: your past, your life. I wasn't part of it. How can I suddenly appear in your past?! Can you imagine me materialising in your Melville tutorial, or sitting next to you in the library?"

He laughed at the prospect; it was delightful.

"I can't," he said, "but it might have been nice."

She blushed. And then a thought struck him.

"But do you know that?"

"Know what?"

"That you can't go through the door too. Do you know what would happen?"

Jen said nothing.

"You don't, do you? Admit it."

Again silence.

Jack stood up. The door was just three paces away, and the remainder of the corridor stretched far away into the distance. He could hear Luke and Matt's machines humming and working away. Overhead, the occasional footfall from the pavement above. Jen stepped back, giving him the physical space to make the decision.

"You will still be here?"

"I'm not going anywhere Jack, until you decide you want to leave."

FOUR

"Where do you want this?" The voice came from somewhere else in the apartment.

"What is it?" Jack shouted back. He was unpacking crockery in the kitchen.

"Small box; heavy. Books probably."

"In the back room."

Jack finished piling his plates in the cupboard next to the fridge, then walked towards the source of the voice. The small entrance hall was still filled with boxes that, one by one, were finding their way into the correct room for unpacking. He and his brother had been hard at work for a couple of hours now, ever since Rick had helped them unload the contents of the van and relocate Jack's furniture into its new home.

Ben was standing by the desk, upon which cardboard containers of various sizes were piled. It would be a small enough room at the best of times, but with his brother and all the boxes in there, it looked cosier than ever. Unable to see how he could possibly have managed to get a bed and sundry furniture into the room without taking up all the floorspace, the decision Jack had made to make it a study rather than a spare bedroom, seemed vindicated - even if it didn't look large enough for that use right now either.

One or two of the small boxes were open, and Ben was looking to see what they contained. A copy of 'Moby Dick' had found its way onto the desk.

"Heavy stuff", said Ben, weighing two volumes of poetry and three Dickens' novels in his hands, "in more than one sense of the word! I've no idea how you managed to get through this lot. I know I couldn't have."

"Sometimes I'm not sure how I managed it myself, to be honest; all things considered."

Jack never referred to his dyslexia directly. It was part of family folklore that now simply required tangential reference to assert its relevance. Ben knew what his brother meant.

"Yes; some effort, pal. More than I could have."

"Come on, Ben; we're just wired differently, that's all. Could I have done what you did - what you do now? I don't think so."

Ben put the books down and squeezed past his brother. "How many more to go?" he asked rhetorically, as he headed back to the hall.

"Too many probably," said Jack, pausing to consider the amount of space offered him by the bookcase leaning against the far wall. He wasn't convinced that should be its final resting place, but it was clearly going nowhere just now given that moving it would have involved turfing everything else out into the hall again. He picked the 'Moby Dick' from the desk and placed it on the top shelf. It was a symbolic gesture - and one that would also lead, he knew, to the bookcase quickly becoming full and thus cementing its final resting place once and for all. It had seemed small back in the old house - too small for all his books - but here, in this room, it seemed larger than ever, even if it was still inadequate.

He had argued with himself about disposing of some of his books; or of finding somewhere else to store them. Ben had plenty of room in that loft of his; that might have been an option. He knew he would only have to ask.

As he left the room, Ben came towards him, struggling with two more boxes.

"I think there's only one more this size to come in here. The rest look too big to have books in them."

"Great." Jack squeezed against the hall wall to let him past. "Fancy a coffee? If I can find the kettle and mugs and stuff."

Although it was a different room - different shape and size, different purpose - the kitchen offered an echo of his study. Boxes dominated all the available flat surfaces including the floor, with little paths left between them to allow access to critical areas. Someone had suggested to Jack (he couldn't recall who) that he label the boxes well, not only stating where they should go, but what was inside each one. Thus the ones in the study just said "Books", whereas those surrounding him now were much more forthcoming. He found the big box labelled "Appliances" easily enough, and once he had shuffled those containing "Cutlery" and "Saucepans", his mugs surrendered themselves readily from the "China" box. Coffee proved to be more of a problem. Only after he had tried all the remaining boxes Jack remembered he had packed some of the contents of his old kitchen cupboards into two large Ikea bags.

"It's black, I'm afraid," he announced as he returned to the study, a mug in each hand.

Ben had been busy unpacking some of the book boxes. Three of them lay empty at his feet, their former contents now adorning the shelves next to 'Moby Dick'.

"I know they're not where you want them," he said slightly apologetically, as if he had crossed some kind of line, "but I thought it might be a help. You can sort them later."

He stood up, straightening his back a little theatrically as he took the mug Jack offered him.

"You're a star. Thanks."

"Are you back at work tomorrow?"

"Unfortunately, yes. I have lots of time in hand, so getting a day out to help you wasn't an issue. If we'd been going to Aberdeen or somewhere, it might have been a different story."

"If I'd have been moving to Aberdeen it would have been a completely different story!"

Jack appreciated having Ben helping him out, not just because he needed the labour to get his move completed in a day, but because it was another step along the road of their reconciliation. There had been a time - and not so long ago - where they would have hardly spoken, the inevitable fall-out perhaps of one brother stealing another brother's girlfriend. As it turned out, in the end they were both losers, and when Mandy also deserted Ben, it was the cue for them to cease hostilities.

"Is work really hard right now?" Jack asked. "I mean, that's the impression I get."

Ben looked up from his coffee having been studying the ripples on its surface.

"Pretty much. We've one or two difficult cases, you know? And I'm not sure one of them is going to end well - either for those involved or for yours truly."

"Why's that?"

"Oh, I don't know. If someone wanted to dig around and check process, if someone wanted to 'find' something in terms of the way the case has been handled, then I doubt it would be difficult."

"Do people do that? I mean, want to dig up dirt on their colleagues?"

Ben smiled ironically.

"Some do, unfortunately. To justify their existence.' He paused. "I can see it coming that's all."

Jack placed a hand on his brother's shoulder.

"Said I couldn't do what you do. All that pressure. And real responsibility."

"Thanks. But I doubt I'd be very good at much else."

Jack smiled and put his mug down on the desk.

"I'll get the biscuits," he said, and walked out of the room.

Outside, Jen was waiting for him in the corridor. Jack paused, thrown by the sudden transfer almost as much as he had been before. He tried to adjust to the subdued lighting. Instinctively he looked behind him to where the door was, where the back bedroom had been, but there was just the plain door he had walked through a few moments earlier, now swinging slowly closed. He waited for it, waited for the 'click' of the latch, then turned back to Jen.

"Was it Maggie again?" she asked.

"Sorry?"

"In the room. Were you back at university with Maggie?"

Jack paused long enough to regain the vacant stool opposite Jen.

"No. My brother, Ben. I was moving house. Funny how you can remember something as if it was yesterday."

"Were you remembering it, Jack? Was that how it felt? Or were you truly there, living it?"

"Or re-living it, surely... I suppose it felt real enough," he confessed, "but it wasn't like the last time somehow. It was as if I was going through the motions but with a little bit extra."

"Extra?" Her forehead furrowed slightly. It was not an unattractive look.

"I don't know. It was almost as if I was able to appreciate Ben just a little bit more than I had in the past. And not just for helping me move house."

"And did you tell him?"

"Tell him what?"

"That you appreciated him? Remember, that's exactly what you didn't do with Maggie."

"Yes, I'm pretty sure I did." He tried to scan his memory. "I made him coffee - and even gave him biscuits!"

"Well then...!"

There was a short silence that Jack instinctively knew Jen was not going to fill unless she absolutely had to. He waited. It was her turn he had decided.

"What happened?" Giving in, she tried to move him along.

"About Mandy?"

"Who's Mandy?'

They were now at cross purposes. Jack had realised too late that she was asking about the scene he had just played out; for some reason, he had immediately focused on Mandy. She had, after all, been instrumental in shaping his recent relationship with Ben - not to mention his own view on women! - and as such, innocently provided the remote backdrop against which his house move had taken place. Having had the thought, Jack smiled at the absurd notion of Mandy and innocence being natural bedfellows.

"Mandy? She was my girlfriend once. And Ben's. It was complicated."

"But before you moved house?"

Jack nodded.

"So how was it complicated? Isn't that a word people use by default when they mean something else - like emotional, personal - or when they don't want to talk about something?"

"You've been doing this too long," Jack said with a laugh. "You're far too good at it."

Jen laughed lightly now. "Not really. I mean, not really very long and not really very good. I've only been here a few weeks, I guess."

"Then you're a natural." Jack paused. "You want me to tell you about Mandy?"

"Not necessarily."

"I know," interrupted Jack before she could conclude, "this is all about me; my journey, my experiences. I can make as much or little of it as I want; distil, replay, reevaluate as I choose." She smiled at this and he knew he had stolen from her script. "Do I want to talk about Mandy; that's the real question isn't it?"

"And do you?"

He thought for a moment. Mandy was, he knew, an unexorcised ghost - and he knew that sitting here with Jen for a few minutes would be insufficient to cease her haunting. But if this vignette was about his relationship with Ben, then Mandy was there, lurking in the historical shadows.

"Not that there's much to tell," he bluffed.

"Even if it's 'complicated'?" Playfulness was evident in her voice.

"She was my girlfriend for a few months. We got on pretty well. I thought it was serious."

"Was she like Lucy?"

Unconscious that he had been looking vacantly along the corridor as he spoke, Jen's question surprised him. He looked back at her.

"No, of course not." He replayed his answer internally. "Well, maybe a little; more than I'd like to admit perhaps."

"Because of lessons not learned?"

"Because I'm a man!"

She laughed at his joke. It was the response he had been hoping for.

"They were alike in that she was pretty, outgoing - vivacious, you might say. I met her in a bar near work one evening. We hit it off. I thought it was karma." He adjusted. "Maybe I thought it was karma. Anyway, after a few weeks we were practically living together. The horizons about which we spoke began to move off into the distance; you know, the way you start out by talking about tomorrow or the next weekend, and then you're talking about next month, and then... But maybe most of those conversations were just in my head. One Saturday we went to a party. We'd been going out for about three months by then. Ben was there."

Jack allowed the story to trail away.

"And after that?"

"The rest - as they - say is history." He paused. "Whatever I thought I had, Ben had in spades. I was always the slightly cheaper version of my elder brother. 'Not quite' in all sorts of ways. Not quite as tall, as handsome, as successful, as solvent, as charismatic... Whatever Mandy saw in me she saw multiplied in Ben. Perhaps I should have been flattered that it was him she left me for - but that's difficult to see now, so it would have been impossible then!"

Jen shifted slightly on her stool, but remained fixed on him.

"And you fell out with Ben?"

"Of course. Big time. We never really argued. Wasn't our style. So when this one broke it was the mother of all arguments! They tried to keep it secret for a while. This was Mandy's idea I discovered later. 'Playing both ends against the middle' was how Ben came to describe it. He and I stopped talking. Avoided each other in as spiteful a way as we could manage. It wasn't healthy. About two months later Mandy 'traded up' again; another of Ben's phrases! It took he and I a while to resume normal relations once hostilities had ceased."

"And by the time of your move?"

"Oh, that was maybe six months later. At least. We were back on an even keel by then. Maybe better than that."

Jen furrowed again; Jack smiled.

"I mean" he said, answering her unspoken question, "that we were probably closer than before. Wounded soldiers, if you like. We could compare scars; we now had a common enemy, after all."

"Mandy," she seemed to hesitate for a fraction, at least to Jack, "or all women?"

"Honestly?"

"Honestly."

"All women I suppose. At least for a short while. Not long after Ben helped me move, one of his cases (he's a Social Worker, by the way) went badly and ended up in court. It wasn't Ben's fault, you understand, but he went through the mill for a while. That aged him. But it also allowed him to find Anne. She was one of his colleagues. Helped him through the court case; gave him a shoulder to lean on. They grew close, quickly."

"More common enemies?" Jen suggested.

"You could say that! But she's great; good for him. Let's say they make a better couple than he did with Mandy. Than anyone could with Mandy, I suspect!"

There was a still pause. Jen looked beyond Jack for a moment, and then down at her hands now resting in her lap. Thinking about Mandy was now easy for Jack. All the anger and emotion had long since dissipated, replaced by something stronger. He wondered why Jen had asked him how totally encapsulating his definition of the female enemy had become. He allowed his mind to begin wandering.

"And when you moved house." Jen brought him back. "How far 'post-Mandy' was that?"

"I don't know. Nearly three years, I suppose; maybe a bit more. I'd been wanting to freshen things up, if you like. Not exactly a clean start - I wasn't in that bad a shape! - but it was time to do something new. I changed jobs; that came first. And then moving house. It was, euphemistically speaking, 'an interesting year' or so!"

Jack could see a question forming in Jen's mind. He wondered if he hadn't been clear about something, or had managed to confuse her.

"What is it?"

She smiled.

"You're getting good at this too!" She allowed a pause. "I was just wondering when you lost your book, 'Moby Dick ."

"When?"

"Well, you clearly had it when your brother helped you move, and you clearly didn't have it when you came in here today."

"Correct."

"And I'm guessing that you didn't lose it from that small back bedroom bookcase. In a way, how could you?"

"Correct again! To be honest, I don't think it ever moved from where Ben put it as we were unpacking. I meant to reorganise my books but didn't manage it."

"Because?"

"Inertia, mainly. One of those things you never get round to... And then my job changed again, and I had to pack up and move once more."

"To where you are now?"

"There was one stop in between - I mean, I've lived in a couple of places since then. But in a way, isn't that the key question? The 'when' of losing it. If I knew that, I'd have something to go on."

As if in response, Jen stretched her legs and then stood up.

"Does it matter?" she asked. "Exactly when you lost your book, I mean. If you knew, would it change anything?"

"Change anything? Probably not - but it would just be nice to pin it down. Of course, if I found out that one of my friends nicked it, that might lead to something else..." He laughed to show her he wasn't serious.

"In a way you can never know, I suppose." She seemed to be theorising as much for her own sake as his. "When is something lost, exactly? Is it when you first notice you don't have it any more? In this case, you only lost your book a couple of days ago when you realised it wasn't there. The alternative is that it becomes lost when it's not where it is supposed to be - whether you realise it or not. What if - for argument's sake - Ben actually removed 'Moby Dick' from your bookcase before he left that day? He might have fancied a read. You would have assumed that the book remained where he had unpacked it, wouldn't you? But if he had taken it, was it then lost?"

"Ben would never want to read 'Moby Dick'!", said Jack, focussing on the concrete.

"But you can see what I'm getting at?"

"I think so."

"What is real to us, how we interpret the world - it's very important, individual. Often I suspect we don't think about things deeply enough. We say 'I've lost my book' without truly trying to understand what we mean."

Jack looked at her with renewed interest.

"Sounds like there's a little more Jen in there than Twerton's," he suggested.

She blushed a little and straightened, smiling purposefully at him.

"So what now?"

Involuntarily, Jack glanced back towards the closed door.

"Is it the same question as before?"

"Of course," she said, touching his arm. He was also standing now. "To leave or not. To accept that we don't have your book in the format you'd want it, that you have nothing further to learn, and that there's nothing else to be gained down here." She moved slightly closer to the wall to give him a fuller view along the corridor and towards the exit. "Your choice."

"Will I find my book?" He asked; then clarified, "Or rather, find out when I lost it?"

She shook her head.

"I've no idea, Jack. Again, does it matter?"

He had already decided to go back through the door at least one more time, of course. His experience thus far had been fascinating, hypnotic. It was - from what he could recall - almost addictive. But splitting the living from the re-living of each scene was impossible. Indeed, he couldn't even explain the relationship between his past and present - if indeed he was still 'in the present' as soon as he walked through the door.

Adam, Matt and Luke - and Twerton's as a whole - had stretched his comprehension already. If it had not been for Jen, he suspected that he would have bolted long ago, and damned himself for a lunatic. But however he chose to explain it, there was something here to be uncovered; something about himself. That was worth something - and who knew how valuable the next experience might be?

He put his hand on the doorknob.

"Maybe at least one more - just to see how it goes..."

FIVE

Apart from a thin spear of light coming through the crack in the not quite closed door in front of him, he was suddenly in darkness. From somewhere else Jack could feel as much as hear the low thud of a heavy bass line; its source was beyond the door and undoubtedly through the floor. So he was upstairs, somewhere. He turned his head slowly as his eyes became used to the black, attempting to recognise where he was.

It was a relatively small room. Against one wall, the wall behind him, a narrow single bed had been squeezed in along with what appeared to be a set of drawers. To his side, he could make out some kind of table, and then ahead shelving of some description. He wanted it to be familiar - he knew that it should be familiar - but he was unable to place it, unable to locate himself adequately. He measured the scale of the room by calculating the effect any movement on his part would have. Two steps backwards and he could sit on the bed; one to the right, and he could place his hands on the flat surface of the table; two steps forwards and he would have been able to examine the contents of the shelves. From where he stood he could make out the tell-tale rectangles of books, but none of the words on their spines.

He should know where he was.

Suddenly he felt a presence outside the room, saw a shadow fall momentarily across the shaft of light, and then the door began to open. Jack wanted to reexamine the room as the new light began to encroach, but was unable to take his eyes from a virtual spot a little above where the light switch now appeared - and where he assumed there would soon be a face. And even though his gaze remain fixed on that one spot, peripherally he took in the colours of the wall - a kind of soft peach - and the vague frames of the pictures that adorned them. Neither were familiar. Yes, it was dark, but Jack was convinced that if he had been in that room before, he would have registered the colour. It was the kind of navigational aid that one took for granted, and one which rarely failed him.

He felt panic beginning to rise from somewhere deep within him. And he suddenly realised that here, in this presence, in this new here-and-now, he was still conscious of the corridor, Jen, Twerton's. He was shocked almost to the beginning of trauma to be acutely conscious of that other reality - and conscious of it in a real, tangible, intellectual way. He felt himself to be in two places at the same time, split between two worlds almost. Previously, when he had returned to university, the library, Maggie, even Ben to some extent - he had returned wholly, in blissful ignorance of his re-living past moments and the corridor he had left behind.

But this was very, very different.

"Jack?"

He heard her voice a split second before he saw her. Like the room, it was a voice he failed to recognise. And when he saw her as she tentatively entered, it proved to be a face with which he was totally unfamiliar.

"Jack!" she said, her voice a mixture of gentle admonition and relief. It was a soft and warm sound, full of a depth that was immediately seductive; a voice that would have been at home on the radio, purring to listeners in the small hours of the morning, introducing lazy jazz classics to a small but dedicated following. And it was a face that would have fitted that profile too. Slim and elegant, with perfectly proportioned features, and long hair that, even in this half-light, was immediately and impossibly blonde.

"There you are," she said, taking a confident step into the room, evidently relieved to have found him there. Her voice broke slightly. "What's wrong, darling?"

He had stepped backwards fractionally as she - this woman who was a complete stranger to him - approached him so knowingly. But Jack knew that it was not this movement that had prompted her question as she stopped still. It was the fact that he was crying. He moved his left hand up to his face and felt the damp stream as it trickled down his cheeks. When he had started crying? And how had he not managed to realise it until she had spoken?

He stepped backwards again, as much to try and retreat from his tears, as if they were located in a fixed part of the room. In her reaction, he could see that she was concerned that his movement was as a result of her presence. Jack's calves hit the side of the bed and he allowed himself to sit down. His hand went to his trouser pocket to retrieve his handkerchief and then back to his face. Once he seemed rested, she moved further into the room and then sat down beside him. Her right hand rested on his knee.

"What's the matter? Has something upset you?"

It was self-evident that something obviously had, so he chose not to answer her question in binary terms. It would have been easier to do so, to simply say 'yes' - especially in his current emotional state - but such a response was pointless. In any event, it was not her question that was uppermost in his mind. What had upset him; that was the issue at hand.

She squeezed his leg gently.

"Have I done something wrong?"

"No," he said, quickly, instinctively. In doing so, he felt himself accepting her presence, his situation, the room, all in one fell swoop. How could he now ask where he was, or who she was? Jack put his hankie back in his pocket. He tried to find a source for his sudden unhappiness, an unhappiness intimately related with a life he did not know he had. He closed his eyes for a moment, trying to block out the physical reality of the room in which he sat and the woman alongside him who was now holding his hand.

"Why am I upset?" he echoed, trying the question out for himself. "I suppose I am suddenly sad; that must be it."

She tried a smile.

"What is there to be sad about, Jack?"

Hearing her say his name rooted him even more solidly into this present. She was leaning against him slightly now, and he could feel her warmth through his jumper, and smell her perfume as it gently assailed him. He turned his head slightly to look at her, something he had avoided ever since she had entered the room. He knew again that he did not know her - and that she was beautiful.

"I feel," he began hesitantly, now looking away from her towards the shelves across the room, uncertain as to the words that would be forthcoming from this new Jack he seemed not to know, "as if I have suddenly found something - but that I know I am going to lose it."

The words fell from Jack's mouth without any premeditation, and he tried to listen to them, to weigh and validate them, in the same way that this woman beside him must have done. They were strange words, and their inaccuracy bothered him. He had limited alternatives.

"Or that I've lost something. And if I have, it's as if I've only just realised it." He felt her stiffen at these words. Was that a good or bad thing? "But it may also be that I've found something, I think. Maybe I'm crying because I'm happy. Maybe I'm not sad at all..."

His sentence trailed away into the darkness. He tried to focus on the two rows of books facing him across the other side of the room. What were they?

"Jack, let's not have to go through all this again." The purr had gone from her voice, and she reminded him of someone from his distant past; a woman in authority, perhaps an old teacher, or his mother. "I thought we had been making such progress. The Doctor was beginning to speak more positively. Please let's not go backwards."

"Back to what?"

She removed her hand from his knee and stood up.

"Back to what?" Her face hardened. "Back to what? Back to all your nonsense about being lost, about not knowing where you were. How do you think that makes me feel, Jack? What do you think that does to me? Or our family?"

He played with the notion of family for a moment, but said nothing. He had no family. Was that what was missing - either in this present or in the other, more real present? And when was this present? How far into the future? Or was it just some kind of projection?

"Are you lost Jack, really? When you have me, your friends, all this?" Her voice tried to encompass something - everything - both seen and unseen, and yet Jack was unable to place it, quantify or qualify it. As she glanced around the room, her gaze rested on the shelves. "You have been losing things for years, Jack. Even if you don't realise it. What did it start with? I can't bring myself to say it - that bloody book! But then again and again, with other things. The Doctor said it had gradually brought pressure to bear. That you were forcing yourself to - I don't know - 'indulge' somehow. He said you were beginning to lose yourself. I thought things were getting better, Jack, but evidently not."

He sensed that she was waiting for something from him to defuse the tension, to ease her fears, to reassure her that he was, in fact, perfectly ok. But how could he when he didn't even know who she was, or where he was? He didn't even know - he suddenly realised - who he was, or who he was supposed to be.

Hearing nothing but Jack's silence, she suddenly turned and rushed from the room.

What should he do now? What could he do now? If he did nothing, if he just sat there and waited, spent the time trying to figure out something, what benefit would that bring him? He would simply be making something up, constructing a story line to fit a situation that was impossible on so many levels. Jack knew that he had to act, and that his first act could only be to leave the room. He stood up, paused, glanced vaguely at the bookshelf and then walked through the door.

Jen stood up when she saw him.

"What's the matter? Has something upset you?"

Jack moved his hand to his face once more, knowing what he would find. Again his hand went to his trouser pocket to retrieve his handkerchief and then back to his face. He paused, waiting for the finality of the 'click' of the closing door before moving to the stool that had previously been his. He sat down.

"Crying, right?"

It wasn't really a question, more a rhetorical statement. He expected no response - but Jen moved her stool closer to his, then sat herself and placed her hand on his knee. Jack stared at the hand.

Jen waited. When he said nothing, when he simply continued to stare at her hand, she gave a small squeeze.

Jack looked up at her.

"I think I may be done," he said; and even though his statement was perfectly vague, it had the effect of making Jen remove her hand. She sat slightly more upright.

"What happened, Jack? Where were you?"

Jen's was not a radio voice - unlike the woman in the darkened room - but it had its place. Jack had always thought that all voices had their place, however humble. Even his own. For a fraction of a second he tried to place it, to transport it to a new home, a new environment, an ideal situation. In Jen's case, the quality of her voice was not actually in the sound she made (no sleazy, late-night jazz here!), but in its cadence and meaning. The woman in the room could have made buying a railway ticket sexy and desirable, but that wasn't Jen's style.

"Where was I? I've no idea. It was somewhere I didn't know, or didn't recognise. A room. It was just a room in the dark."

She looked concerned.

"And you don't know where it was?"

He shook his head.

"I think it was supposed to be somewhere I lived; I'm not sure. It was as if I was expected to be familiar with it, those surroundings. And I had no sense at all that I might have been some kind of visitor."

"Who expected you to be familiar with it, Jack? If you didn't know it, who did?"

Jack paused to put his handkerchief away. He noticed a small table now beside the stools, and on it was a pitcher of water and two glasses. He started to fill a glass.

"A woman," he said as he poured, "though I've no idea who she was. She clearly knew me. We were" - he hesitated over the words - "a couple."

"But not Lucy or Mandy? Or Maggie?"

"No. I'd never seen her before."

"What was she like, this woman?"

"I don't know. Blonde, pretty - very pretty. She had a voice like honey; that was the first thing I think I noticed. Thinking about it, in many ways she was an amalgam; bits of all three of those and more. And she cared for me, that was obvious. It was also obvious that I had been - difficult."

Jen frowned, and Jack saw another echo.

"How so?"

"I get the impression that I hadn't been well."

"And you've never been ill?"

"Of course - but not mentally. That was a new thing for me, a new history if you like. So, a bit like the room, the woman, it was something I simply didn't recognise." He paused. "And you know the scariest bit?" She shook her head. "It was as if I was looking into the future rather than re-living my past. How else is what I saw possible?"

"And was that why you were crying: because you thought you were staring into your future?"

"Staring into the abyss!" He deliberately tried to sound melodramatic, as if doing so would help them to lighten a mood that had become quickly sombre.

"So not a future you want then?" she replied, picking up on his tone and smiling.

"You might say that - in spite of the perfect blonde companion!"

He drained his glass.

"There is one question," he resumed, slowly. "I think the only question I really need to ask."

"Which is?"

"If what I saw really was my future. I mean, is it inevitable that I will end up in that room, with that woman? Will I become ill, unstable? If so…"

Jen placed her hand on his arm briefly and then withdrew it.

"People - in my experience - rarely see into the real future. At least here. I mean, how can they? That's what I'd ask. Of course, we'd all like to be able to see it. On one level anyway. I would. But the future is always changeable; that's what Mr Twerton says. It's one of the reasons he places so much emphasis on looking back at the past. Doing so allows you to shape tomorrow, the next day, the next month. It gives you choices."

"So that wasn't me in that room then?"

"I think it obviously was, Jack. But maybe it was just one version of the future, who knows? Perhaps there's a path you could take that would lead you there."

"It was a warning then?"

"I wouldn't describe it like that personally, but I know what you mean."

"But I don't see how it helps me," Jack said. "There was nothing concrete to help me out. I was just in a room I didn't recognise, crying. That was it."

"And why were you crying?"

"That's what she asked me."

"And?"

He tried to remember; tried to reflect backwards, to overlay this present with that future present; to see where there were connections. And then he found one.

"I told her that I was crying because I was sad; because I had lost something."

"And she said?"

"She said that I was always losing things. She talked about 'that bloody book'. I remember that. She said that's where it started." He paused to allow Jen to interrupt, but she did not. "Isn't that the link, Jen?"

"Sounds too much like a coincidence to be anything else..."

"But not enough to make me cry!" Jack said, suddenly animated. "Not enough for that. Not enough to make me cry here and now." He took a breath. "It's not about the book, not really. Is it?"

They both allowed a silence to fall. In Jack's case the silence represented less a dawning realisation, but rather recognition of something he had known all along - or at least been aware of. It had been about the book of course, at least when he arrived, but as soon as Jen took control and brought him downstairs, then the focus changed. If there was a pivot point, a fulcrum where the balance changed, then surely that was it - and if so, her role was surely in focus too.

"Does it matter?"

"Does what matter, Jack?"

"The book. 'Moby Dick'. Does it matter whether I find it, or that I lost it in the first place?"

"I can't answer that."

"Because you can't or because you don't know the answer?"

Jen looked suddenly troubled.

"Both. And neither. In a way I don't know if I can't or if I don't know; does that make sense? I mean, I could guess - but that would just be me guessing. It wouldn't have the same kind of -

what should I say? - 'authority' as anything Adam or Matt or Luke might say. 'Unofficial', if you like. And I don't want to lead you astray, or lay false trails; anything like that..."

It was inadequate and unhelpful; at least that was the impression that Jack gave. He looked at her, simply not knowing what to do next. As he did so, he tried to imagine the picture he presented, how he must appear to Jen. If he was indeed 'done', as he said, then surely there was nothing left to do, no remnants to be tidied away. And yet the feeling that he wasn't finished, that there had to be some kind of closure, was suddenly undeniable and irrepressible. And then a thought struck him.

"How long did you say you had been working here?"

She shifted a little on the stool.

"Why?"

"I'm curious, that's all. Just trying to get a sense of that 'authority', I suppose."

"A few weeks." Her reply came slowly and cautiously. Jack had only seen her calm and confident, sure of herself, but now she appeared nervous.

"And how many people have you helped? People like me?"

"A few. Not too many. Does it matter?"

"And when will you stop, Jen? At what point do you call it a day, go back to your studies full-time and stop coming down here?"

"Jack," her voice was less confident now, "this isn't about me; it's about you. I'm just trying to help."

"I know that; really." Jack leant forward and placed his hand on her arm. 'My turn', he thought. "I'm not questioning that, not at all. I was just wondering..."

"Wondering what?"

The idea had occurred to him that perhaps Jen was not that different to him. Here she was, repeating her own scenarios, helping people out. It was not too great a leap from there to an assumption that she would stop when she had found what she was looking for. Indeed, if that was anywhere near the truth, then he was potentially helping her as much as she was helping him. He thought about the notebook she carried with her and that now lay beside her on the small table. Jack had assumed that she had been making notes about him, but what if she were working other things out for herself?

"I suppose I was wondering what you needed. Don't we all need something? Aren't we all searching for something? I started out with a lost book I wanted to replace, and now it seems I may be trying to both find myself in my past and locate myself in my future. The question keeps changing; at least for me. Now 'what next?' seems so much more important. I hadn't walked in here this morning thinking 'what next?'..."

"And isn't that a good thing? Progress?" She tried to re-establish their default relationship. Jack could see that. But now he'd had the idea of her being, in a profound sense, no different to him at all - well, that changed everything.

"If it is, then it's actually nothing to cry about, is it?" he offered.

"Exactly!" She smiled, then leant forward to the table and started to fill the second glass with water.

"I guess," Jack said, trying to choose his words carefully, "that I was simply wondering what 'progress' looked like to you. I mean, if I've learned something today, that's great; but you've seen a few people like me, haven't you? Do those experiences help you to learn something? To move forwards somehow?"

She took a sip of her water and then replaced the glass on the table.

"Sometimes - but not often. I've seen how people react, watched them. I've seen their struggles and dilemmas. I've seen people just walk out of the shop, or refuse to extend their search down here. Some have left after seeing Adam, or Matt and Luke. Some have just given up. One or two make it through the last door and nothing happens to them. Those people tend to leave then, assuming that we're just a con, after something."

"And people like me? Is my reaction typical?"

When she frowned again, Jack realised that there were parts of Jen that contributed to the amalgam of the blonde woman in the room. He didn't need to be surprised.

"No, I wouldn't say so." She was weighing her words; he could see that. "If anything you have been very - receptive."

"Odd word."

"Yes, sorry; but you know what I mean." She carried on, serious, but her smile not far away. "When you came into the shop, I had a sense that we might end up down here; but my instinct told me that it might be a waste of time, a failure. Obviously that's not how I see it now."

"Me neither," he said, reassuringly, wondering if the 'waste of time' was referring to him or herself. "In fact, thinking about it, I reckon I need to go back through the door one final time. Now I have a better sense of things. And no tears this time."

When he stood, Jen accompanied him to the door. He paused, grasping the handle.

"Would you do me a favour?" he asked.

"Of course."

"Would you given me a hug - just to wish me luck, if you like. I'd like to thank you for helping me out too, but don't really know how."

She smiled broadly and walked up to him, placing her arms around him, her head towards his shoulder. Then, as soon as he had his free arm about her waist, Jack tightened his grip, pulled upon the door, and flung them both through it.

SIX

It was beyond dark. It was profoundly empty. Jen's brief struggle subsided as soon as the door closed behind them and they could see nothing. More than that, they could feel nothing; there was no sense of any kind of physicality at all. No walls, no boundaries. For a split second Jack wondered what they were standing on - or if they were standing at all! - and shifted his weight from one foot to the other to test the invisible floor.

He had expected - something. A room, probably. He had assumed that they would have been placed in a situation that was somehow relevant. Jack knew that it could not be from the past as he and Jen did not share a past; at least, not one of which he was aware. His action had been predicated on taking a step once again into the future; a projection that might be more illuminating - or at least different! - from the room with the blonde woman. Or if not that, it would be an insight that might be of more relevance to Jen, for he had manage to convince himself that he and she were basically not different, each searching for some kind of answer. And he had been serious with himself about helping her.

"Jack, what have you done?!" There was more than a little fear in the timbre of her voice.

"I thought I'd try and help you," he said, somewhat lamely.

"But this isn't how it's supposed to work for me. I'm not supposed to go through the door…"

She loosened her grip but did not let go altogether.

"Perhaps we should just go back," Jack suggested, now a little embarrassed that his plan had immediately - and disturbingly - backfired.

"We can't," she said without moving. "Something has to happen first."

"Happen?" he echoed, then looked over his shoulder expecting to see the door through which they had come, but finding only nothingness. How was that possible? They had taken two, maybe three steps at most.

Jack looked ahead, into what should have been a room; something. It was as if they had materialised in the greatest, deepest fog known to man. Visibility was perhaps a few feet at best, though divorced from any sense of true presence, it was impossible to judge even that. Feeling Jen at his side was the only thing that even started to suggest any kind of reality at all.

"Perhaps it's thinking," she suggested nervously.

"'Thinking'? What's thinking?"

"I don't know. The room. Something. Maybe it doesn't quite know what to do, what to present. We've confused it. One person, that's the norm; and that's what it relates to, responds to. But now there are two of us..."

She allowed the phrase to fade into the fog. Jack tried to associate some kind of sentience with an inanimate room, but was failing. He turned to say something to her when pressure on his arm stopped him. Jen was staring intently ahead.

Jack followed her gaze. In front of them, slowly and with an almost imperceptible vagueness, the density of the fog appeared to be changing; and in the bland greyness that faced them, shades of colour appeared to be materialising. Simultaneously, he had a sense of breeze, movement.

They watched. Shapes of grey and green began to emerge, slowly solidifying, taking form. Jack looked down at his feet. They appeared to be standing on some kind of path, the edges of the paving slabs beginning to become clear. The green nearby became darker but remained blurred. It was grass. Slightly further head, the form of a bush. The greys solidified further and were complimented by other colours; russet, some off white rectangles. A building - a large building - was manifesting before their eyes. They were outside.

"It's the library," Jen whispered, as if she were afraid that her voice might disturb the illusion.

"The library?"

"At the university. Can't you see?"

Jack leant forwards fractionally, as if doing so would make all the difference.

"It looks like it, yes. But there are elements I don't recognise; those bits over there, or the entrance doors."

"The things that are still indistinct?"

"Exactly."

Jen let go of his arm but not his hand. She moved her right foot forwards, as if to test the integrity of the path they were now clearly standing on. Ahead of them, the library building continued to distinguish itself from the fog - or at least most of it. It looked like a strange semi-abstract painting with picture-perfect detail alongside loose impressionistic brush strokes. It was both real and unreal.

"The things that are indistinct..." she began again.

"Yes."

"I bet those are things that have changed since you were here."

"Really?"

"The doors were replaced about three years ago. And they remodelled the windows in the east wing at the same time. They're not clear, are they?"

"Not at all. But most of the rest of it is."

"Those are the things that haven't changed. What is the same today - when I'm here, in my time - as it was when you were here, those elements are rendered perfectly aren't they? The walls - or most of the walls - the footpath, the steps. We don't have a shared history, Jack, not in the sense of living coexistent lives in the same sphere at the same time, but we do have a shared sense of place. Maybe that's what this is. Maybe that's why we're here."

Jack tried to absorb what she was saying. There was a certain logic to it, of course. He ignored the surreal; he had too. If he had been challenging the surreal, then he wouldn't have made it beyond Adam's room - maybe not even that far. He was normally a profoundly logical kind of person (or at least that was how he saw himself), and yet somehow he had been able to suspend belief from almost the instant he entered Twerton's. Because of that, why should he not now openly engage with the diorama that was now before him? It was, after all, not a little liberating.

"And the greens? Why are they not more distinct? There has always been grass there - and that big tree near the entrance, I remember that."

"But they're not constant, are they Jack? They grow, get cut; bud, shed leaves. Perhaps in a specific instant for a specific life they can be rendered perfectly, but when we're sharing…There is no true form."

Jack tried to recall his first regression, when he went back to the library and met Maggie. Nothing was blurred then, not that he could recall. And he was sure he would have noticed. It supported Jen's theory.

But then was that Jen's theory, he suddenly found himself asking. What if all this were just part of the play, the act. What if he had been led inexorably and inevitably to grab her and pull her into the room? What if she had been dissembling then and was dissembling now? What if she always went into the room?

"What do we do now?" Jack asked. If this were not unusual for her, if this were part of the plan, then she would know.

"I guess," she said - though without any conviction Jack could discern - "I guess we should move. Somewhere. We can't just stand here. Perhaps we're supposed to go inside."

She took a step forwards before Jack stopped her by tightening the grip on her hand.

"Have you noticed?" he said, cryptically. "There are no people."

Jen looked around - a full three hundred and sixty degrees this time.

"No. But how can there be, Jack? We have no shared contemporaries."

"Then what," he said, pointing towards the library steps with his free hand, "are those?"

Ahead of them, vague shadows appeared to now be moving to and fro, a flow of current centring on the library doors, like a chain of ants viewed through misted glass.

"Ghosts."

"Ghosts?!"

"Echoes, Jack. Echoes from your past, from mine. Perhaps one of them might even be Maggie. After all, how can they be drawn perfectly? Just like the grass, the tree." She paused. "In fact, I suspect that the shadows I see are different from the ones you see. There! Coming out of the library now. You can just make out a lurid pink colour moving. Do you see that?"

Jack leant forward again. Took a single step. He could see no pink.

"Nothing. Some blue and a flash of red, but no pink."

"I see no red, Jack…"

"So that's it then," he said, offering closure to the debate. He moved a single step forwards. "Shall we?"

They moved towards the library steps silently and without hurry, looking at the shadows, relating to the distinct and guessing at the indistinct. As they reached the bottom step, Jack felt a bump on his shoulder.

"Sorry," he said, thinking he had knocked into Jen.

"What?" she said.

Jack had assumed that she was still close beside him, but even though they were still holding hands, there was a meaningful gap between them.

"I thought I bumped you."

"No, not me."

And then Jack felt something brush his other shoulder.

"It's the shadows. They're bumping into us."

"Or we're bumping into them," Jen offered. "And whose are you bumping into?"

"Whose?"

"Yours or mine? What does logic dictate?"

From the look on her face, Jack could see that she wasn't sure. He thought for a second.

"Must be our own, surely. In any event, I think we should try and avoid them, don't you?"

They mounted the steps cautiously, and in swerving to minimise contact with the nebulous shapes they were forced to loosen their hands. For a moment, the main entrance lobby of the library seemed less busy, more calm. Jen took a step towards him then froze.

"Look out, Jack!"

Suddenly, from each wing of the library that radiated out from the central foyer, dozens of shadows came rushing towards them in a coordinated wave. There was no way they could be avoided, and Jack had no time to devise any kind of plan.

"Try and get to the far wall," he said quickly - but as the mass enveloped them, Jen began to become slightly blurred herself, her very real image fogged by the movement in front of her. It was light trying to discern her through frosted glass.

Jack felt himself propelled sideways. With the mass of movement around them came a low hum of sound. He guessed it was chatter; talking that was also defused by the lack of definition. For a second he thought he could make out the muffled sound of a bell. Unable to now see Jen, he focussed on his nearest escape route, a small corridor near the main check-out desks. He tried to move purposefully towards it, just as one particularly solid contact nearly knocked him over. Regaining his balance, he moved forwards again. In five strides he was at the desk, and moments later had made it into the corridor.

It was quiet here. He looked back into the lobby. The throng was still there, moving inexorably towards the exit, but he couldn't see Jen. He wondered if she had managed to find sanctuary somewhere. As he resigned himself to sit it out and wait for the tumult to subside, he heard movement somewhere in the corridor behind him. It was not loud, but it was distinct and clear. Perhaps Jen had managed to find her way to his side of the building after all.

Seeing no shadows ahead of him, Jack began to walk along the corridor. There were various rooms off to either side, and through their open doors he could see desks strewn with papers, computer screens, mugs with steam rising from them. This was clearly where the library administration people worked; the desks looked recently abandoned. He was about to go into one of the rooms when he heard the sound of movement again; it was close enough.

Still hoping to find Jen, he tried to use the sound as a homing beacon. It was coming from one of the rooms at the far end of the corridor, beyond where he could now see it shifted to the right. Was it possible that it doubled back on itself or had a second entrance and one that Jen had managed to find? He quickened his pace a little. Just as he turned the corner and had begun to form her name on his lips, he stopped.

Ahead of him was a long bright room; it was a room in which the corridor morphed and terminated. At the far end of the room, some thirty feet from where he now stood, a single desk - and behind the desk, a man sat.

"Hello Jack."

Even at this range, Jack could see that the man was old - old, yet somehow familiar. His hair, thinning yet still allowed to grow long, collar length, was white, and his small, unfashionable moustache of slightly darker grey turned upwards slightly at the ends, driven by the man's smile. The voice was old too; gravelly from either decades of use, or ruined by smoking. Instinctively, Jack tried to find the scent of tobacco in the air, but all he could smell was the neutrality of the library offices. No tobacco, no books.

"Sorry about that," the man said. He motioned to the empty chair on Jack's side of the desk.

"About what?"

"The fire alarm." So Jack had heard a bell. "It was necessary to find a way to separate you and Jennifer. I apologise for the crudeness of the device."

"Where is she?' Jack had yet to move.

"Please." The man motioned to the chair again. "She is perfectly fine, of course. Your concern does you credit."

"Is she here?' Jack asked, trying to be authoritative - but knowing he was failing.

"You'll see her again, soon enough, Jack. But please sit down; just for a few minutes. Humour me."

Jack walked towards the desk, the age of the other man becoming ever more evident as he did so - as was the sense he had that he recognised him from somewhere. On reaching the chair, he stood behind it for a moment, his arm holding its slatted wooden backrest, expecting the old man to say something further, but it was evident that he was going to offer little until Jack had sat down.

"So," said Jack, once he was seated.

"So," the old man echoed.

"Who are you? I mean, based on what I understand, given that you don't look fuzzy means that you are real and from my past."

"Oh, I wouldn't worry too much about rules, if I were you! After all, you've broken so many just recently."

"Rules?"

"No, not exactly 'rules'." The man paused. "Perhaps 'laws' is a better term, isn't it? I mean the things you've done and seen shouldn't really have been possible, should they? But your logic is sound enough, even saying that. Though I tended to keep in the background, as it were, I suspect you might have seen me just a few times - years ago, of course - whenever you came into my shop."

Jack felt a very large penny drop.

"Mr Twerton?"

"Guilty as charged!" The older man laughed. There was a pitcher of water on the table and two glasses. Twerton moved to fill the glasses. "What do you think of my little emporium? Seems a bit different now than it used to, eh?" He pushed one of the filled glasses across to Jack and raised the other to his lips.

"I used to love your shop when I was at college. Here, I mean. I spent ages in it."

"Yes, I know. Shame we had to - I believe the term is 'downsize'. But the demand just isn't there like it used to be."

"But I never realised... Has it always been as it is today? I mean, with all that's going on downstairs?"

"Pretty much. Adam's been with me from the beginning, just about; he's only just younger than me really."

"And you've had this little sideline - been helping people out - all that time?"

"Time is such a difficult concept really," said Twerton, evidently trying to find the best reply, "as you are now finding out, I suppose. But yes, I've been doing what I can, lending a hand if you like, for - well, forever it seems."

"So all those years ago, when I was upstairs browsing..."

"Or buying 'Moby Dick' perhaps," the old man suggested.

"...yes. All that time, downstairs there were people..." Jack was unsure how to conclude the sentence.

"People downstairs meeting Adam and Matt and Luke, and walking through that magic door at the end of the corridor? Just so."

"And what about Jen?"

"Ah. She is good, isn't she? A natural, in many ways. New in her role, of course, and still finding her feet, but very sympathetic."

"Is she searching for something too - like me?"

"In her own way, yes I suppose she is. Aren't most people? But it doesn't involve little trips to the past - or future come to that. She isn't supposed to go through the door, Jack. You can see what happens as a result, can't you? All this confusion. Things that need to be sorted out, unravelled."

Twerton looked evenly at him, the slight benevolent smile still on his lips but seriousness in his eyes. Jack felt guilty; as if he was being gently scolded by his paternal grandfather.

"Yes. Sorry. I just thought..."

"Oh, don't worry about it. She's fine. No harm done. I understand your motivation, really. And that's noble of you, of course. And I did know that you were going to try to get her to come with you. It was obvious from very early on, so I had a chance to prepare."

Twerton sipped his water. In spite of his age, his hands were rock steady. Jack would have expected to see some kind of ripple on the surface of the water as the result of a degree of shaking, however limited, but there was none.

"The main question, of course," said Twerton, gently deflecting the younger man's examination of him, "is what about you, Jack?"

"Me?"

"Indeed."

Jack thought for a moment. Finding another copy of 'Moby Dick' - a replica, if you like - no longer seemed as important as it once had. It was impossible for him to say what had replaced it in terms of importance however, assuming that there was some kind of 'law', as Mr. Twerton might call it, that always ensured we all had a certain stock of importance in our lives; there must always be things we cared about, and those things filled some kind of capacity we had for them.

When he looked back at Twerton, the older man was nodding subtly.

"What is it?"

"Oh, I was just following your logic," he replied.

"I wasn't aware I said anything," said Jack, confused.

"Just a trick of the trade really," Twerton assured him, moving a conciliatory hand towards him across the desk. Even though it stopped some way short of his arm, Jack felt the gesture. The old man carried on. "Yes, logic again on your part, and one of your strengths, if I may say so - though a strength can sometimes be a weakness too, of course. As you say, we each have a capacity for 'things' of various nature - and not all of them good, mind you. Importance is one, of course. If something - like your book - becomes less important, then it's logical to assume that something has taken its place or become more important. There are other capacities too. Love is an obvious one; or compassion; or generosity - you understand I'm concentrating only on the positive ones..! But we have an overall - what shall we say - 'bucket' into which all of these things go. A totality of ourselves that we each divide up in our own unique way."

"So we can trade between them? Have less love and more compassion; is that what you mean?"

"Exactly so," Twerton moved to refill his glass. "There are various labels people have given to this overall capacity; like 'spirit', or 'soul'. And some people are richer than others, of course."

"What about me?" Jack had the inescapable feeling that Twerton knew more about him than he did himself; that this strange old man appeared, not only to be able to read his mind, but see far more deeply into him than he could himself.

"You?" He laughed softly. "Oh, you have nothing to worry about on that score, Jack! You are a perfectly healthy specimen in terms of your 'bucket' - even if you have perhaps become a little, 'unbalanced'. Think about how you were concerned for Jen and wanted to try and help her out. People who are weak in spirit would never have been able to make that leap. Of course, she could see that in you herself, obviously. Otherwise you would never have been taken downstairs."

"Her being 'sympathetic'?"

"Precisely!"

"So if my finding my book was important but is no longer, what has replaced it? What has taken up its space in my bucket?"

The smile on Twerton's face broadened and he began to giggle. Soon the giggle became louder and more infectious. Jack started laughing too. For a few seconds they were both fighting back the tears. The older man then coughed and shook himself to try and break the spell.

"I do apologise," he said, still fighting to restore equilibrium, "it was just so funny, what you said: 'What has taken up its space in my bucket'. Most amusing! Of course, of course... Of course something has, but I'm afraid I can't tell you that. Something for you to work out; your 'homework', if you like. Losing the book - or finding the book - was never actually that important; Coral was right about that."

"Coral?"

"The lady from the room. When you were crying. Remember?"

"She was called Coral?" It seemed a preposterous name to Jack. "I didn't know."

"Well there it is. She was frustrated by the importance you placed on that book. All disproportionate. And she was right really."

"But I don't know her."

"And never will, I daresay. But an important lesson nonetheless - from that little peak into a potential future."

"That's what it was? A potential future?"

Twerton suddenly stood up and started pacing. Jack shifted slightly in his chair, taken aback both by the fact that, firstly, the old man had moved at all, and secondly by his size. He was quite tall; Jack had, for some reason, assumed that he would be small, small and frail. He recalled the rock-steady hands. Twerton was neither of those things.

The older man looked at him and smiled.

"If you like, yes; a potential future. But there are millions of those, aren't there. Unaccountable millions. All deflecting from each other based on the most minute decisions, changes in direction. Deciding to get a bus rather than a train; cornflakes instead of toast; wine instead of beer; Lucy instead of Maggie." Twerton paused to see what affect his words would have on Jack, who remained motionless. "I daresay there would be a combination that would lead you to Coral, yes. But then," here he stopped and looked at Jack square on, "that's a route you are now highly unlikely to take, correct?"

"If I can help it, yes."

"And you can help it, Jack; you can!" Twerton, suddenly animated, walked over to him and placed a hand on Jack's left shoulder. Jack glanced down at the thin, bony, wrinkled hands, and marvelled at how solid and strong those same fingers felt. "Do you begin to see that? To get a sense of it?"

Did he? Had he wanted to, it would have been all too easy to just say 'yes' as a means of bringing the interview to a close. Indeed, Jack truly felt that his answer could only be a positive one, and yet he was struggling to articulate exactly why he knew that to be the case.

"I get a sense of it, yes," he said finally, "but I don't think I could describe how I know that or what that might feel like. I mean, what I might do next."

"I think its difficult for most people to truly know what comes next," Twerton had released his grip and was now resuming his seat behind the desk. "Of course there are plans made - but that's all they can be. But don't despair, Jack, I think you've made a start already."

"I have?"

"You need the evidence?" This was accompanied by a slight furrowing of the brow.

"It might help - to give me a steer, maybe…"

"The fact that you're here, that you made it downstairs, passed Jen's sensibility test, met Adam, Luke and Matt, made it through the door, are talking to me… All that's truly something, Jack. Then your lessons - if you want to call them that." Jack had made no such allusion. "You were nice to Maggie, saw her in a new light almost. That was a change for the better, wasn't it?"

"But too late," Jack interrupted, "I mean I saw it through the replay, if you like, but it was too late then to make any difference wasn't it? I can't go back and do it all again differently. Too many - what did you call them? - 'deflections'."

Twerton smiled again.

"That's an interesting word, 'replay'. You have assumed that you just saw the same experience all over again, relived it in exactly the same way, said exactly the same things, and all because the past is immutable… That's right, isn't it?"

"Isn't it?"

"Normally, of course. That year, hour, minute, second has gone; lost forever. You can't get it back or do anything about it. A miracle or a tragedy, depending on your point of view."

"Or a bit of both?" Jack suggested.

"But what if that wasn't entirely true, always? After all, you've done some things you shouldn't have been able to, as we've already said. Why shouldn't your reliving the past break some laws too?"

It was a notion that floored Jack. Simultaneously, he was hit with both the impossibility of the notion and its enormous potential.

"Wasn't it the same?" he asked the older man.

"Was it?" Came the reply. "Do you know that it was? Or wasn't, come to that. You don't have any kind of script to refer to, do you?" Twerton allowed a few seconds for his suggestion to sink in. "What if you had done or said something slightly differently this time? Obviously not enough to change the course of history - of being here, for example - but what if you had said something different, or the same things but in a slightly different way? How do you know, sitting here now, that when you returned from the lavatory and went to the bookshop with Maggie you didn't say something that made her feel good about herself?"

"That I didn't say first time around?"

"Or that you did, in fact, say 'first time around'." Twerton shrugged his shoulders. "It's just a suggestion. And what about 'I couldn't do what you do'? Did you say that to Ben just in your 'replay', or first time around too?"

"I don't know," Jack said, feeling uncomfortable all of a sudden, "How am I supposed to know?"

"You're not, Jack; you're not. But when you said it, it made him feel good, appreciated. And even if you did say it originally, part of the 'new Jack' may simply be an ability to recognise it now; just as you can see Maggie in a slightly different light."

They both allowed silence to fall. In Jack's case it was a pause to allow Twerton's notion - the illogical, impossible notion - to filter through. Yet, no matter how hard he tried, he found it impossible to reconcile the suggestion with reality. Indeed, even the notion of reality had begun to blur at the edges - a little like the shadows in the library. The only way Jack could keep a hold on things was to regard those two past episodes as mirrors, genuine reflections on what happened. How could things have changed, really? His sense of practical and logical reality got in the way.

And if he did start to question - really question - what had happened to him, what he had done or said, on some kind of cosmic scale, where would that lead him? Was it, for example, significant that he had lost 'Moby Dick' as opposed to, say, 'Bleak House' or 'The Tennant of Wildfell Hall'? Was there a message there? Or was that going too far, making things too complex? Perhaps the critical thing was that it was less important now, not more so. Perhaps he had been given an opportunity to sift and analyse and recognise what was truly important. Maybe he should leave it at that. After all, if that were the case, wasn't that something worth having?

Twerton was smiling again.

"So Jack, what next?"

"I need to find Jen and then go back."

"Back?"

"Back to your shop; back to my life. I need to stop worrying about what I have lost and concentrate on what I have found, I suppose. And even though it may not be much - or may be something that I can't quite put my finger on - then perhaps its enough to ensure I avoid a future with Coral."

"Now that," said the older man, "is probably something worth avoiding!" The laughter was gentle enough, but it had the ring of closure about it somehow, as if the episode was over.

Jack stood, not waiting to be invited.

"Going back?" asked Twerton.

"Yes."

"Don't go back along the corridor. Take that door over there," he indicated a door camouflaged in the wall panelling that Jack had not previously noticed. "It will take you back to where Jen is waiting. No more shadows; no more confusion."

Jack stood for a moment, uncertain as to whether he should offer the other man his hand. But it seemed an unnecessary and inappropriate gesture. Instead, Jack nodded, and walked over to the door.

"Take care of yourself." Twerton's voice came to him over his shoulder as he placed he hand on the door handle.

Jack didn't look back, assuming that when he stepped through the door he would find himself in the basement corridor of the bookshop and that Jen would be there waiting for him.

SEVEN

The shop had always possessed that unique, old bookshop smell in spades: the aroma of tired leather, fading paper; it was almost as if the store itself was going brown and curling at the edges. It had been a smell that had delighted him and, stepping into the 'front room', he was pleased to be greeted by that particular old friend. His optimism increased.

The old, dark wood counter had been replaced by something a little more stylish, and he could see that the old prehistoric till had been replaced by a more modern equivalent, including card reader. Behind this new desk, a youngish person sat, working hard at her mobile phone. She glanced up at him and then carried on. Sometimes old Twerton himself would man the front desk, though he was probably long gone now, either retired or dead. He stood looking at those same old bowed shelves that had enchanted him many years previously. The catalogue had clearly changed and they had moved sections around - there were books here he would have expected to find on the top floor - but essentially the place appeared to be in a time warp.

"Can I help you?"

The young lady behind the counter had given up on her phone and was staring at him smilingly.

"It has been years since I was last here," he said, then added, "Sorry."

"We get that sometimes. Can I help you?"

He smiled, aiming to look totally comfortable and at home.

"I think I'm fine," he said. "I'll just start on the fifth floor and work my way down."

"Fifth floor?!" she said, in surprise. "There's no fifth floor, I'm afraid. Haven't used it for as long as I've been here. Years, probably. We only go up to the second."

"Really?" This was disappointing. He felt his optimism begin to fade. "I'm looking for novels. Paperbacks."

"Right. Second floor; room at the front."

"Just one room?"

"Sorry; sign of the times maybe. Anyway, if you need any help from me, you know where I am." Satisfied he was now sorted, she returned to her phone.

Well at least the stairs still creaked. In places it used to feel as if they were just about to give way - and he was reassured to get that same feeling again.

The window of the second floor front room looked out onto the street, as did all the front rooms windows (except on the fourth floor, where the window had been bricked up for some reason in the distant past). He recalled that there used to be a hard chair in front of this particular window, which had been a boon after three floors of browsing with still three to go. Although here too the shelves themselves appeared to still be the ancients from his earlier days, they appeared slightly less dense than he remembered them. Perhaps that was just a sign of the times with people eschewing the printed word in favour of the electronically delivered. Either way, it was a sad state of affairs.

He started immediately inside the door expecting to find 'A' and then working his way from there - that was the way old Mr Twerton used to like things. However, he found Joyce and not Austen, so had to trace his way around the room backwards to find the 'A's. Of course, Joyce was much closer to Melville, and he could have taken perhaps a step or two to his right and found himself where he needed to be, but he had long since decided that if he was going to do this he was going to do it properly, and that meant trying to recreate something for his past along the way - an acceptable by-product or bonus, if you will, from his excursion. Once he had found the 'A's, he started scanning the shelves as if generally browsing until, a few minutes later, he found himself back at the door and back with Joyce.

Going methodically row by row he was there soon enough, and the first thing he saw was a copy of 'Billy Budd, Sailor' in the same Penguin livery as his own. Then, immediately alongside the first, were another two of the same. And then... 'Moby Dick' - and in the Penguin edition! Just one copy before 'The Woman Upstairs' by Claire Messud.

Jack picked it up carefully. It was clearly not that old, but old enough. He checked the frontispiece for any owner's name that had been written in and found none; then he flicked through the book at random to see if there were any annotations. Again none. Back on the first page, the words 'Call me Ishmael' stared back at him, and Jack knew that maybe he should give Melville another chance; it might be better second time around. He might be ready to read it now.

Back down at the front desk, the young woman looked up from her phone long enough to slip the book into a simple brown paper bag and take his money. Then Jack walked out, down the steps, and into the afternoon sunlight a happy man.

*

WRITING TO GISELLA

PROLOGUE – August 1987

Jackson always seemed out of place there, his Wear-side accent cutting through volleys of imperfect Tuscan Latin. He was tall, angular – too many bones and sharp corners – and seemed to grate against the marble smoothness of Lucca. And yet here he was, sauntering along ancient streets, holding court in cafes and ice cream bars, dedicated to his life and somehow taking it all too seriously.

And he <u>had</u> taken it seriously. Having made the decision to go to Tuscany to teach English (and I never quite found out how this opportunity arose or why he had taken it) he put himself through a crash course in Italian – without any of us knowing – and then one day just disappeared. It was not a romantic gesture for him – he managed to avoid romance in all of the conventional senses – but to his new students, this slightly wild-haired, gangling young Englishman (with the impossible accent!) possessed a degree of charm, even as he murdered their native tongue.

In the same way as his being there was not about romance, neither was it about adventure. He understood no sense of the dramatic; if anything, he was a little timid, shy even – which made the whole escapade even more incredible. For him it was, at some profound level, 'logical'; the chance to experience, to add to his life's store. And he did it without planning or goals of any kind. In many ways, it was an ultimate expression of naivety. And yet. And yet…

But this isn't about Jackson.

"You should come."

He had phoned the house out of the blue. If I hadn't been the one to answer the call, would he have made the same offer to whomever he happened to speak to? I don't know. I prefer to think not, but with Jackson, well... Maybe for him it wasn't about <u>me</u> being there; maybe he just wanted <u>someone</u> there. Not to boast or to show off. Just to share perhaps.

"What are you doing? Nothing! It won't cost you much to get here. I've got room at my place. You should come. Next week."

The timing was never critical; I discovered that. It wasn't that he had a plan in mind, events to attend, things to schedule. For him it was more a question of 'why not?'. He had always been inclined to live in the moment, but not from any great philosophical design. Indeed, almost the complete opposite. There was no method. You could have called it logic. Maybe that's all it was.

I didn't go the following week, but I did find myself on a plane to Pisa the week after that. Jackson had been right, it wasn't expensive (though some years on and it's even cheaper now!). It was easy to arrange – both the going and the leaving behind. I had been searching – without any great lust – for my first real job, Not only did I have no irons in my job-hunting fire, the few coals that were there were pretty cool. My house mates would look after things for me – "It's just a holiday. A week, maybe two, tops" – and they had Jackson's number if they needed me (though I couldn't imagine why they should).

Being able to remove myself from my life in Bristol was less traumatic than I had imagined; disturbingly so. But I was not a seasoned traveller. Far from it. My only previous excursion outside of the UK had been a rather disastrous trip to Paris when I had been too young an adult to appreciate it. Maybe that's why Jackson invited me: because he knew that; because he thought I needed something – enlightenment, or having my mind broadened? Maybe he wanted more than just to share what he had found. I'm ascribing motives.

The one thing I was certain of, however, as I flew at 29,000 feet over France and towards Pisa, was the unnerving sense of limbo in which I suddenly felt. It was only for a short break, I knew that, but I had left behind something that was safe, comfortable, known and unchallenging – and I was about to experience something totally new and alien to me.

"Just bring shorts and t-shirts."

That had been the totality of Jackson's preparatory advice to me.

✼

And what did I find? Heat, sun, noise, confusion – and then more noise. Nothing seemed to happen – at least not at the airport – that didn't involve too many decibels or too much passion. Everything was over-emotional: the greetings, the lost luggage, the queuing for hire cars, the exchanging of currency. With my rucksack slung over one shoulder, I emerged from baggage collection into a wall that stopped me dead.

If I'd had a notion of what would meet me, then those first few minutes blew it away. The picture postcard, renaissance, terra cotta image that I had perhaps unconsciously gleaned from occasional ventures into literature and art over the years was suddenly obliterated, rudely ripped from me and leaving nothing but discomfort. Perhaps that was to prove beneficial, both in starting to strip me of my voyager naivety, but also to allow Italy to re-image itself for me – and for Lucca in particular to set the true standard by which I would eventually come to judge all places.

A shout broke through that wall I'd hit, Jackson's accent slicing into cacophonous Italian as easily as the proverbial knife through butter.

"Here, man!"

His hair was wilder, his skin darker; he not only looked tanned, slimmer, more healthy, but he looked in part like a different man.

119

How long had he been here? Just a few weeks? It felt as if I had suddenly come across a castaway I had not seen for years. And if I had expected him to be English – to be the Jackson that I had shared a house with in Bristol for the best part of three years – then I was immediately disabused as he dragged me through the crowds, talking at a million miles an hour, pushing through taxi queues and then throwing us into the back of a creaking Fiat that was suddenly off into the hot, noisy, confusion of traffic lurching around the airport environs.

"Hungry? That plane food's rubbish! We're going to meet some friends of mine who are going to drive us back."

I tried to absorb Pisa as we drove, but my ability to take it in was compromised by a certain nervousness brought on by a concern for self-preservation. Between car horns and lunges round corners, I sensed colour above all things: a patchwork of ochres, yellows and oranges, and a unique shade of green from the trees and sparse grass. Occasionally there would be a splash of vibrancy from flowers or a building, but this seemed the exception. Even now I can recall little of that first journey, perhaps the most abiding memory being its ending and then the freedom of stepping out onto the Lungarno Pacinotti by the river and breathing in what seemed to be suddenly fresher air.

"The river goes all the way to Florence. You should have been here last week; there was dragon boat racing. Coffee?"

Jackson took me into a small café over-looking the river that perhaps anywhere other than Italy would have seemed run-down. The volume ramped up again thanks to the stereo behind the counter and numerous enthusiastic conversations amongst the clientele. Rather than talk much about himself – despite my questions – he gave me a quick guide to Italian coffee, including an apocryphal story about a Brit he had heard of who had, on first arriving in Italy, consumed Espresso in the kinds of quantities he was used to drinking Nescafe at home and then failed to sleep for two days! He persuaded me to try a 'short' coffee rather than a Latte, and told me that real Italians drank Ristretto – which, from his description, sounded like distilled caffeine syrup!

After a short while we were out into the heat again, turning to the town and away from the river.

"We're meeting Mita at the university refectory. We'll eat and then head off."

I wondered how either of us would get in given that neither of us were students there. He laughed.

"They let anyone in. You'll see!"

We waited at least a quarter of an hour outside the restaurant entrance. There was a constant flow of people coming and going, like slightly manic worker ants on a break. It was funny how snapshots like those fifteen minutes taught me things about life in this strange new (old!) place that I was to find endorsed again and again. Little vignettes, or a peep through a curtain at another world.

I learned that time didn't really count here. It was little more than an approximation. If you agreed to meet at a certain hour it was just a ballpark, an indication of when you might be there – give or take. This used to be as foreign a concept to Jackson as it was to me, both of us historically proud of our punctuality; but as I grew slightly frustrated, I watched him. He had adapted already.

I also got an inkling that the passion I had seen at the airport wasn't passion or excitement for its own sake. As I watched these young people (my age!) greeting each other or saying goodbye, I realised that, like the friendly earnestness in their interactions, it was all part of a portfolio that was based on the joy and pursuit of immediacy. Of being in the moment, if you like. For a place swamped in history was that ironic or inevitable? I didn't know. Maybe that was why time failed to matter too.

Mita arrived in a whirl. Suddenly she was there with two others in tow. The way Jackson greeted them belied his nationality. There were brief introductions and then we went inside the building. I could hear the noise rising as we climbed two flights of stairs before bursting into a vast chamber filled with tables, chairs, people and, most of all, sound. Jackson said something to me I couldn't hear and after that I tried to stick to him like glue. Somehow I managed to get a tray with some food on; somehow I managed to exchange some Lira for the food; and somehow we managed, the five of us, to find somewhere to sit.

As I sat there, listening and unable to listen – because of both the language and the background volume that accompanied any conversation – I had a vague sense of what it was like to be an alien. I was there yet somehow not so. If I had been suddenly vaporised, no-one would have noticed; there would have been no difference. It was a strange sensation of other-worldliness, of not belonging, maybe of worthlessness even. It took all my discomforts from the moment I had retrieved my bag at the airport and multiplied them a million times. What the hell was I doing there?!

All of a sudden I was aware of someone by my elbow, leaning in to me slightly. I could hear them murmuring something. It was not a loud voice, but it was insistent and unavoidable. I looked round. It was a vagrant, begging. Possibly three or four times older than anyone in the entire place, in rags, unkempt, smelling. She carried a small bag on one arm and in the other she offered me one of the refectory plates with a few coppers on it. I was paralysed.

Then there was shout from my right – Mita – a short exchange, and the woman shuffled off to the next table. Jackson smiled at me.

"I told you they let anyone in!"

*

Mita's car – small, compact, but very nice – was parked just around the corner. She was, I discovered later, the daughter of a man who had made his fortune in olive oil. The family was wealthy enough to have a large house on the outskirts of Lucca; tennis court, swimming pool and domestic staff. One of the guys – confusingly called Luca! – sat up front with her, leaving Jackson, Roberto and I squeezed in the back. Jackson made sure I had an outside seat – "so you can get a look at the place" – although by this time the light was beginning to fade just a little.

We started our journey in boisterous mood, Jackson attempting the tour guide role, pointing things out to me as we left Pisa. Occasionally Mita would contribute. The fact that she seemed considerably more accomplished on the road than our earlier taxi driver allowed me to relax a little as we moved away from the city and onto a route that began to wind up a steep valley.

"There are two ways to go; this way and the autostrada. Normal thing: autostrada longer but faster; this way more direct, but you travel more slowly. Takes about the same time. We thought you might like this way better."

And for a while I did. The colour palette changed dramatically from earlier as we moved further into the valley. The trees were darker and more dense. There were fewer buildings so less terra cotta except when we passed through small villages, though soon dusk was falling and just about everything lost its hue.

As the road continued to wind and the scenery became lost in darkness, the talking in the car stopped, and the tiredness from my journey began to overtake me, in spite of the coffee! I'm not sure exactly how long I had slept, maybe not that much, but I was woken by Jackson tugging on my arm.

"We're here."

As I regained focus all I could see were anonymous roads, cars, street lights. It was clearly not England, but to be honest it could have been anywhere. The guys in the car were talking again in the way that people tend to bookend journeys with conversation. After a few minutes we pulled into a lay-by and Luca left us. Jackson eased himself away from me a little. Apparently we were next.

A few minutes later we pulled into a bus station and Jackson and I got out. As we retrieved my bag from the boot Mita joined us. She kissed Jackson goodbye, gave me a smile and said "See you later" in a way that suggested either inevitability or a plan. I suspected the former.

"Don't expect too much" – this from Jackson as we walked along a narrow street, lined on either side by a mix of slightly tired residential and commercial buildings – "you'll get a better sense of the place tomorrow."

He stopped by a nondescript door and pulled out a key. I followed him in.

I don't recall much of my first impression of Jackson's first floor flat. It was suddenly cooler, that's for sure. And it seemed extraordinarily long and narrow. We walked along a corridor to the far end; the kitchen. I could see the bathroom beyond.

"Do you want a coffee, or just to crash?" – but before I could answer – "Crash. I can see that! You're in here."

He led me back along the corridor to a small room where he had set up a bed for me. It wasn't large or elegant, but it was just what I needed.

*

It helped that the day dawned perfectly blemish free. The blue of the sky was something I would get used to over the coming days, and I would begin to handle the heat too – even well enough to play tennis with Jackson at Mita's house. Standing on the city wall looking inwards took my breath away. Here was the Italy of my vague imaginings! A mass of terra cotta roofs, pale ochre walls, church towers, and roads and passages that seemed to define the city in a haphazard fashion. There was some of the usual hubbub – mainly from outside the walls and the newer parts of town to which my back was turned – and everywhere the sound of scooters and mopeds.

"I have to teach this morning", Jackson had said over our simple breakfast. "Here's a map. I've marked out where we are and where I'll meet you for lunch. It's a small café, but you can't miss it. To start, the best thing you can do is to go up onto the walls and just walk round."

He was right. And when he said 'walk round' that was literally what he meant. The city's walls were entirely intact and enclosed the old town. At the top, they were wide – many metres wide – with a continuous path lined by grass verges, benches, trees… perfection! Although it was mid-morning, the path was busy with joggers and dog walkers, but there seemed few people like me; few 'tourists'.

For some minutes I just stood and looked, captivated. I orientated myself with the map and tried to pick out some of the landmarks: the Duomo di San Martino, the Basilica of San Frediano, San Michele in Foro, the Anfiteatro, and the remarkable Guinigi tower – a medieval tower with trees growing on the top of it. Over the coming days I would get to know all of these – including the Guinigi trees! – and begin to find my way around the city on foot: the Via Fillungo, Via Roma, Via Santa Croce. Not once did I choose to leave this wonderful ancient city except for an excursion to Florence by coach.

When I had got my breath back (for that was how it felt!), I tucked the map, folded, into the pocket of my shorts and just followed the path. I tried to stroll rather than walk. Occasionally

I would stop and look, always inwards! Once or twice I found a bench and sat with a drink bought from one of the few little cabins on the wall. About an hour and a half later (though I can't be sure), I arrived again at my starting point and just marvelled again.

As I described my morning to Jackson he just listened and smiled. It was a new smile, filled with understanding, humour, fellow-feeling, compassion, maybe even a little pity. We talked about Lucca – or rather I asked questions and Jackson answered. Unlike those first couple of hours in Pisa the previous day, he was more than happy to answer questions about the city. He became voluble, enthusiastic, animated.

"I'm not working this afternoon. We'll take a wander; I'll show you some stuff."

And that's what we did for a couple of hours. We planned over the coming days to establish a pattern where in the mornings Jackson would work and I would explore, and then after lunch we would spend time walking the city together. That first day though things were still much of an unreal blur. After all, just two days previously I had been in Bristol living an existence without light, colour, poetry; without brilliant coffee and ice cream; without the melody of the Italian language. Essentially without beauty.

As a novice explorer, I tired early that evening, still coming to terms with the effects of the travel and the considerable walking I had done during the day. Jackson cooked a carbonara which we ate in his kitchen, drinking a little wine.

"Tomorrow, we're going out to dinner with a few friends of mine. Mita and Luca will be there, so you'll know more than just me!"

As I snuggled down in bed that evening trying to concentrate on my book, I wondered how I could introduce myself to people I met in a way that would be meaningful and understandable to them. Even spending time with the 'new' Jackson was enough to highlight how far he had come – and how far I had to go. 'My name's Richard – but call me Rick, all my friends do. I was at university with Jackson and I'm rigidly British.'

Rigidly British or not, I set out the next morning without consulting the map (though not leaving it behind!), trying to take a less structured approach to my exploration. At lunch Jackson told me he had been asked to give some extra private lessons that afternoon, so I went back to his flat alone. I read for a little and then slept a little. When he arrived later in the afternoon I was making coffee, English-style, in the kitchen.

We set off for dinner around eight thirty. Jackson explained how people in Italy ate later in the day, and very often many would go out for a stroll around the town and eat ice cream at eleven o'clock or beyond.

"This street we're on," this just after we had left his flat, "they say that once Julius Caesar walked along here. Can you imagine?! Bet he wasn't eating ice cream though!"

We passed through the Duomo square and walked on a little further, then we turned into a small side street I had not yet explored, and off that into a tiny piazza. In the far corner was a restaurant and outside perhaps ten or twelve people, talking loudly. Clearly the definition of a 'few friends' Jackson and I had once shared seemed to have now diverged somewhat. One of them shouted out to him as they saw us approach. I saw Mita, who waved, and Luca made a point of coming out from the throng to shake my hand. It was a small gesture I guess, but at that moment it made a colossal difference. I tried my warmest smile and Luca laughed and put his hand on my shoulder

It appeared they had been waiting for us – our tardiness was Jackson being Italian! – and once there, we filed into the restaurant. I stuck to Jackson wanting to ensure that I was sitting next to him at the table, not least because I needed someone to interpret the menu for me. With Jackson on my right, I think Luca made certain that he was on my left, Mita beside him. It almost felt as if he had decided that it was also his job to look after me. Jackson introduced me to the rest of the people around the table. They waved when he said their name or tried some broken English on me. I smiled and laughed as I thought fit. Jackson said something in Italian – probably at my expense – and everyone burst out laughing, at which Luca slapped me on the shoulder again.

As it turned out, my concern in relation to the menu was justified in spades in that there was no menu! When he eventually appeared the waiter simply recited what was on offer and then what seemed like chaos ensued. From three sides, people tried to translate what the waiter said for me: Jackson, Luca and the young lady sitting directly across from me. In the melee of those initial moments I had noticed her no more than anyone else around the table, but now she was talking to me, she had my complete attention. Her name was Gisella.

"No, not that!" she said in her very good, but heavily accented English. "Is horse! Don't listen to Luca!" And then a volley at my new best friend who this time gave me a pally hug.

I recognised a word.

"Pollo. That's chicken, right?"

"Si, si," said Gisella, smiling. "You are safe there."

"Pollo", I said when the waiter looked at me at which there was a general eruption of laughter around the table. I blushed uncontrollably and looked across at Gisella who was laughing too. Suddenly I never wanted to go home again.

I suspect we probably shared no more than a few dozen words for the rest of the evening, though I caught Gisella's glance often enough. Apart from an attempt by Luca to discuss English football with me, I was always the interloper, the odd one out.

Jackson tried his best to keep me engaged, but it was me against eleven people from his new and exciting life. I didn't really stand a chance.

In the end the meal passed without drama or me eating anything that was psychologically unpleasant. I kept my alcohol intake down to two bottles of beer, though one or two – Luca included – made short work of a little too much wine. For all the lack of discipline around the menu and food ordering, for all the shouting and laughter, the splitting and paying of the bill was smooth and seamless. After a couple of hours, we found ourselves back outside, milling quietly waiting for the party to break up.

After one last handshake and a hearty cry of "Manchester United!", Luca and Mita were first to leave. I watched them disappear out of sight as Jackson and Gisella arrived at my side.

"You like Lucca?" she asked, smiling.

"It's like nowhere I've ever been," I said. She frowned a little. I tried to keep it simple. "I think it may best the best place in the world." That seemed to work.

For most of the way back to his flat, Jackson and I walked in silence. It was a silence he broke eventually.

"Did you mean that – about Lucca being the best place in the world?"

I laughed. I said I didn't know; that I couldn't know. But it had to be right up there.

"I think it might just be, you know," he said thoughtfully.

We had one last glass of wine in his kitchen before lights out. He suddenly smiled.

"You should come to my class tomorrow morning. Just to sit in. You might find it interesting."

❋

The language school where he taught was beyond another nondescript door, this time in the Duomo piazza. We climbed up two flights of elegant marble steps into another long, cool corridor with a large window at the far end overlooking the cathedral square. I followed Jackson into one of the teaching rooms.

"I just need to go and pick something up. You can wait here."

The walls were filled with pictures and words: the pictures were from Lucca, Italy, England – almost anywhere and anything; the words were nearly all in pairs, the Italian and then the English. I thought of 'pollo = chicken' and smiled to myself. As I was browsing the posters and displays I heard a sound behind me and turned. It was Gisella. She reddened slightly. I said hello.

"You take the class today?"

"No," I was amused at the thought of me standing up and teaching – or of being taught by Jackson! "Jackson suggested I just come along."

She put her bag down. In the dim light of the restaurant the previous evening I had only managed to get an impression of her; that impression was now enhanced and endorsed. She had dark brown hair, slightly longer than shoulder length, that had a subtle wave to it. Her face was very slightly on the round side of oval; her flawless eyes were just beginning to tip from brown into hazel. And she had wonderful lips. Average for a young Italian woman in many other respects – height, physique, tone – she was striking rather than stunning, and in a quiet way. She wore a simple t-shirt and blue jeans.

"Jackson's just popped out. Said he had to go and collect something," I offered, to try and stop any awkward silence.

"Si. Yes, I understand."

She paused and then went out into the corridor. I waited, expecting her to return immediately for some reason, and when she did not I followed her. She had opened the window at the far end of the corridor and was leaning out onto a minuscule balcony overlooking the piazza. As she stood there, her back to me in semi-silhouette, I told my brain to take a photo of the moment and never lose it.

I walked towards her. She looked over her shoulder and smiled.

"Jackson. He is coming."

Like many Italians she struggled with the 'j' sound, which often turned it into a long 'y'. In Gisella's case this made Jackson's name sound heavenly. She edged left slightly to give me room to stand next to her even though there wasn't really space there. I tried to lean out against the railing too, my shoulder brushing hers as I did so. Beneath us, my friend was making his way towards the building.

"Yackson!", Gisella called, and he looked up and waved.

Two other students appeared with Jackson in the classroom. I did not recognise them; I was pretty sure they had not been at the meal the previous evening. As for the lesson itself? It was quiet by and large, and studious. Jackson was surprisingly good, ensuring he got his point across, ensuring that everyone contributed. Even once or twice he got me to chip in. Having said that, I can remember very little of the session and none of the context; my only focus was Gisella. At one point Jackson wanted people to work in pairs, so with just three students there he had me help Gisella. To this day I can't remember what the subject was!

After about an hour or so the lesson came to an end. The mood in the room lightened a little. The two other students – both male – introduced themselves to me as they packed up their things. I walked out into the corridor to wait for Jackson, and looked out from the balcony onto the cathedral again.

Once she was ready to leave, Gisella came out and joined me.

"Rick, what do you do tomorrow?"

"Tomorrow? I'll probably go for a walk in the morning while Jackson's teaching. Do you have a lesson tomorrow?"

She shook her head, then paused nervously.

"Can I show you the Orta Botanico Comunale?"

"The botanical gardens? Yes, I would like that. Very much."

When Jackson joined me at the balcony, Gisella had left. He put his hand on my shoulder.

"Ready?"

I told him that it appeared I had a date for the next day.

"Of course you do," he said, flashing that new smile again. And then, in as warm a voice as I can ever remember him using: "Rick, you do know you're an idiot, don't you?"

❁

We arranged to meet by the cathedral steps at ten the next morning. We were both early. It was another glorious day, and Gisella was wearing a white, fitted v-neck t-shirt, a long peach-coloured linen skirt, and some simple white shoes. If hearts do truly miss a beat, mine did then. She looked like a young Claudia Cardinale.

I now knew enough of the city to be able to go about without a map, but I had made sure I had a picture in my mind of where we would be headed before I left Jackson's flat. Those first few minutes were a little awkward for both of us, I think. I found it difficult enough to think of things to say to girls under normal circumstances, never mind the additional challenges of culture

and language. I quizzed her about what she did and she asked
me likewise. At least it was relatively easy talking about a subject
I knew reasonably well!

The botanical gardens were accessed through a tiny wooden
door in a long white wall. There was no grand entrance, no
glossy shop selling 'tat', no café; just a man in a small wooden
hut beyond the door who took the money and handed out the
tickets. Gisella insisted that she pay. As we wandered the
deserted garden paths, I learned that she was a year younger
than me and a part-time student hoping to go to university in
Pisa. Her studying English was to improve her chances of
getting into college, but also because she wanted to travel once
she graduated – "Like you, Rick". She worked in her family's
shop when they needed her or when she needed the money. It
seemed to be an arrangement that worked. In the same way as
she had yet to decide what subject to take at university, I told
her I was in pretty much the same place: graduated, yes, but
with no idea what I wanted to do next. A job, for sure – but
doing what?

By the time we left the gardens all the awkwardness had gone. I
suggested a coffee and we went to a small place near the walls.
Laughing, Gisella made me drink espresso – I still found it a
little difficult – and I threatened to make her drink tea! It was a
good sign. It was nearly twelve o'clock when we finished our
drinks. This was where the plan ran out for me – but not for
Gisella.

"Would you like to walk some more?"

"Maybe the walls?"

"Si. Of course."

So we left the café and walked up the incline from the Via
Francesco Carrara to the top of the walls. I had always walked
clockwise, but Gisella headed in the opposite direction promising

to point out where she lived. After a short while we arrived at the spot where I had first stood and gazed into the city. I was compelled to stop and look again.

"You like our city?"

"It's beautiful." I smiled at her. "You are beautiful."

She took my hand and gave it a gentle squeeze. For the next hour, she didn't let it go.

✲

Is there such a thing as a chaste but passionate kiss? I can't say for sure, but that was how it felt when we separated mid-afternoon. That first nervous moment; the feel of her as I held her close to me; the smell of her skin. We had smiled, laughed, trembled and maybe even cried a little all in the same blissful moment. My head had spun. It felt as if I hadn't taken a breath for minutes.

Her house was on the northern side of the city, just outside the old town. I watched her as she walked beyond the walls – what a strange sensation that was! – and waved every time she looked back until she was beyond the big roundabout and out of sight. Being suddenly alone felt instantly confusing. What did I do now? What <u>could</u> I possibly do now?!

I made my way back to Jackson's flat through the town, going via the Anfiteatro to get an ice cream and watch the tourists and the children chasing pigeons. Tomorrow was Friday and Gisella would be busy all day with her family, something from which she could not excuse herself. On Saturday, Jackson and I had already booked coach tickets for our day trip to Florence, so I wouldn't see her again until some point on Sunday. As I realised that, it hit me that within a week after that I would be back in England. It hit me hard.

Jackson was already back at his flat making dinner when I arrived. We had planned to eat early and then go out to a bar where one of his students gave impromptu gigs some Thursday evenings.

"There was a phone call for you," he said as I sat down in the kitchen. "From your new friend..!"

I must have blushed royally because he burst into laughter. Then he poured me a glass of wine.
"You probably need this! Anyway, she said – what was it she said...?"

I threatened to stand up and punch him.

"OK, OK! She said to tell you that she'd had a wonderful day and was going home very happy. They're so emotional, these Italian women! And blind too, half of them! Only kidding! She said – oh, some soppy stuff that she'll tell you on Sunday probably. And she said not to call her back, but that I can give her a message for you; her parents know me, that's all. So, let me know Romeo, OK?"

I couldn't think of very much other than to tell her that I was very happy too. At some point before we left to go out I heard Jackson on the phone, so I guessed that was him being Cupid. The concert was fine, but I struggled to concentrate. The next day was dreadful. Suddenly I didn't know what to do with myself. Jackson was teaching all day, so I was bereft of company. I went for a walk, but even that had lost some of its magic because I didn't want to be walking Lucca alone. So I read and drank coffee and walked and read some more. By the time Jackson came back from teaching and closed out his week, he was tired and I was in a foul mood. We didn't have a great evening.

At least Saturday would occupy me. We were up early for the coach and arrived in Florence mid-morning. Given that we had a finite time there before our early evening coach back, Jackson had taken the trouble to craft a plan of all the things he wanted me to see in our time there. Planning not being his strong point, he actually did a pretty decent job. Occasionally we had to whizz through somewhere – Michaelangelo's David, for example – but it was a pretty successful day, assuming success can be measured in tiredness and cultural overload! I probably only thought about Gisella fifty times a minute…

We got back to Lucca late and ready for bed. There was a note waiting for me in Jackson's mail pigeon hole at his flat. From Gisella. Could we meet at the Duomo just after lunch? We hadn't made a plan when we parted on Thursday, so it was good to have one – but it wasn't the one I wanted. I now had another whole morning to kill.

After breakfast, Jackson suggested we go for a run. He and I had jogged together occasionally in the past. I protested that I didn't have any suitable kit, but he leant me some shorts and said my trainers would be fine. It wasn't as if we were Olympic athletes anyway, and it would take up time. So I found myself, along with many others, running the walls that Sunday morning. It was a good thing to do; a release; a way of relaxing. When lunchtime came, my tautness had left me and I was back to plain old excited.

Once again we were both early. I had wondered what that first re-greeting would be like, and perhaps not surprisingly it was a little awkward. Gisella – looking divine again! – gave me a short peck on the cheek and brushed my hand, and we then walked on without contact. Unconsciously I suppose, I had decided to make my lead from her. She seemed a little nervous, preoccupied; as we walked she was glancing in the café windows. Once I saw her wave to someone.

Almost without thinking we headed for the walls again and began to stroll. After a short while she suddenly stopped, grabbed me by the arm and kissed me. I held on to her for all I was worth. She eased herself away.

"Hello," I said as she took my hand. Suddenly we were all right again, picking up from where we had left off two days previously.

The fact that I was flying back to the UK on Thursday was a subject that couldn't be avoided; certainly it was one I didn't want to ignore. Only by recognising it could we make the most of the rest of my time there. So we sat on one of the benches and talked about what we would do together between now and then.

Gisella was adamant that she would not come to the airport to watch me leave. That, she said, would be too hard. For both of us, I thought. She was busy on Monday and Tuesday mornings – one with lessons, the other in the shop – so we agreed that we would see each other those afternoons and as much of Wednesday as we could. I wanted to have my last meal to include Jackson somehow, and it was Gisella who suggested that the three of us should go out together. I had already sounded Jackson out on this possibility and he was fine with the idea. On Tuesday morning Jackson and I had already arranged to go to Mita's house to play tennis and have lunch, so things seemed to dovetail nicely.

We spent the rest of that Sunday walking, with Gisella showing me some of sights I had yet to see, including the Guinigi Tower. When we were in town proper she seemed more reserved, cautious again; she was not inclined to hold hands, and pretty much avoided any contact. But on the walls it was different – and when we reached the top of the tower and were briefly alone, she kissed me with passion.

I found out that she was nervous about being seen in such a way with me. She said her parents were often in town and she had not told them about me yet. They rarely walked the walls anymore, and never went up the Guinigi Tower! I pointed out that other people would see us together; her friends out jogging or walking their dogs perhaps. But she trusted her friends; they would say nothing.

We finished the day with a quiet meal in a small pizzeria and once again we said goodnight in the same place on the northern side of the walls. When I got back to the flat, Jackson said nothing; he just smiled and poured me some wine.

The next two days went by too fast. Monday afternoon Gisella took me on a local bus to Viareggio where we walked barefoot along the beach and ate an early dinner at one of the seaside restaurants. She looked simply spectacular. I asked her to pinch me to make sure I wasn't dreaming. I explained the phrase to her and she laughed – then she pinched me anyway. I told her I simply couldn't understand how all this had happened to me; how much I felt I had changed and grown since coming to Lucca. I made her promise that she wasn't a mirage or an illusion, that she was real and would not suddenly disappear.

Mita's house was enormous and Jackson thrashed me at tennis. As I spent a little more time with her, I grew to like Mita much more. She was a very pretty girl, classically Italian. I watched her watching Jackson. As we went back into town that afternoon I told him that I thought she had a soft spot for him, but he said he couldn't see it – and anyway, she was going out with Luca.

That Tuesday afternoon we went back to the botanical gardens again and mainly sat and talked. I asked her if she would come to England. That was a difficult conversation because it posed the 'what happens next?' question I think we had both been avoiding.

"I have to find a job, and you have to study and go to university. I know that. But there is no way on this earth that I am never going to see you again after Wednesday. I promise you that."

"I promise too, Rick."

That evening I sat up late with Jackson, talking. Oddly, we spoke a lot about him, about what he wanted to do, where he was going. He talked about his philosophy – "If you can call it that!" – and he tried to apply it to me and my new 'situation'. He challenged my notion about going home and getting a job. Why not do what he had done? Why not do something somewhere else?

"Surely," he argued, "you are heading towards having more ties in Tuscany than you are in miserable old England."

As is often the case in such circumstances, it was a conversation without a conclusion. Maybe it was just talking for the sake of it. I suspect it was me trying to work things out and using my friend as some kind of sounding board. As I went to sleep that night I was acutely aware that I didn't know what was going to happen beyond Thursday.

I was getting ready to go out Wednesday morning, Jackson having already gone off to teach, when there was a knock at the door of his flat. I opened it. Gisella was standing there in a long pink summer dress and carrying a small handbag. Instinctively I took her into my arms.

We made love twice. The first time was haphazard, uncoordinated, fumbling, frenzied almost. It was as if we were both releasing the frustrations of the previous days and also cementing what we had come to feel. Then it was more measured, harmonious, considered – but no less passionate. We were neither of us proficient I guessed, but we managed just fine. And Gisella had clearly come prepared.

"What do you like about me, Rick?" she asked as we lay on my bed in the back room. She was on her slide, looking at me.

I sat up slightly.

"Your ankles," I said, brushing one of them with my foot. She laughed. "And the shape of your hips. Your perfect nipples. The nape of your neck, and the small of your back. And your skin. I love your skin."

On her left side she had a small birthmark, and on her belly a small scar from the appendix operation she had undergone two years previously. Her skin there was slightly hard yet remarkably sensitive. I touched it gently with my fingers and she trembled slightly. She took my hand and placed it on her hip.

"Love me again, my Rick."

When we eventually left the flat to go for a late lunch, she put her arm through mine and held me close.

"I have told my parents that I have met a lovely English boy," she said, "who is going home tomorrow and is going to break my heart."

I stopped and kissed her.

The rest of the afternoon passed. I can remember so little of it, the emotional haze I spent it in. We talked and walked the walls (for one last time), and then went back to the flat to collect Jackson for dinner. He had booked a table at a restaurant called Puccini, named after the composer who had been born in the city. Compared to my first restaurant experience, this was quiet, sedate; more the kind of restaurant I guess I would have expected.

I was concerned that the meal would be difficult. There were three of us; it was my last evening with Gisella; the fretting over the following day; the uncertainty about what happened next. But, in its own quiet way, it was a blissful evening. There was nothing in the way between Gisella and I now, and Jackson – as our erstwhile Cupid – was charming, up-beat, positive, even jokey. He also acted as a translator when I was struggling to either understand the menu (I was getting better!) or to express myself to Gisella. Occasionally they would break off into a little conversation of their own in which I could play no part, but that was fine.

We drank a little too much wine, I suspect to make the evening last as long as possible and to delay the inevitable. But eventually we had to move on. We walked into the Duomo square and, holding Gisella's hand, I took a final look around. I looked up at the balcony of the language school. Jackson made to walk away.

"Jackson, per favori," said Gisella, asking him to stay. "Now I go home. To my cold bed. My Rick, do not forget me."

I went to speak, but she put a finger to my lips. The she spoke, rapidly, to Jackson in Italian, before removing her finger, kissing me quickly, and then turning away. I felt Jackson's hand on my arm as she started walking.

"Let her go Rick. She said, please let her go."

I watched her walk away out of the square and disappear into Via Arcivescovado, and even after I could see her no longer, I did not move.

LONDON – September 1991

Gisella,

I received your letter a couple of days ago and to be honest I didn't really know what to do with it. I know you sent it a while back and I guess it only managed to catch up with me thanks to people forwarding it on. I haven't lived at the house in Bristol you sent it to for at least a couple of years now. Luckily the people who now live there are still in contact with one of my old house-mates and he sent it on to my parents… Anyway, I got it on Thursday.

The not knowing what to do with it part… I read it several times over. It was probably one of the biggest surprises I'd ever had; I mean, I was never expecting to hear from you again – certainly not after all this time. What is it, four years nearly? And I wasn't sure if I should reply or simply… But then I decided I couldn't ignore it. So I woke up this morning – Saturday – with the express aim of writing this letter back to you. Even now, I'm not sure where it will take me…

So many questions. So many questions.

But then maybe just one real question, when you boil it down. What happened? What happened after I left Lucca?

I came home like a man reborn. It was a Thursday, wasn't it? The plane was late leaving Pisa, which meant I was stuck in the airport for hours; then it was really rough flying on the way home. They nearly diverted the flight, though God knows where to. Given the emotional state I was already in when I awoke in Jackson's flat (after an awful night of not sleeping), all I needed was a dreadful journey. By the time I got back I was shattered.

The next morning I wrote to you. Probably the letter had a longer description of my travels from Lucca to Bristol. Maybe it was abominably boring, I don't know. I sent it to the address you gave me and then waited. I know I included my address (again) and phone number (again). That weekend I rang Jackson to let him know I was back safely – and to ask if he'd seen you. I knew my letter wouldn't have arrived with you yet, but I just wanted some kind of confirmation I suppose. And Jackson was my only conduit. He seemed fine, but said he hadn't seen you.

I waited a few days and wrote again. Was that unreasonable of me? I'm surprised I waited that long to be honest. I felt suddenly like I'd been cast adrift, a lone sailor with no sight of the shore and longing for home. I rang Jackson – at least I tried to ring him – that following weekend. I eventually got hold of him a few days later. Had he seen you? Yes, you had been in lessons. How were you? Did you get my letters? He couldn't answer the second question – and answered the first one pretty badly too. I asked him (maybe begged him) to get you to contact me.

I have wondered often – and four years ago, nearly all the time – what happened. The simplest explanation would be that you didn't get my letters. Is that it? If you didn't get them, did you assume that I didn't care, that I was going to break your heart after all? (Mine was already crumbling!) But that notion didn't work for me. If you hadn't heard, then why didn't you get in touch through Jackson? Why didn't you call me? Or write to me?

And then that led me to my second explanation: that you didn't care. That _you_ were the one who was going to do the heart breaking. But somehow I couldn't believe that, not after our last day together. I couldn't.

So what else did that leave? You'd had an accident – or been captured by white slave traders – or you'd won the Italian lottery or met a millionaire and didn't need me any more... I came up with all sorts of permutations. But none of them worked. And the reason they didn't work was that Jackson would have told me: "Gisella's been in a car crash", "Gisella's been smuggled out to Algiers", "Gisella's run off to Milan with a Prince".…. But he didn't say any of those things.

Actually – and I don't know how much you are aware of this – after a while Jackson stopped saying anything at all. Oh it was months later, but he went silent on me too. He'd said a couple of weird things about Mita, and made reference to wanting to see what the rest of Italy was like – but I've no idea what happened to him. Someone told me that they'd heard he was in Florence – or was it Rome? Anyway, when he was no longer in Lucca, and no longer on that phone number, my only link to you – if you weren't talking to me – had vanished. I was no longer a lone sailor out of sight of shore, I was now a castaway on an uninhabited island…

At some point I gave up. You may think that was wrong of me, I don't know; that if I cared as much as I said I did, then I wouldn't have given up. Ever. But what was I supposed to do? I'd tried the avenues that were open to me – other than jumping on a plane and wandering the streets of Lucca until I found you – and they were all now dead ends. I didn't decide one day to not care, to give you up; it was never that calculated. You just get worn out.

And I got a job. You asked in your letter about my job. I kind of fell into one, maybe about 3 months or so after I got back. It didn't look like much at first – a nondescript role in a marketing company – but it was the first real offer I'd had, so I took it. The fact that it was based in London meant I had to leave Bristol, so I was breaking ties there. Maybe the job was coincident with me assuming I would never hear from you again. Perhaps I thought the job and London was the ideal 'fresh start'.

I lived in Greenford for a while (I know the place names won't mean anything to you… it sounds nice, but it's a dump!) and then to Kensal Rise (another dump!) and then to Camden –

which is where I am now. The job actually went pretty well. I seemed to find a niche for myself supporting promotional road shows for our customers, working on the technical side. This has meant that I'm rapidly becoming a seasoned traveller: I'm off to Amsterdam and Sienna before Christmas (my first time back in Italy) and then for sure New York in the new year. Sounds more glamorous than it is: airport, hotel, venue, hotel, airport is usually the routine, though I try and get about as much as I can.

I'm still young. It's a life. It's not a career; I'm going to get bored with it in a while I'm sure, but for now it's kind of fun and interesting. I've idea what happens after.

You didn't say anything in your letter about what has happened to you. I see the postmark is Lucca, so does that mean you didn't make it to university in Pisa yet – or that you've finished there? There's part of me that would like to know if Luca's OK; do you know? And Mita too. And maybe you can shed some light on what actually happened to Jackson; you're my only source for news on him now, much as he was my only source for you...

And I am interested to know how you are and what you are doing. A lot can happen in four years. And I know it's a long time... You may not want to tell me, I don't know. But you did write to me. Why <u>did</u> you write to me Gisella? There must be a part of you that wants – I don't know – to know something about where I am and what I'm doing, even if it's just for old time's sake. You asked about my job...

So if you want to write back, then that's just fine. I'll put my new address at the end of the letter so anything can come straight to me next time. And if you do write back, I'm going to keep asking you what happened four years ago; asking until I know. So at some point you'll need to tell me. Not next time maybe, but when you're ready.

I'm sure there's a lot that's happened to both of us since I was there. I guess we both need to work out how much of it we want to share.

Take care,

Rick

AMSTERDAM – October 1991

Gisella,

So you did write back, and quickly too! I have to confess that I wasn't sure what was going to happen next, or what you would do. Your letter arrived a couple of days ago – the morning of my current trip with work – straight to me this time, and not via some complicated, third-hand route!

I'm actually sitting in my hotel room in Amsterdam. Have you even been to Amsterdam? This time of year – that nasty bit at the end of Autumn and just before Winter – Amsterdam can be horrible. Today it was really cold. Freezing. There was a fog or low cloud or something all over the city that seemed to cling to the buildings and burrow through your clothes to your bones. You can't actually see very much when you're out on the streets walking, and it's strange how the restriction in visibility robs the place of its identity somehow; it doesn't look Dutch any more, if that makes sense. And you get no view of the canals, of where they are or how important or picturesque they are.

Last time I was here it was summer a couple of years ago. It was a stag do for a friend of mine. Does that translate? Basically it's a thing that happens before a man gets married when all his mates take him out, get him blind drunk and tie him naked to a lamppost. Or they all dress up as women. Sometimes both. Do the guys do that kind of thing in Italy – or is it a traditional, quaint old English custom?!

The first day of the conference has gone pretty well. The client seems happy enough. My bit went smoothly; all the computers and screens worked as they were supposed to, and the sound system was pretty loud. We're here for another couple of days before we dismantle our stuff and head back to the UK. It'll be cold and miserable there too I expect.

Thanks for starting to fill in some of the blanks created by the passage of time. I now know that you did get to university in Pisa - I guess in '88. I can't remember if that was what you planned. I think you were a bit vague about when you were going and what you were going to study. You didn't mention that. You must have carried on with your English as it's really good! I suspect you found living in Pisa completely different to living in Lucca – or maybe you didn't. I'm just saying that because to me – based on my brief visit – they seem like completely different sorts of places; Pisa is more frenetic and 'modern' somehow. Not that I'm saying that's a good thing..! And 'frenetic' is relative! Anyway, you went to university and now you're back home. That's a start.

I have to say that the news about Jackson and Mita came as no surprise to me at all. I told him when I was there that I thought she had a thing for him. He denied it, but I could see something in the way that she looked at him… You were a bit vague on timing; was it around the time you left for Pisa? Was Luca distraught or was he already history by then?

It sounds as if it was a bit wild and passionate – and that it didn't last very long. Thinking about it, when Jackson started going with Mita was pretty much when he stopped communicating with me, I think. Maybe earlier. It was around that time anyway. If there was talk about them leaving Italy and going off together (though I do find America a bit hard to believe!) it must have been pretty serious for the time it lasted. You suggested that the first couple of months was a real whirlwind for them, more from Mita's perspective, naturally. I wonder what brought it all crashing down. Do you know? I can imagine her family wouldn't have been too thrilled – though I'm not sure why I think that, seeing as I never met them properly.

I guess the ending of their relationship was the thing that made Jackson leave Lucca then? Or was it the other way round: he wanted to leave and when she wouldn't...? In any event, the pieces are starting to fit together, at least from my perspective. In a way that's kind of comforting. I mean, there's been a slice of life – OK, maybe not a huge slice – that's been absent of any reality or fact for four years. It's good to get something plugged in there. Maybe that's true from your perspective too; I don't know.

I do have a girlfriend, yes. Debbie. Though I'm not sure if its serious or not. I somehow doubt it. In fact I don't think I've had what might be termed 'a serious relationship' for a while. We met at a friend's party. Usual kind of thing. Drink was involved, of course! I actually fancied her friend, Mary; an Irish girl. Even now I'm not entirely sure how I managed to transfer my emotions to Debbie. I'm sure there's a logical explanation - and one which probably doesn't reflect too well on me. Anyway, we've been going out for a little while. She works for one of the big UK retailers in some kind of administration function relating to their warehouses. It doesn't sound too exhausting to be honest. We do the usual stuff: dinner, films - that kind of thing.

What about you? I can't believe that there isn't someone who is in love with you! I'm guessing that they're not from Lucca for some reason - but you don't have to tell me if you don't want to.

My trip to Sienna next month is still on, but the way. The job is similar to this one, but the conference will be considerably smaller. I think I fly in on the Monday and then out on the Wednesday: set-up, do the job, pack-up and fly home. Hopefully I'll get the chance to see something of the place, even if it's only the square where they race the horses.

I think that's about it for now. We have our final session here tomorrow and I need to grab some dinner and then check that everything's ready and working for the morning.

Hope to hear from you soon.

Rick

SIENNA - November 1991

Gisella,

I'm really sorry it has taken me a little longer to reply to you - especially as you wrote back so quickly again. Things have been pretty grim here for the last three weeks or so, and it's only now - sitting in my hotel room in Sienna (not so very far from Lucca!) - that I find myself with the time to put pen to paper.

Actually, my mother died a couple of weeks ago. Not that it was a surprise, really. She hadn't been well for some time and I knew it was serious. The doctors had warned us that, although she seemed stable enough and able to hold her own most of the time, there was a real possibility that we might see a sudden deterioration. Which is exactly what happened. Just after I wrote to you last she seemed to have a particularly bad night, and then that was it. Weight just fell off her over the next few days; she slept a lot. By the weekend they had taken her into hospital, and then on the Tuesday she died.

Knowing it was coming helps you prepare for the event, but nothing can help you with the suddenness of it all. One minute and the next are completely different.

We weren't that close, I suppose. I get a sense of how critical the family is in Italian life, and maybe that's true for many people here in the UK, but just not for me. Or not for my family. We tend to deal with each other in a rather detached and matter-of-fact way. That can make us a bit distant I suppose. But at least you managed to see through that!

Michael, my brother, handled most of the arrangements. He's something in 'The Law', and so getting stuff like funerals sorted was right up his street. I helped out where I could, offered suggestions, dealt with some of the mail and phone calls. We buried her the following week. It was a small enough service; not too many people, simple, a bit antiseptic I guess.

Then I went back to work. My Boss asked me if I wanted more time off, to duck out of this conference in Sienna, but I said no. I thought getting away and being occupied would be the right thing to do. And have I been busy!! We've run into all sorts of problems here. Only just managed to get them sorted in time actually. It was a long old day today!

Of course there was another reason I didn't want to miss this one. It gave me the chance to come back to Italy. Did I say that I hadn't been back since I left Lucca? I wanted to find out if it held any magic for me still - or whether my visit to see Jackson had ended up being just a remarkable one-off... Did I end up with an over-romanticised view of your country?

I needn't have worried. Sienna - what little I've seen of it - is wonderful. The colours, the streets, the sounds and smells - Italy as I remembered it, all bringing back echoes from Lucca. I'm glad, of course. Late yesterday afternoon I managed to get a little 'me time' and wandered down into the main square (the hotel's not that far from there). Most of the trappings from the last

Palio have long since gone of course, but a few remain; enough to get a flavour I suppose. And just walking around the 'course' and those tight bends… I can't imagine how the riders manage to stay on the horses for a couple of those turns. I know they don't always! I've seen photos of the race; it would be great to see it for real some day.

There was a third reason for wanting to make the trip too. Debbie and I split up. It was the day before Mum's sudden decline. If I'm honest, initially I think that hit me harder. I had assumed that we were OK, but apparently not. And there was no Doctor on-hand to give me warning that the end was coming. She said that it was nothing to do with me (whatever that means!), and that she'd found someone else. But of course it had everything to do with me, didn't it? I mean, why did she need to find someone else if there were nothing wrong? Anyway, getting away for a few days seemed like the perfect opportunity to think about things there too.

Truth be told, I'm not sure how I feel about splitting up with Debbie. I didn't get much of a chance to think about it given what happened with my mother. All my emotional energy went into that; I postponed thinking about Debbie until the last couple of days. I say 'postponed' as if it were some kind of calculated thing on my part - which it obviously wasn't. But there's only so much capacity for serious stuff and I instinctively prioritised. I thought about her on the plane over, and a bit yesterday when I was out walking. If there's any conclusion, then I guess its that I'm OK with it. Deep down I knew it wasn't perfect, that Debbie wasn't "The One". Maybe there was something inevitable about what happened - it was just the timing that was a bit shitty. Or maybe it wasn't…

So, as I said, not a great two or three weeks. And I'm sorry that this letter is all 'me' and that I've dumped a load of stuff on you.

Let's put that right, shall we? After all, you answered some of my questions from last time with enough to tease me and keep me interested! Piecing some of that together I'm getting a sense of your timescale; like the fact that you started at Pisa University in '88 - which was what I'd assumed. And that you had chosen to study languages - which also explains how your English is so brilliant! I can't remember exactly what you had been hoping to study when we met, but I'm pretty sure it wasn't languages, though I might be misremembering. I thought it was history or something. In any event, you've certainly learned a lot! If it was a three year course (that's how long courses are in the UK) then you will have graduated last year.

What have you done since then? Is there much demand for a language grad in Lucca, or have you taken up teaching like Jackson? Presumably with your degree you could have gone anywhere: stayed in Pisa, gone to Florence - Rome even! Were you never tempted?

But then maybe Roberto had something to do with it? You were a little coy when you introduced him - "a nice boy who still loved his mother"... He must have had more to him that just loving his mum to win you over! Was he on the same course as you? I have an image of him in my mind and I assure you that it's almost certainly very unfair, so you had better put me straight! How is he? Would I like him if I met him? (Better not answer that!)

Sounds like I was right about Mita and Jackson - the fact that it was a brief flame that burned brightly but for only a short while. You say Jackson left Lucca in the second half of '88; so you'd already started at university by then. I think the last letter (or anything, come to that!) I had from him would have been around May time probably. He didn't say very much that I can recall. Briefly mentioned Mita; didn't mention you at all. If things were starting to go sour with Mita and he was already thinking about escaping... Thinking about it, there was something not quite right about those last missives of his, even the ones before he hooked up with Mita. I'm not sure when they started changing, probably not that long after I visited. Anyway, if you don't know where his is now then all I can do is to wait and see if he shows up one day, either in person or 'virtually'…

I've just checked the clock and it's really late. I should be getting some sleep. One last session in the morning, then we pack up and get the train to Florence and fly back from there. I'll get reception to post this for me first thing, so hopefully you should get it at the weekend. How long does the post take in Italy?

It's been good, us getting back in touch. Hopefully my next letter will be slightly more upbeat on my side. I'm still due to go to the States after Christmas; maybe I'll write to you from 'the Big Apple'!

Take care.

Rick

NEW YORK - January 1992

Gisella,

I'm sorry if the tales of woe in my last letter made you re-live your father's death in any way. I wasn't to know, obviously. Given that it was such a shock and drama for you puts my own experience into some kind of context; gives it a sense of relativity. I don't know how I would have reacted if my mother or brother or someone I loved had been involved so tragically in road accident. And getting close to Christmas too Had the weather been bad; snow or anything like that? I assume you can get snow in Lucca?

From what you say, your sister suffered even more than you. (I didn't know you had a sister, by the way. I don't think you mentioned Paola before.) You had your studies and Roberto to fall back on and support you, but it sounds as if Paola had very little to help her through it - other than you and your mother, I guess. But if you were away most of the time, then I don't suppose you could have helped that much. I know Pisa is not a million miles from Lucca, but sometimes the shortest distances can be the hardest to travel. I confess that I'm struggling to picture what a young Italian woman - you sister - would look like if she were "going wild". I can't picture that in you is what I'm saying I guess.

The tangible outcomes - drinking too much, staying out a lot, taking off somewhere (anywhere!) at the shortest possible notice - I have seen in others occasionally. I would have had cause myself to go down that road just a few short weeks ago I suppose, what with Debbie and my mother... But it just never occurred to me. I don't think that's saying anything profound of course, just how I'm made.

How is Paola now? You didn't say. It was, what?, about fifteen months ago, so I assume (hope!) things have changed for the better.

Of course it would have been even harder for you to help given that you also had to work part-time to fund yourself through college. A lot of students have to do that in the UK, just to make ends meet. Some of them find it really hard, and their studies must suffer. If you were having to work most weekends in Pisa, then it would have been even harder for you to help your sister out. Clearly not all young Italian women have the kind of advantages that Mita undoubtedly enjoyed being the daughter of an olive oil magnate, or whatever he was!

But at least you had Roberto, didn't you? He was on the scene before your father's death wasn't he? He would have been some kind of help to you I imagine. For some reason I had assumed that you would have met Roberto on the course you were studying. Well, at least I was right about it not being in Lucca. And partly right in that you did meet him on university grounds, if not on your course. I'm not surprised how you met him by the way. Did I tell you about my experience of Pisa University refectory when Jackson took me there? It was my first exposure to the real Italy in many ways; a kind of baptism of fire. I'm pretty sure you could meet almost anyone in that canteen!

Well, as expected - and as I'd hoped - I'm actually writing this in New York. Don't I get about the place?! I'd never been here before; in fact, nowhere in America. In many ways it has met all my expectations: big and brash, neon lights and yellow cabs everywhere, harsh accents, everything rattling along at a million miles an hour. But one thing has surprised me: it's not as noisy as I'd expected. I'm guessing that's because of the snow that fell a couple of days before we arrived; that seems to quieten things down a little and must keep a few people off the streets. Having said that, they are clearly geared up to deal with inclement weather - which is a bit more than can be said for the hotel hosting our conference. It was a good job we came over early as things were a shambles first thing; something else that surprised me.

According to the guys on the reception at the hotel, the snow they've got at the moment is "nothing". I know three inches would be a big deal in the UK, but here it almost doesn't get a mention!

Hopefully you won't think there's some kind of sad trend in that I use my work to run away when things get a little tough. (I'm thinking of my last letter.) But, truth is, Christmas was 'personally eventful' for me. When I got back from Sienna it seemed as if party season was already in full swing. After my mother and Debbie, I felt determined to try and enjoy myself as much as possible. The result of that was I suddenly found myself hooked up with Mary, Debbie's Irish friend, remember? It hadn't been planned or premeditated; just kind of happened.

But it didn't last long. I feel as if I should add 'of course' to the end of that last sentence… And I'm worrying that I shouldn't be telling you any of this. You might be getting the wrong impression of me - or right impression, who knows? Doubt I'm living up to my original billing as being "a lovely English boy"… And this kind of flitting about really isn't like me, honest. Maybe it's some kind of reaction to my mother's death; some kind of unrealised desire to 'live in the moment', or to 'take opportunities'. I don't know. "You're only young once" is the kind of thing my mother would have said - though I doubt she would have been that approving of me just now.

No-one got hurt, which is one consolation. I think Mary saw it as what it probably was, just a Christmas fling. She clearly didn't invest anything major in me, so that's good. And I didn't have the time, I guess, to make any such investment either. But I do feel as if there's a void in my life now that needs to be filled. Perhaps that's too dramatic. Not a void so much as a longing, desire; something missing, in any event. Maybe it has been there for a while and I'd just not seen it because I had things to paper over the cracks - like my globetrotting job! If so, then I've been stripped back a little. Bouncing around. And I'm pretty sure I'm not yet finished…

Sounds like a confessional! If you'd like me to shut-up, then just tell me. But please don't be so disappointed that you don't write back. I'll try and behave - promise! I've a couple of weeks back in the office and then we're off to Barcelona for a few days - which is about as far from the snow of New York as you can possibly get! I went there once a couple of years ago and am looking forward to going back. Have you even been to Spain? I've only been to Barcelona and Madrid, and have steered clear of the party islands like the plague. Not my scene, although the way things have been going... Only kidding!

Anyway, please write back soon. It's great getting your letters.

Take care,

Rick

BARCELONA - February 1992

Gisella,

There's a cable car in the middle of Barcelona! How cool is that?! I'd forgotten about it to be honest. I mean, I must have seen it the only other time I was here, but somehow it had completely slipped my mind. It goes from the western side of the city up to a castle called Montjuic - and it's some ride! High over the roads and paths that lead up to the castle, close to the Olympic stadia and the botanical gardens. And when you're up at the top, the views over the city are spectacular.

We've been really lucky on this trip. Not only were our hosts supremely well-prepared, but because we'd allowed extra time ourselves (after that nightmare in New York), we suddenly found ourselves with almost a whole day free. Raul, one of the guys from our local office here, offered to take a couple of us around and show us some of the sites, which was brilliant. So we saw the Gaudi Cathedral (unfinished and a little bit weird, if awesome), and then the Parc Guell, more Gaudi. Then Raul pulled this little cable car stunt on us. Marvellous! We've come back to the hotel before going out for dinner. Conference tomorrow. Makes a change to have a bit of time in a place, and to be able to spend it not on my own. Don't like that too much I find. I remember a day in Lucca - maybe just my second or third day, just before we met - when Jackson was teaching all day. I was on my own. Not great. Maybe I'm not that good at being lonesome...

All of which - the being alone, the Spanish connection (not to mention some of the contents of my last couple of letters) - leads me to one final confession on the relationship front. Don't worry, this isn't another sad tale of something else I've managed to stumble blindly into on the back of feeling sorry for myself! This one's a bit older. About a year after I left Lucca, so before Debbie.

There's something that makes me want to just be honest with you; to not have any secrets. I don't know why. It's not as if I have a specific reason for telling you all this. I'm not after any kind of forgiveness or absolution. After all, what possible interest could you have in me now? I guess I just feel the need to be totally honest with you. Maybe its cathartic for me, you know? Cleansing...

Anyway, her name was Maria. She was Spanish. (I say 'was', but she's still alive as far as I know - and therefore, still Spanish!) I can't actually recall how we met - which sounds dreadful doesn't it? Those first few months after I came back from Lucca went by in a bit of a grey fog to be honest. I'm not sure how conscious of anything I was. Like being on automatic pilot. The job helped of course. I became one of those anonymous London workers in the cycle of home-tube-work-pub-home-sleep. There wasn't much to it, and that meant there wasn't much to think about.

At some point during the second part of '88 (maybe even around the time Jackson was leaving Lucca, who knows?) I met Maria. She was studying at the LSE. Economics; just starting her last year. It didn't really suit her - neither Economics nor the LSE. Still she was happy enough being over in London on her big adventure. Being from Madrid, she was used to big cities, so

London didn't daunt her. There were a group of us that used to go out drinking on a Friday night; she became attached to that group somehow - and then subsequently attached to me.

She was pretty in that typically dark Spanish way. Bright and witty, but not loud. I knew there was some kind of spark between us, but I was scared; I distinctly recall that. Since Lucca I'd kept myself to myself; deliberately walled off from other people, I suppose. One of my Friday night buddies saw what was going on and gave me a nudge - a bit like Jackson maybe. But that's history now. The short version of the story is that Maria and I started going out together. It was vaguely surreal at first, but it worked well enough. I became a little more normal; got some zest back in my life.

We were together until the middle of '89, which was when she had to go back to Madrid. I was sad, but not heart-broken. We knew it was coming far enough in advance to allow us to prepare for it. We wrote for a while afterwards, and made promises to visit. I went to Madrid once towards the end of that year, but without realising it I think we had both already moved on...

That's it. No more confessions! No more skeletons in closets! You know have all the high - and low - points in my adult life, pretty much. What's the verdict?!

At least my story is nowhere near as tragic as Paola's. No; that sounds wrong and selfish, sorry. I don't mean tragic. Difficult, perhaps. Hard - though emotionally that's certainly an understatement. I had no real inkling from your last letter that her life would spiral the way it did after your father's death. I mean, you hinted... But bouncing into that relationship and then becoming pregnant... That must have been so, so hard for you and your mother to deal with. I can't really imagine what it must have been like. From what you say at least the father didn't desert her. Did he have a choice? I can only imagine the kinds of pressures Italian social custom puts on young women in such circumstances.

Did Paola have any choices? I suspect the UK may be a little more 'liberal' in such matters (righty or wrongly). No. None of my business. Ignore that.

All of that going on at home would have coincided with your second year at college, wouldn't it? Another strain on you; must have been. I don't know, maybe just having the routine of Monday to Friday classes, part-time work, knowing that Roberto was around, all helped you to get through it. It would have given you some kind of structure or framework to rely on; something 'normal' to go back to and lean on. A chance not to think sometimes is important I've found.

Having said that, right now there's something that I very much need to think about. I found out last week that I'm being considered for promotion. It's not something that I've sought in any way; I've just been getting on with my job. But apparently, I've been doing it pretty well. Rumour has it that the Powers-That-Be were impressed with the way I'd pulled the fat out of the fire in New York last month. I'm not sure exactly what they've got in mind. The usual next steps from where I am right now would either be a permanent desk job in London, or a posting to one of our European or American offices. I suspect - and a couple of my colleagues have told me - that I shouldn't turn down the offer if promotion comes my way. 'Career limiting', they said.

I'll try and get my head around the possible options and see if any of them truly appeal. They won't make any proposal until after the company's financial year-end - which is the end of June. At least that gives me a bit of time to mull things over. And I'm not supposed to be gong anywhere again until May in any event; Paris this time...

All for now. Look after yourself,

Rick

PS: Please tell me Paola's OK and that it all worked out for her... x

LONDON - March 1992

Dear Gisella,

I seem to be alternating between hot and cold environments...
(I'm English, so I'm allowed to talk about the weather!) Cold in
Amsterdam and New York, warm in Barcelona, now cold in
London. Its that damp, bitter British cold that eats through your
clothes - no matter how many layers you have on! - and burrows
into your bones. We had some late snow here last week, and just
when everyone was beginning to think hopefully about Spring
we get a slap in the face. I think the only place recently where
the weather was nice was Sienna. Big surprise.

One of the things I like about your letters is how open-ended
they are. You never give me whole stories, but rather things by
instalments. At first I confess that I found this a little frustrating,
but not any more. Its nice to have them spread out in chapters; it
gives me something to look forward to - and sort of ensures or
confirms that there will be another letter to come.

Like your story about Paola. I get the feeling that there is an
ending you could reveal to me now (in as much as anyone's story
ever has 'an ending', I suppose), but rather than jumping to that,
you give me the next step on the journey. So I find now that she's
had the baby - Sophia - and that all is well on that front; and that
she is reconciled with your mother (I think that was the word

you used). But that her boyfriend, whose name you have never given me (and that's just fine!), has started to behave badly.

Actually that's a bit of an understatement isn't it? I don't mean to belittle how bad the situation must have been, sorry. He seems to have become less reliable, less 'there'. Disappearing for hours if not days on end. Growing distant; showing no interest in his daughter. If I'm honest, I wonder if this was something that might always have been going to happen, and that Sophia's arrival just sped things up. Apologies if that's judgemental or unfair, but by and large I don't have a particularly positive view of my fellow man when it comes to relationships with women (including me!) - especially when they are in the wrong. Compounded, I guess, when I've some kind of attachment to their victims - even though I've never met Paola.

And there's an undercurrent to the story that worries me a little. I'm slightly fearful of your next update. But at least you've given me enough hope that Paola comes out of this in one piece, even if she's still struggling a little to get herself back on a good course.

The one thing I wasn't expecting in your last letter was to read that you and Roberto had split up. For some reason I was reading about him with an assumption that he was a kind of constant for you; that after you had met him in Pisa, he was always there. Was still with you now. I should say that I'm sorry things didn't work out for you.

Was that about a year ago? Did your changing work have anything to do with it? You said you were doing something new, but didn't say exactly what. I suppose with you back in Lucca after your degree finished, his staying in Pisa (was it because of his work?) could only put a strain on your relationship. Those long-distance things can be very difficult to make work, as I'm sure we might have found out. But the way you portrayed it, it sounded more like a drifting apart than anything specific that triggered it. Is that right?

Anyway, I'm sorry it didn't work out in the end. I now have an almost certainly imperfect image in my head of both you and your sister now 'man-less' and a little solitary, which is sad. But you're back together in Lucca at least, and I guess with your mother the three of you have been able to get the beginnings of a return of equilibrium. I hope so. Certainly your letters suggest a kind of clarity or calm focus and determination, the way you write them.

Your interest in Maria is sweet. There I am giving you the whole story in one chunk - not really like your style at all! - and in consequence you ask me to go back and fill in what, for you, are gaps. I guess my style is a little more perfunctory - especially where I'm the subject. A then B then C; done.

As with Maria. We met, we got on OK, she went home; end of story. But you want to know what she was like - something more than "pretty in that typically dark Spanish way", or "bright and witty". And the $64,000 question: did I love her? <u>That</u> surprised me!

What can I tell you? Maybe something about her habits? Well, when she was working on assignments for her degree she used to sit at the kitchen table talking to herself in Spanish. Understandable, I suppose. And when she got angry, she used to shout in Spanish too. We didn't argue that often - not in the beginning - but when we did, and when she struggled for the English words or was frustrated by an inability to say what she wanted as quickly as she felt she needed to, she would lapse back into Spanish. At that point I could only tell what kind of trouble I was in by how long she spoke before I could get a word in, and how loud she was shouting! When she turned native they were funny arguments that we could never resolve conventionally.

We argued a little more the closer it came to her going back to Madrid. I think that was just pressure; I don't think our affection had diminished any. It was a way, I suppose, of making the separation easier to take, as if we were edging towards being gradually less happy with each other to soften the blow.

What else? She was very tidy, very organised. She said she needed to be as she was working in England and in English. It would have been different, she assured me, if she had been studying in Madrid. She didn't like meat very much, but loved Roast Beef and Yorkshire Pudding. She tried to like English football, too. I took her to an Arsenal game once, but apparently it was nothing like Real Madrid - and I can see that. Easily.

Does that help?

And did I love her? I don't know. I don't think so. Is it all relative? Individual? I didn't have a whole lot to compare it to, to be honest. I know I didn't love either Debbie or Mary (obviously!). Maria? Close, but no cigar…

Are you doing anything special for Easter? I suspect its a bigger thing in Lucca than in London. Over here its more about Easter Eggs and superficial bunnies and flowers than anything else. Just like most public celebrations these days, its all commerciality and what companies can get out of it. We get a couple of days off work, and that's about it for me. I might go to Edinburgh and visit an old friend for the weekend, just for a break.

Anyway, that's about it from chilly London. Say hello to your family from me, maybe.

Take care,

Rick x

PARIS - May 1992

Dear Gisella,

So my fears were realised! I had a sense that Paola's boyfriend
was a little darker than you were painting him. It must have
been quite hard for you to try and depict him as even-handedly
as you did. Especially when he turned violent. In a way it doesn't
matter how violent he was nor how many times he hit her. Once
is once too often. I can understand why she didn't react
decisively against him straight away, what with the new baby.
She was probably hoping that it was a minor aberration, and
that he would see the error of his ways and turn out all right in
the end. But obviously not.

I assume it was threat of going to the police that eventually
brought things to a head. It sounds as if your mother played a
major role in that, not surprisingly. Reading between the lines, I
suspect that she might not have approved of him from the very
start, is that right? I guess given what happened to your father,
she was still in a pretty dark space of her own, and so Paola's
trials and tribulations would have been heaping more
unhappiness on her. But she did act, that's the most important
thing. I hope she's OK now. You've never really talked about her
that much. I have this picture of her now, standing guard over
you and Paola like a sentry; challenging the world to make
things tougher. She will have had a pretty horrible year back in
1990; I hope she's happy enough now...

You didn't indicate what role you played in the final scenes of
Paola's relationship. If I read it correctly, this also happened
around the time that you and Roberto split up, so you would
have had a lot on your plate too, adding that to the impact of
your father and then Paola's problems. It must have been
incredibly hard for you, looking in from the outside as it were,
still away from Lucca most of the time and thus away from your

sister. And then the pressures of the last year at university too. It's a pretty worthless statement now, but I wish I had been able to help somehow.

I couldn't help but notice that there was no further elaboration on your split with Roberto. That's fine of course. Perhaps there's a mirror there with what happened between Maria and I, I don't know. Did it take you long to get over him? Was there anything to get over, come to that? If it ended up being a slow but natural transition away from each other, then maybe there wasn't that much trauma involved. I hope that was the case.

But then you haven't told me what happened in your final year at college either. I think we've reached that stage in the approximate chronology we're following. I assume you passed or graduated or whatever you do in Italian universities. Is that correct? I hope you got what you wanted out if it.

Of course then you went back to Lucca - and knowing what I now know, I'm not that surprised. I think I asked you if you had thought about going to work in Rome or Florence or somewhere, but now I have a fuller picture of the end of the eighties, I can understand why you would want to be home with your mother and Paola, at least for a while.

Your new job sounds like fun. And there's a certain symmetry about it, isn't there? You teaching English in Lucca... Where do you work? I don't suppose you're in that building overlooking the piazza where Jackson used to teach, are you? That would be too spooky! From what you say, the volume of work and class sizes seem just about perfect to start out with. Hopefully that gives you the right kind of balance, time-wise. I don't think I would have the patience to be able to teach. And in a way, I'm probably not academic enough. Hopefully it's not that I'm not bright or intelligent, but that I seem to be missing that special gene you need to be good at studying - and teaching, come to that. That was another of Maria's criticisms, by the way; that I couldn't take academic or theoretical subjects seriously enough. She was probably right. I'm much more a practical, hands-on kind of person; or at least, that's where I feel most at home.

Mentioning Maria brings me to the next $64k question you asked me: did I want to have children, and Maria not? I really hadn't seen that one coming! You were wondering if that wasn't the real reason we split up - or why she didn't stay in London; because we wanted different things. I can honestly say that we never talked about it. And, more importantly, that it never even crossed my mind - at least, not to my knowledge.

So the simple answer to your question is 'no'. Have I thought about it subsequently, in a vague and abstract kind of a way? Probably. But doesn't everyone of a certain age? I bet you've wondered about having children, haven't you? One day the time will be right, I suppose. And, more importantly, the person will be right too.

Edinburgh at Easter was fun. I hooked up with two of my old friends who had moved out from London a couple of years ago. One was working in Scotland for a software company, the other is doing a PhD at Manchester University (no issues with academic capability there!). We didn't do much: went out for dinner; went to a football match; drank a little too much whisky... By and large it was too cold to do much else. We'd talked about going over to Loch Lomond for a walk, but chickened out. Certainly it was nowhere near as pleasant weather-wise as it is in Paris right now.

Early May, Paris in the spring! Isn't that the biggest cliché? But it is lovely here - which is something of a pick-me-up, to be honest. I haven't been feeling too well recently. Not entirely sure what it is, I'm probably just a little run down. Tired a lot, off my food a bit - but only since Edinburgh. My boss suggested that I miss this conference out; he had noticed that I wasn't looking 100%. I said no, of course, hoping that the change of scenery might buck me up a bit. Perhaps it has helped a little. Inadvertently I think it may also have cemented my chances of being offered promotion. People might choose to see it as dedication, loyalty, or some such. Of course its none of those things; purely selfish really. Anyway, we'll see where that road leads soon enough.

I have a little holiday due. Well, quite a backlog in fact. Maybe once I get back to London and I've shaken off this bug or whatever it is, then I'll take myself off somewhere for a couple of weeks. Might be the ideal time to think about if I want this promotion, and what sort of opportunity I'd be happy to take.

For now though I think I'll just get a hot drink and have an early night. Back to the UK tomorrow and I don't want to be flying with a sore head.

Rick x

LONDON - June 1992

Dear Gisella,

I'm sorry it has taken me a little while to replying to your last letter, things have been slightly surreal here. And I was more unwell than I thought...

A couple of days after I wrote to you, I started getting stomach pains. I assumed that it was something I'd eaten - my friend's cooking in Scotland probably! At least I was in the office when I passed out and not home alone at my flat. One minute I'm walking back to my desk from the photocopier, and the next I'm lying on the floor with two paramedics tending to me and a crowd of people looking on! Not only wouldn't they let me get up (I've no idea what I looked like that persuaded them to keep me still), but not too many minutes later I was being wheeled into the back of an ambulance! I tried to tell them that it was probably nothing - but thankfully they didn't listen to me.

The next two or three hours saw me examined in A&E, then examined again, then admitted. Just as I was scheduled to give a presentation at work, I was lying in a crisp, clean bed on Ward 57 listening to Dr. Booth as he rang through both my symptoms - to reconfirm them with me, I suppose - and then the possible causes. From causes he went on to describe how they might fix me depending on what was wrong. That was when I knew it wasn't an under-cooked haggis that had done for me!

Two days later I was still lying in a hospital bed, but now recovering from major surgery.

To cut a long story short, the doctors discovered that I had something called Meckel's Diverticulitis. (You can look it up on the internet...) As I understand it, it's a small anomaly in the intestine that apparently lots of people can have - about 1 in 50. In some cases, like mine, it can flare up, or burst or something, and when that happens it has to be taken out. That means removing the offending section of the intestine. About three inches in my case. Serious stuff. I was in agony afterwards. And because of where it was, just being mobile as you recover is really difficult. It's not a quick thing to get over.

They kept me in hospital for nearly two weeks - which is probably longer than normal, but because I lived alone there was no-one at home to look after me. My mother was no longer an option, of course. Eventually we sorted out that I would spend a few days at my brother's and recover there. It wasn't the most convenient thing for him or his family, and the 'few days' turned into over a week, but to be fair he stepped up to the plate, and his wife - Gina - was brilliant. When I left to go back to my flat I was reasonably mobile, but still not quite well enough to resume my normal life.

Work were brilliant - not they had much choice in the matter. My boss told me not to rush back, that they would miss me but could cover for me. Obviously I would not be able to attend a couple of events that had been added to the schedule at short notice - Munich and Venice (and I've always wanted to go to Venice!) - but they told me not to worry, just to get fully fit again. This week was actually my first week back after, what?, six weeks or so away. I've just enough time to get things ready for a session in Switzerland next month.

When you go from what you don't realise is fundamentally quite an active and busy lifestyle, to something completely different - in my case sitting on my bum in front of the TV for far too long! - it does something to the way you think. I mean, I spent a lot of time reading, which is a luxury I had not experienced in a long while. I remembered how much I used to enjoy it, and by last weekend, I was getting through a book every couple of days - and watching far less telly! Novels mainly, but the odd travel and sports book.

And I re-read all your letters. At least twice. In fact, I thought about you an awful lot. I thought about other people too, of course. But my reflections on Maria and Debbie and Mary were all about the past; about things that were finished. Closed episodes, if you like. And I guess I came to the conclusion that's one thing our relationship never was - closed. It's more than it being a 'loose end'; and I don't mean a lack of closure in the sense of needing it to be finished or something. I think I mean in the sense of missing an equilibrium somehow. We never really found out our potential to be friends, if that makes sense? I'm not suggesting anything, by the way. I would just like to settle on our friendship. How it is. The terms of it…

I'm conscious that I'm probably not making much sense. See what hospital food does to your brain! The bottom line is that I think I'd like to see you again. It has become important to me that I can place the real, physical, today you to give your letters context. In many ways I suppose I am currently writing to a memory; I'm engaged with a past that needs grounding in the present to make it real. When I open one of your letters I want to be able to see you now, and not through some slightly blurry, rose-tinted image from over four years ago.

And I'd like to meet Paola and your mother. I'd like them to be 'real people' to me too.

What do you think?

Even though I've lost time at work through being ill, they're still fine with me taking some holiday soon. Indeed, my Boss (who's called Jim, by the way; did I say?) is keen I take a break straight after the Basel trip next month. He doesn't want me 'over-doing it', he says. "Get some sun and warmth" he said - and Lucca will be both of those things in August!

So, what do you think? Should I plan on coming to see you? If you don't think that's such a great idea, then please just let me know...

All those conversations with Jim, the way the company has behaved, has made me think about work too. Jim confirmed that they intend to make me a promotion offer at the end of the month, probably just before Basel. And he confirmed that the likely options are those I'd anticipated: fixed in London, or a spell abroad. If I was interested in neither, he said they'd still give me a raise, but if I wanted to progress then I should accept the promotion. It's all a little binary when you look at it like that...

The overseas options are more varied than I'd anticipated. America is the usual primary route - either west- or east-coast -

but the European options include France, Germany, the Netherlands, and Scandinavia. Often with more than one location in each. In France, for example, you could be based in Paris, Lyon or Nice. And yes, Italy is on the list too.

During those quiet evenings recently I came to the conclusion that I like my job - and I grudgingly acknowledged to myself that I'm good at what I do. And I like the company, and I like the people. It will never make me rich and famous, but for now it fits me pretty well. So on balance, I'm not sure I want to think about changing just yet. In that case, it would be all about direction…

Sorry it has been all me, me, me this time! Hope you understand. Looking forward to your next letter as usual - and now, a little nervously!

Rick x

BASEL - July 1992

My Dear Gisella,

Just across from the main railway station in Basel is the Hotel Victoria. It's a large imposing building that overlooks both the station and the myriad of tram lines that serve it. A much nicer hotel than Jim usually finds for us. Maybe he's trying to look after me!

It is getting darker now. The rest of the crew have gone out for dinner. From my window I can see the commuters hurrying about and hear the bells of the trams as they weave amongst the pedestrians. Your letter, thick and heavy, sits open in front of me on the small desk at which I sit.

I'm not really sure where to start.

It must have been really hard for you to write it. Perhaps I should start by saying that. Hard, not because of its size or complexity, but because of your desire - or need, maybe? - to be totally honest. I can imagine that, even though you <u>had</u> to write it, you would be nervous about how I was going to respond. Was I going to respond at all?! After all, when you have been consistently lied to over a number of months, when you have made a certain set of assumptions - begun to construct... something, I don't know - then doesn't one have the right to be upset or angry?

But I'm not. Let me say that first. I may be later on, but now, having read your letter more than once, I'm not angry. My first reaction was one of confusion, I suppose. You were turning just about everything you had said upside down. It was probably only after the third run-through that I was able to grasp the facts as they now clearly were - and then to begin to decipher your motivation for laying it all bare. And your motivation for lying in the first place.

Throughout this entire process of interpretation, I have tried to be kind; please be assured of that. I have tried to see things from your perspective. To try and understand. First and foremost, that. Perhaps the best way for me to be certain - certain that I now have the facts; that I do understand - is to replay what I now see as your history since I left Lucca all that time ago. There will still be gaps, of course; details that require finesse, or questions that remain to be asked, but if I get any of this wrong, then you must tell me. I need to be as sure as I can that there is nothing left unsaid.

[I have just opened the mini-bar and removed a far too expensive miniature of Scotch. It is open beside me now.]

The only logical place to start is with Jackson. When I left Lucca I truly believe what you say about where your heart was, what your intentions were. You surely know by now that from my side I was completely head-over-heels about you. I was already constructing probably impossible future scenarios in my head as I flew home.

But it seems that in stirring me, you stirred something in Jackson too. Maybe he had never seen you in such a radiant light as during those few days. Maybe he had been harbouring feelings for you that he simply did not recognise until - when? That last evening dinner with just the three of us? I can only ascribe motives to him as he has chosen not to speak up for himself. The fact that he made an advance to you within a couple of days of my leaving is… I'm not sure I have the words. Despicable is too soft, but it is in the right general direction. And, from what you say, it seems as if it was a very direct, passionate, uncompromising approach. Over-powering probably. I can see how he can be so utterly charming.

Yet I struggle with how he can possibly have been successful. How you could have succumbed so quickly? It is clear that you can't really answer that one yourself either. Had you feelings for him that you didn't realise? In those first 24 hours without me, did you suddenly come to some realisation that nothing with me could work because I was so far away? Or that, given the choice, Jackson trumped me in almost every department? That you didn't like me as much as you thought? Was it that, having been 'roused' somehow, you had a need to be satisfied immediately?

I don't really know how to process this. Like you.

But what is clear is that you and Jackson quickly became an item. This must have been the reason for him to gradually drop all contact with me. He couldn't be honest. His guilt got in the way. Of course, your relationship with Jackson had a knock-on effect. Mita. Relations with her must have become very strained; I know you sensed that. And from what you say, it seems clear that she wasn't going to take it lying down. From her perspective (and ignoring poor Luca!), you had stolen Jackson from her - in much the same way as he had stolen you from me. But she was there, local; she was in a position to fight back. And fight back she did!

Whether she trapped him, or blackmailed him (emotionally, of course!), or simply 'won' him, I don't know. But she did triumph, didn't she? And I get the impression that, after just a short period, you were OK with that. My interpretation of what you wrote is that it was a brief flame, and that what you had with Jackson was already effectively spent. And I believe you when you say how sorry you are that it happened at all.

But by then - early 1988 - you had university to look forward to; to occupy you. At least partially. You could afford to let Mita have him couldn't you? But clearly that didn't last for long either - and maybe that says more about Jackson than anyone else.

[There was a brief pause there. Room service just delivered my dinner, so I took a break to eat it, flicking through the TV channels - nearly all in either German or French - to try and occupy me while I ate. I'm finished now. It's even darker outside, but the tram bells are still ringing.]

I suppose if that were the extent of it, that would be enough. But to discover that you don't have a sister, and that Paola is just a fiction, and that you and she are one and the same... That Paola's boyfriend was Roberto, your boyfriend... That Sophia is real, but that she is your daughter... Again, I just don't have the words.

You said that you created Paola to give you an opportunity to tell me your story without jeopardising my reaction; in a way, to find out about me somehow, as a person. Did you think I would be judgemental, or disapproving? Did you want to know if you could trust me with the truth - before you broke it to me? Of course we don't know each other very well at all really, and if you were scared that the truth would somehow drive me away - especially when you had reinitiated contact...

I have a big unanswered question right there.

So you went to university to study, as you had said you would; as you wanted to. And things were fine for the first year weren't they? I guess after me - and then Jackson - that getting away from Lucca was probably a blessing in a number of ways. The chance to start afresh perhaps. And then you met Roberto at the start of your second year there. It must have felt as if things were beginning to fall into place. Even though he was from outside the college - more 'humble' is how you describe him, but I think I know what you mean - it sounds as if you were happy for a while; as if your life had taken a new road, one that was 'acceptable' and 'normal'.

But your father's death - the remaining major truth - hit you terribly. When you described how Paola was affected, it was perhaps a way of not only beginning to tell your story to me, but also it allowed you some distance from it so that you could work it out for yourself. Although I still cannot conceive of any 'wildness' on your part, I can appreciate the slide into recklessness - if that's not too strong. Based on the way Roberto turned out, he was never the kind of selfless character who was going to protect you from yourself.

So you partied more, neglected your studies and your work. It sounds as if you were hanging on to your place at college by a thread by the time you fell pregnant. That must have been a sudden and extreme alarm call for you. From what you say, it sounds as if you were shaken from whatever malaise you had fallen into; it was something that forced you to stand back and take stock. And just when you needed that support again, so Roberto's true colours showed through. I cannot comprehend what it must have been like to have him become harsh, unloving, violent... I am sure you tried to win him round, to salvage something - but I am equally sure that was never going to be achieved.

Suddenly, your perfect Pisa world was in tatters. How could you continue with your third year at university under those circumstances, being in Pisa with him still there somewhere? And being pregnant. I can see that going back to Lucca, reconciling yourself with your mother - and deciding to keep Sophia (if you ever really had the choice) - was the only option for you. There must have been a turbulence in your life that you needed to be rid of; an equilibrium you needed to re-establish. That whole year - 1990 - must have been crushing for you; and for your mother too probably. But when Roberto was finally dismissed from the scene, did that give you the chance to truly recover? A new family, a new set of rules? A chance to embark on a different journey?

In spite of everything you have been through, there is a calmness about your letters now. I feel it in the words you use, the phrases that make up your sentences. It is almost as if there has been, from all your trials, a bequest of self-knowledge, awareness, perception. When you write about the Christmas just gone, I can even feel a sense of joy in what you say, how you described that first yuletide with Sophia and you mother. It feels like a re-emergence somehow, or a resurrection (though I'm sure that's not the term I should use). And I'm guessing that working again, doing something positive, teaching English, engaging with other people, re-building friendships - all of that must be such a relief and comfort to you.

But still there are two big questions aren't there? One is yours, the one you've more than hinted at: how do I feel about all of this? About you?

The other is mine. Why?

Why did you decide to write to me? Why, having got back to some kind of peace by the end of the summer last year, why did you want to risk that by getting in touch with me? After all this time? What was there to be achieved? Wouldn't it have been better to let sleeping dogs lie and not disturb the past? (And I'm only thinking about you here, not me.)

But you did get back in touch; you did have a reason for doing so. What was it? I can see that it might be because you wanted to apologise, or set the record straight. That you needed me to understand. That there was a gap in my life - that there <u>had</u> to be a gap in my life - and a story that needed to be finished, an ending offered. I can see all of that, I truly can. But then you could have just told me the truth, without fiction or elaboration. That would have satisfied most of those ambitions. But you say there would have been a risk - but a risk to what? Wasn't making up Paola and not telling me about Jackson adding in even more risk? But a risk to what?

I have another answer to 'why?' in my head, and I just don't know if it is the right one.

And yet I suspect this will be the answer to your question too. In fact, I know it is. On the surface how I feel about you is how I felt about Paola; compassion, sympathy, caring. All those sort of things. I am not furious or angry. I am not - cannot - suddenly become a different person, a person without feelings; cold, heartless. I would not be writing this is I were. I believe I have tried to empathise and feel your pain. I believe I still do. None of that has changed.

But on another level…

I am trying to understand what it all means; what 1987 meant then, and what it might mean now. I am trying to decipher today, 1992, and a bundle of letters from someone I once fell hopelessly in love with… And it is really hard. Really hard. I am rephrasing your questions in my head - inventing them almost. I need to answer them for you, because that is what you want. And I could be wrong on so many levels, and misjudging and misinterpreting… But now I have no choice. And I am OK with that, I think, because I need to answer them for me too…

It is very late now, but the tram bells are still ringing though less frequently. Looking out of my window, there are fewer people on the streets but there is still movement, people going home, leaving or entering restaurants. On my desk there are now three empty mini-bar bottles.

As I finish this letter, you are not so far away from me here. Perhaps 400 miles? This evening, that is a strange thought. I will write again when I get back to London, and when I have an answer to our questions. Please wait for that - unless you think I have missed the point completely and am barking mad. That wouldn't be the first time such an opinion was held about me!

Much love,

Rick xx

LONDON - August 1992

Dearest Gisella,

Since I last wrote to you just a week or so ago, I have done little else but think about you. I have been wrestling with all those questions that I posed - both to you and myself - to see if I could settle on any kind of answer or uncover the true meaning behind, well, everything really. And I simply can't. It's just impossible. There are two conclusions that I keep coming back to, inevitably, without fail, and the first of these is that I cannot truly know the answer to all those 'why?' questions based on our letters alone. There is a gap - in understanding interpretation, nuance, meaning, everything - that can only be bridged by dialogue, and seeing, and feeling.

The second conclusion is one I think I was already forming as I sat in the hotel in Basel, and which was confirmed when I asked myself a subsequent question - this one hitting me suddenly, violently almost, as we flew back over the English channel the following day. Did I care? Really?

And the answers came flooding to me then: by the time we had landed, next day at breakfast, on Monday when I returned to work, five minutes ago…

I do care.

And there is a gap in my life, a part of my story - the story with you - which is unfinished, open. It is a story that needs closure. Or it is a story that needs picking up again, dusting down, and resetting in motion. A story that needs to run its course - however long or short that course may be.

And I believe - I hope - that these are your answers too. That these are the reasons that you wrote to me nearly a year ago now. The very same. That you care. That you have an open-ended story too.

Whether these conclusions, beliefs, assumptions - hopes and dreams, even! - are right or wrong, can only be decided in one way.

I am coming back to Lucca.

I have arranged to take next week off from work. I have already booked my flight on Sunday morning. I've found a hotel for the week; the Universo. I will get the train from Pisa. If everything is on time, I will be waiting for you on the steps of San Michele at 5 p.m. Sunday evening. Waiting and probably looking up at that little balcony of the old English language school building…

XX

P.S. You will probably have been surprised when the postman delivered this 'special' letter you had to sign for. For obvicus reasons, I needed to get it to you quickly, and to know that you have received it...

See you Sunday...

LUCCA - November 2015

My Darling Gisella,

The weather was spectacular today; a perfect blue sky, really warm, yet with a subtle breeze that stopped it being too close. You would have loved it. I had been hoping for something else, of course; perhaps a little rain overnight or some fine drizzle, enough to darken the stone, the marble, and the streets; and some cloud to make the mood more sombre. There was a slight jarring in the juxtaposition between feelings - internal and external, if you like - that meant I could never quite embrace what was going on.

And of course, 'embrace' is totally the wrong word, suggesting as it does the positive coming together of two people, when in fact what we were facing was the complete opposite. What I mean is that I wanted to feel more than I did, I wanted the day to be profound as well as sorrowful; a celebration in the right context. But when the sun is shining and there are people on the streets laughing and eating ice cream, well, it's difficult. Or at least it was for me.

I wanted to say goodbye in the right kind of way, but I was deprived of that. Not only because of the weather, of course, but because in so many ways I was the focus of the day, constantly needing to alternate between efficient organiser and the person suffering the most, between needing to be strong and just wanting to be weak.

So I thought I would write you one last letter, sitting outside our favourite cafe at San Michele.

It is early evening now. Most people dispersed after lunch, and I was able to change, ensure anything else that needed sorting was in order, and then make my way here. You might have guessed that I would have chosen to be here at 6 o'clock. It seemed appropriate somehow...

Sophia looked wonderful, by the way. Perhaps more womanly today than I have ever seen her. Maybe that's not such a surprise. And I saw more of you in her than even before, as well. Yes, she cried unconsolably, but she was also strong, resolute, brave. Perhaps you sensed that. She has gone now, away on the train back to Firenze a couple of hours ago, leaning heavily on Toni as they boarded, looking glorious. 'Radiant', we would say in England. I think knowing that you would never see your first grandchild was perhaps the hardest thing of all for her.

And it was so unusual to see Giorgio in a suit. He borrowed one of mine and gave it a certain élan that I could never have pulled off! I'm glad he chose to come down from Pisa on his own. As I stood beside him, I was acutely aware that we have simply never seen enough of him in the last couple of years. But he has his own life to lead now, of course.

Who else? Your mother was unusually quiet, arrived last and left first. I know she found it very difficult. I will talk to her later when I go back to the house, just to make sure she is all right.

Poor Luca was in pieces! He seemed to be relying on that stick of his more than ever - but perhaps that's just my imagination. He embraced me about once every ten minutes it seemed! I think, after all this time, he is the one person I am attached to more than any of our other friends. But then I'm pretty sure you won't be surprised by that! Mita was still away. She sent me an e-mail to let me know that she would not be able to make it back from America. But that was fine, of course, and I think an encounter that neither of you would have relished.

The fact that Jackson turned up also made it fortuitous that she was away. I don't know how he found out (probably though Luca, though he denied it), but I had word from him three days ago that he had heard the news and would like to attend. He wanted to know if I would mind, after all these years. He ghosted in (from where I've no idea), stayed in the background, then left equally anonymously. We spoke, of course. He looks much older now - don't we all! - and time has not been that kind to him. He still has that certain charm, but it feels a little careworn now. In a way, even though our meeting was a little cool, I'm glad he came; and though its most likely that I will never see him again, it was good to be able to finally close that chapter face-to-face.

It's funny, thinking about people moving on. Sophia soon to be a mother; Giorgio graduating in a few months and then starting his career in the Carabinieri...

And then there's me. What do I do now? It's a question I have not had to ask myself for twenty-three years. Yes, in a minor way of course, but now we're on a scale of decision that reminds me of Basel. Neither Sophia or Giorgio need me now, and your mother is settled and secure.

Seppi has just brought me another tea, and I asked him what I should do now. He said I should eat some of his extra special cake to make me feel better! I don't think there's a cake in the world that could do that...

I'm going to take some time off and do a little travelling. Not too far, as I want to be able to get to Firenze within a day, so that I can be with Sophia and Toni when needed. I will probably go back to Genoa or Verona for a few days, or to our favourite hotel in Viareggio. I expect I will need to return to London to decide what to do about work and the business, but there's enough time for that.

Above all things, I need to face up to the fact of being without you. There can be no second magical reunion, no floods of tears on meeting again, no immediate certainty of what is the right thing to do. There are people standing outside San Michele just where we stood all those years ago. They are laughing and taking photographs. They will stay perhaps a few more minutes and move on. And a part of me wants to tell them not to go, to remain here, to find joy and happiness in this wonderful place as I have done.

Perhaps I will come back every year, to this same spot; to tell you what is happening in my life; to tell you about Sophia and Giorgio. To write you one last letter.

All my love, forever.

Ciao,

Rick xxx

RIDING THE ESCALATORS

1

He had been sitting in the cafe between H&M and the Apple store, overlooking the main atrium of the mall, when the idea came to him.

'How long do you think it would take to ride all the escalators in the mall?', he asked Chek as they sat at the bar of "The Inflatable Frog" later. Buried invisibly in the black décor of the walls and ceiling, ageing speakers offered up a stream of old 80s' and 90s' music in a bid to invest some kind of atmosphere in the place. It was an environment most people either loved or hated. Mitch hadn't made up his mind yet, even after all this time. That it was convenient was the best attribute he could currently come up with, sitting as it did half way between where he and Chek worked. Not quite on the way home for either of them, it had still become a haunt they used perhaps two or three times a week. Often their conversation contributed nothing to their well-being or progression through life, especially after a few drinks.

'What?' Chek put down a lemon-infused beer and stared at Mitch incredulously.

'The escalators,' Mitch repeated. 'How long to ride them all? In one go?'

'You're crazy!'

'No; I'm serious! How long?'

Watching the shoppers cross his line of sight, travelling diagonally floor to floor, had been mesmerising. Pale Caucasians looking out of place in their t-shirts and shorts (except for those who had been there years and simply looked like prunes past their "sell by" date), their shapes generally not in step with the slimmer, more compact locals, whose variations on straight dark hair and flat faces marked out their origins for the informed observer. Mitch was equally comfortable – or uncomfortable – with both; an Asian Mother and European Father had blessed him equally, and his breadth of geographical experience had given him what others might have considered an "edge".

But he was fundamentally uncertain about white women; unsure as to whether he was attracted to them or not. It was a strange sensation. Part of him wanted a European girlfriend (not one from Australia or New Zealand, you understand!), but another part did not. He had tried to acquire one more than once, singularly unsuccessfully. When he did make progress, he eventually found himself up against an invisible barrier; something he had been unable to fathom until he realised one day that they were equally unsure about him. Half-and-half was a complex cocktail.

'There are loads of them. As I sat in the coffee shop today, I could see eight just from where I was – you know, that little row of bench seats right against the glass? Had to crane my neck for the two down near M&S, but there were definitely eight. And that's just in that section of the mall.'

'But why? Why the hell do you want to waste your time going up and down in a bloody mall? What's the point? If it was to pick up girls, then that might be different – in fact I might just join you! – but it isn't, is it? Can't be.'

'Why not?'

Chek laughed.

'Because it's you, dimwit!'

Chek was all too aware of Mitch's 'conversion ratio'; of how successful (or not) he had been with girls in the past. It was almost as if he kept a log so that he could torture Mitch with his catalogue of disasters whenever he wanted to extort a beer out of him. Failure was not in Chek's own vocabulary, and had he maintained his own list it would be populated almost entirely with the green ticks of conquest. Mitch comforted himself with a belief – not profoundly held, it had to be said – that Chek was not happy.

'Look', he ignored the barb, 'there must be at least three dozen in there. If not four. The place is huge! How many escalators are there in the world? Millions probably.'

'And what's so special about these then?'

Mitch pictured them. They were the colour of burnished bronze that, when the sun shone fully through the glass pinnacle of the atrium roof, became almost iridescent. And they were spotless; quiet; efficient. Somehow an almost perfect embodiment of functionality. People got on them at one end and got off at the other. They were transported from one place to another without moving. It was almost serene.

'Nothing, Chek; there's nothing special about them, OK? I just wondered how long it would take, that's all. Like a kind of challenge.'

'But not a very dangerous one! I mean, you won't be risking life and limb, will you? Unless you get tired and fall off one end!'

His friend had never been impressed by safety – at least on the face of it. But if you dug a little into his past, Mitch knew there was more show there than anything else. His parents were wealthy; he had been to a good school; he chose a safe course at a prime university, and followed that with a solid junior management job at a blue chip firm. Mitch had once asked him why he had not taken the opportunity to take a year or two out, go travelling, see Europe, but Chek's response had been evasive and unconvincing.

'That's not the point. I just thought… I just thought that it would be great, just for once, to be able to say that you had done something that no-one else had done. Maybe that's the extent of my modest ambition.'

'Like a world record, you mean? You get loads of nutters doing all sorts of things to try and get into that Guinness book: stack paper cups; eat hot dogs; sleep naked on a bed of snakes – all sorts!'

Chek laughed again, but to Mitch his statement was the beginning of acceptance.

'Not a record, no. But then kind of. And there would have to be rules.'

'Such as?'

'I don't know. Not riding the same escalator more than once. Not going on the up escalator immediately after using the down one that's paired with it. That way you have to plan your way around it bit more.'

'Sounds like orienteering!'

For Mitch, as the idea grew on him, he began to see his attempt more like a crusade. He would be there riding the escalators for a real purpose, not just to help him shop. He would have a goal, a challenge. It was something that he could fail at; surely that implied a degree of risk? How would he feel if he found himself with one escalator left but no way of actually getting to it?

'You couldn't use stairs.'

'What?' Chek's interruption surprised him.

'I said, you couldn't use stairs. If you were going to do this thing then it would have to be escalators only; no stairs, no short cuts. You would have to start and end at the same place – my rule, this one – and you'd need to somehow prove that you had been on each one.'

'And I would need to avoid getting arrested!'

'Yeah! Security will think you're a nutter if you're not careful! So you need to watch that one.'

The Mall employed an army of people – men and women – smartly dressed in beige shirt and pants, whose primary objective was to act like high-class bouncers; but this objective, as well as their muscles and innate aggression, was submerged beneath a veneer of tour guide helpfulness. They looked innocent, but Mitch knew he wouldn't want to get on the wrong side of any of them.

'Carry a bag,' Chek suggested.

'A bag?'

'Yes. Maybe not a rucksack; a bag. Small enough not to appear dangerous. You'll need one anyway, to carry water, supplies. And your log book.'

'What log book?'

Check had suddenly moved into practical mode. Mitch assumed it was his management training.

'It occurs to me that the only way you can prove you actually rode the damn things will be to keep a log of which one, when you got on and off, and something about what you saw or did when you got off. Either that or take photos – but the guards might not like that.'

'Guards?' The work surprised Mitch a little. 'You make it sound like I'll be trying to escape from somewhere!'

'In a way you will.'

Chek paused. Mitch could see he hadn't yet finished so he waited, downing the last of his beer while he did so.

'And you'll need somewhere to keep your map. I can get you a map of the place.'

'You can?!'

'Floor plan. All the rides; all the stores.'

Suddenly Chek had become an ally.

'How?'

'My Dad knows the guy who manages the centre. They belong to the same … club. Let's just say that. I'm sure I can get you a map. Come up with some crazy story. Would that help?'

Five days later, Mitch had a photocopy of the mall's entire floor plan spread out across his bed. It was time to get planning.

2

She had always considered what she did to be an artistic endeavour. It was, after all, akin to taking a blank canvas, a limited palette of colours, and transforming them into something else. Often, particularly when she became completely absorbed in what she was doing, time would steal away from her, leaving her behind, wrapped – and enrapt – in a private cocoon shared by no-one. Eventually, of course, she would let them all in – let anyone in, indeed; but then her creativity was over, and she simply bequeathed to them what had come from that momentary spark. It was surreal, but there came a point where she could sense the instant of transition between unfinished and finished, and at that moment she would stop immediately, no matter what she was in the middle of, sigh, invariably stretch, stand-up (she was usually prone, it seemed), and simply tidy-up and leave.

'Done', she would say to herself. Rarely was there a second glance.

In her own way, she had gained a little notoriety for her work. The window displays at "Cinderella's" were widely regarded as amongst the best in the mall – if not in the whole downtown area. But it was notoriety and not fame because she had established for herself a reputation of sorts, not as a difficult or aggressive person, but rather as someone who was a little weird.

'Eccentric' and 'precocious' were the words people used most about her. Privately she quite liked the thought of being 'precocious' – but she knew what they meant.

If she had possessed any truly close friends, she would have happily tried to explain to them what it was like to be her, and how she became transformed once she was faced with a new challenge. The constituent parts were nearly always the same: the bare canvass of perhaps two to five metres of window display (initially covered, floor and walls, with untainted white canvas), the sheet glass that protected her domain from the outside world (again, pristine and unsullied), and her props.

Apart from her private collection of paints, inks, glues, paper, and fabrics, accumulated over the first two years of her profession, in the beginning the props were always the same: a number of mannequins, a range of clothing and accessories that the management needed to promote and sell, and some additional accompaniments for her to weave in. At first, these were traditional items, like suitcases or umbrellas, but as she became more proficient, and as her talent became more evident, the Manageress began to experiment too, throwing in a few 'whacky' items to see what Suzi would be able to do with them. She never failed, no matter how bizarre these additional props might be, nor how tangential or unnatural their association with the image the clothing range suggested.

She was glad to be working for a woman. She felt certain that a man would be less creative and give her less freedom; she was convinced that she would be told what to do, where to place things, the colour the backdrop needed to be, and so on. Jasmine allowed her to be free.

'Left-centre display' – this was how the briefings normally began. There were three window areas: left-centre, centre (the big one), and right-centre (overlooking the escalators). Jasmine always started with location. 'Swimsuit range for this spring, men and women. I thought perhaps three to five mannequins, but see what you think. At least one man (but probably only one man).'

'Of course!' Suzi laughed; the number of men involved in "Cinderella's" window displays was a private joke between them. 'There's only one Prince!', they used to say.

'I thought for props, some of the usual things from either our storage or the shop out at The Point. You know, deck chairs, sun shades…' – and then the pause that Suzi looked forward to most of all – 'And I thought we might throw in some model aeroplanes – flying off to holiday, that kind of thing – and perhaps some animals. Not sure what, or why, but I'm sure you can work something out. When you've got an idea, speak to Derek.'

Derek was the shop's general assistant; Jasmine called him her 'gopher' – though she never explained why. During the early months, he was in the habit of challenging Suzi when she would ask for slightly oddball or esoteric things for her displays; but as he too began to appreciate the uniqueness of her talents, he stopped challenged and started clarifying. It became a matter of pride to him that he got Suzi exactly what she needed. He turned into a vital ally.

'Animals?' he checked, when she told him.

'Not live ones, obviously', said Suzi, 'but they need to be realistic and life-size. And I'm not going to do anything to them, like paint them or anything. They might just be…"adorned"…'

Derek rolled his eyes in mock horror at the challenge she had given him. Like Suzi, Derek was beginning now to get a positive reputation too. Suzi's demands had challenged his ingenuity and resourcefulness – sometimes even to the extent that he actually made the things she had asked for. Jasmine has noticed this too, and in consequence she had given Derek a little more general responsibility in his own role, even deputising for her in looking after the store for short periods.

'I suppose you know what animals you would like?'

Suzi had handed him a slip of paper.

'This is my ideal list; the top four. But any I could make any on the list work – but I need at least three.'

He had said nothing. Suzi remembered that he had shaken his head slowly and then folded the paper and put it into his shirt pocket.

Contrary to what you might have expected given her talents, Suzi's apartment was minimal and unadorned almost to an extreme. On the twenty second floor of a condominium building about thirty minutes from the mall, it was painted entirely pale yellow; indeed, the yellow was so pale that it was almost white. When her mother visited her once, just after she had moved in, she asked her why everything had been painted white.

'It's not white, it's yellow.'

'Complete rubbish. Any idiot can see it's white! What did they teach you at that college of yours?'

The answer to her mother's question was "Art with Graphic Design". But Suzi had struggled. She had difficulty working within the structure that was demanded of her, both in terms of her formal education as well as the way in which her teachers seemed determined that she should explore any talents that she might have lurking. In general, the staff seemed dismissive of all their pupils, their default line being that none of them could possess any skills unique enough to either compete with what they were being taught or that would warrant them wasting any of their precious thesis- and treatise-writing time.

Mr Henrik was a little different. From an un-disclosed European country, although his official role was to teach "etching and monochrome", it was clear to many of the students that his talents were so much broader than that – and his interest in his pupils much more sympathetic than that of his colleagues. Occasionally he would offer what he termed "extra classes", but these were not classes at all, just an opportunity for students to spend a couple of hours on college premises in a safe environment expressing themselves without any direction, constraint or restriction. Suzi had loved Mr Henrik's "extra classes".

In terms of her domestic arrangements, Suzi would not have preferred a white apartment – though clearly there was no way should could have said so to her mother for whom that's what it was already! But she knew that if it were white, then she would be forced to change it – just like her blank canvasses at work – and at some point inevitably get the sense that she had finished something, so would have wanted to pack up and walk away. But this was her home, so that would hardly have been practical. So the colour was just not-white enough for her to accept that it had its own identity and that she didn't need to tamper with it.

The only creative indulgence she allowed herself at home was to decorate t-shirts. In the tiny second bedroom, she had set up a small workbench. There were drawers underneath filled with dyes and inks, fabric pens, beads, sequins – in fact just about anything she could lay her hands on for material design. On a chair in a corner of the room was a pile of plain white t-shirts (of various sizes), and each weekend her escape was to take one of these and decorate it. Occasionally she would try and accommodate a theme in what she produced, but more often than not her work was flowing, freeform and abstract – after all, she had nothing to sell and no instructions from Jasmine to follow. The conclusion to her efforts – that moment of transition to "finished", the sighing, the stretching – was exactly the same as at "Cinderella's", but these products were never seen. She would simply fold them and place them on another pile in another corner of the room.

If she had possessed any imagination about herself, she might have thought differently about her clothing designs – indeed, she might have actually thought about them in the first place! Others pursuing a similar hobby to Suzi might easily have been overcome with their burgeoning talent, assuming it to be greater than it perhaps was, and consequently seeing themselves with their own clothing range, hosting catwalk shows, drinking champagne at expensive media parties. But Suzi harboured no such self-perception. Indeed, it was almost as if, had she stood in front of a metaphorical mirror to examine her talent, she would have seen nothing reflected. Perhaps that lack of self-awareness contributed a little to her eccentricity, and to why she felt no desire for a wide circle of friends – and why others found it difficult to get close to her. There seemed nothing to hang on to.

3

If Mr Lee had a defining characteristic, then it was probably that he had a persistent habit of answering questions no-one had asked. Or, to be more precise, had not yet asked.

'Is should be sunny tomorrow,' he might suddenly say, just as your mind was heading towards the weather. Or, 'I doubt the government will win the next election,' just as your thoughts were turning political.

Indeed, so often did he display this trait that many people found him a little difficult to get along with, not to say disturbing – especially when he seemed to be at least two steps ahead of where your own mind was. This was unfortunate in the extreme, as Mr Lee was a polite, kind and considerate man whose intent toward flies never went anywhere near harm.

Not surprisingly he lived alone in a small apartment not far from the centre of town. His flat was crammed full of the relics and mementos of his life, and if he ever had more than two guests at a time (which was very rare) they would have struggled to find space to stand up in, never mind to sit down and relax. Although his taste was eclectic, he had a particular penchant for wood carvings, glass paperweights, and old leather-bound books – in spite of the fact that he was no longer an avid reader. It was indeed some of the wood carvings that made the greatest inroads into the little space he had available in his apartment, especially a pair of giant frogs that stood on guard at either end of his lounge.

If you stood at the main window of the flat (having moved a mountain of books and paperweights to get close enough), you would look out on the suburbs of the city; a veritable mountain range of condominiums defined by roads and punctuated by assorted green spaces. Mr Lee knew his neighbourhood well. Apart from his collecting, he was also an avid walker and would think nothing of spending two hours strolling into town – a journey of perhaps a quarter of that by taxi, bus or metro. If he were indeed a taxi driver himself, his knowledge of the streets, avenues and cut-throughs of his district would have been second to none.

Occasionally he would spend a quiet evening hour sitting at the bar of "The Oyster Catcher", a small drinking establishment located in a tiny row of stores near the foot of his building. There he would chat to the barman, people he knew, strangers passing through, usually on any subject and always answering the questions in advance. He never held an audience for very long, for no matter how fascinating, erudite or perceptive he was being, people always reverted to a distrust of a man who seemed to know what they were thinking.

'If only he knew the winners at the race track, or the lottery numbers,' the barman once said to a customer as they watched Mr Lee's back as he left to go home, 'then that would be worth something! Then he would have all the friends in the world!'

As for Mr Lee, he had friends enough. He was happy sitting in "The Oyster Catcher", or chatting to people as he walked downtown; his need was now only for wood carvings, or glass paperweights, or leather-bound books.

It had not always been thus of course, and in his past Mr Lee held a secret that he had divulged to no-one.

He had come to the city from far in the south where he had been born and brought up. After leaving school, he had established himself in the local library and quickly rose to become the Head Librarian. He was kind and very focussed on those who visited his library. He used to call them "fellow travellers". A great deal of his spare time was spent reading, and he establish a wide encyclopaedic knowledge that was invaluable to both the library and its clientele. It was perhaps in this that his ability to answer the not-yet-asked questions was born.

One of his fellow librarians was particularly taken with Mr Lee. So much so, that when she declared herself to him, he was truly astonished, and had to take a two-day leave of absence from work to recover. Catherine was by far the prettiest, quietest and most intelligent of his staff. A little younger than he (but not too much so), Mr Lee was already convinced that she must have had a steady boyfriend, for how could someone as accomplished as she remain single for very long?

Their courtship was at first painful and clumsy; some might even say cumbersome. When he was nervous – as he often was during those early days – Mr Lee's tendency to pre-answer questions came to the fore. It was something Catherine, having been alarmed by at first, learned to live with, assuming that over time he would grow out of it, as much as a child grows out of sucking his thumb. To a degree she was correct, but she found however that his pronouncements, when he made them, became deeper and more profound – and not occasionally a little frightening.

Then, one day, as they walked home together from the library, Mr Lee suddenly stopped dead still, frozen to the spot.

'What is it?' asked Catherine, looking instinctively around for signs of danger.

Mr Lee stared at her.

'Because you are going to leave me,' he said.

Catherine, eyes now wide with panic, grabbed his arm.

'What are you saying, dearest?'

'That's why I have to go. Because you are going to leave me.'

'Go?!' She had begun to sob a little, her grip on his arm stronger. 'Go? Go where?'

'Away,' he said, now slightly calmer. 'I have to go away because you are going to leave me, and I want to make it easier for both of us.'

He managed to catch her as she started to fall, and cradling her in his arm, got her back to their apartment where she promptly ran into the bedroom and shut the door behind her.

Even though anything had yet to happen, from that moment on, Mr Lee managed his life as if the cataclysm of Catherine leaving him was already fact, and even if the emotional residue of such a momentous event was completely absent, it seemed to make little difference to him. She had tried to persuade him otherwise when she finally emerged from the bedroom, but to no avail. She could see that, in his own way, he too was in total shock and trying to cope as well as he could. Needless to say, the nature of their relationship changed instantly, and when, three days later, Mr Lee and his immediate personal effects left Catherine behind in the flat she was already glad. Would she have left him? At the precise moment he closed the door behind him for the last time, her unequivocal answer would have been 'yes'; perhaps not then, but certainly within the week. But if he had never answered the question that had never been asked..?

He had found himself a small apartment in the north (where he still lived) and set about rebuilding his life. It was not difficult to find a librarian's job given his exemplary professional record, but this time he made sure that he kept himself in check. Thus he showed no sign of ambition, and when the Head Librarian left, he chose not to apply for the post, even though many of his colleagues were expecting him too. With them he remained a little more cautious, detached, aloof; the last thing he wanted was to replicate his experience with Catherine, and so he tried to ensure that there was never even the slightest hint or possibility of intimacy with anyone.

His love of books did not diminish, but his desire to read left him – so he started collecting. That this new found habit then spread to paperweights and wood carvings came by accident, following chance purchases and the realisation that collecting gave him something of a quiet purpose that he could indulge in without the need for others. Mr Lee was aware that people found him a little strange – especially as his defining characteristic never went away – but he did nothing to deter it; in many ways it offered him the security of a shield from others, and he had to do nothing extraordinary to maintain it. There were times, of course, when he was particularly moved by something or someone, that he felt his guard being lowered; but he had developed his self-control to such an extent that he could almost always mitigate against the threat of exposure such vulnerability implied. He knew that it would take something extraordinary to shift him from this sense of security.

4

At night time the mall is eerily quiet. The only sounds come from the constant ultra-low hum of the cooling systems and refrigeration units as they ensure equilibrium ready for the morning. Most of the shops are in darkness, though a few choose to waste money by burning some of their window lights and signage, as if they might be surprised by a sudden coach-load of shoppers at 4 a.m. and didn't want to be caught with their pants down. Regularly – perhaps once every thirty minutes in any one location, and at every minute somewhere – the footsteps of the night watchmen, the guards who patrol the subdued mall with their flashlights and batons, just in case.

Occasionally there will the sudden roar from a lift shaft as a guard traverses between floors, though many prefer the automated escalators, now still and silent but always waiting for the footfall that will set them going.

It seems twice the size at night; the definition it is normally awarded is removed by the absence of blazing neon. Shadows are more vague, edges less well defined, and despite the hardness of everything – the floors, the walls, the glass, the frames of doors and furniture and general hardware – it is a softer place; a place where the rigidity of rules is no longer sacrosanct. It becomes, for a short while, a place for ghosts, uncertain images, and memories and dreams. It could almost be a place of escape.

Around five thirty the cleaners arrive, armed with their polishing machines and dusters and mops; and gradually the mall is brought back to life by the injection of light and sound. And voices begin to echo again, and occasionally laughter. At first distinct – a call on level five can reverberate and echo all the way down to a different lobby on level three! – these sounds themselves then blur and become absorbed into the overall thrum.

Yet when the first shoppers arrive as the doors open at ten o'clock, they marvel at the peace and serenity of the place, unaware that in this relative quiet the pulse of the mall has been beating loudly for the last four hours or so.

5

For the next few days after the arrival of the floor plans, Mitch became absorbed in their study. He carried them wherever he went; he even made a reduced size photocopy so that he could read them on the bus or train. More than once Chek found him bent over them in "The Oyster Catcher", oblivious to all around him, his beer hardly touched.

'I'm going over there tomorrow afternoon, just to check a few things out,' he announced one Tuesday evening.

Check was a little surprised.

'You mean in the evening, right? It's work tomorrow.'

'No, afternoon. I've got some time owed to me, so...'

'So you're going to blow it by walking round a mall?. Man, you're sadder than I thought!'

In reality Chek was quite envious of his friend, although he wouldn't admit to it; and once Mitch drew him in with his plans and ideas, he too found himself absorbed by the challenge.

'See, it's not as easy as you think,' Mitch said one evening. 'The first part should be simple enough. I reckon in about half an hour you can cover quite a lot of ground. But then it gets harder to make the changes in levels without walking miles.'

'Leave them until later then,' Chek suggested.

'Tried that,' said Mitch, indicating the sheets of note paper upon which his right arm was resting, 'but that only helps to a limited degree. And you know the two big ones?' Chek nodded. 'Well those are the real bastards.'

In the central core, there were a pair of escalators that traversed all four floors, from the basement to level three. Young kids loved riding them because they were so large; it was like a really safe ride in a really safe theme park. Because, in Mitch's challenge, they were equivalent to four standard escalators, as soon as you took one – down, say – you had to catch up with four in the opposite direction. In this case, you would burn four 'up' rides. That took some planning; do you do that all in one go, or spread the deficit reduction out – four lots of two-up-one-down? The rule about not riding them in pairs, one immediately after the other, made the whole thing so much more of a puzzle.

'I thought it would be easy', Chek said, 'I mean when you said what you wanted to do. A breeze! I had no idea it would be so – well, difficult.'

'Neither did I.'

Mitch had, thus far, calculated that he would probably need somewhere in the region of two or three hours to complete the circuit – once he had worked out his route. This would allow him some time, he hoped, to get a coffee or take a leak. He knew he had as much time as he wanted, but had no desire to dawdle. Once he had his plan then it was just about execution.

'It seems to me that there are a number of key locations on the route; places where you have to make the right calls in terms of next steps, where the impact of going wrong could be fatal.'

'Fatal?!'

'You know what it mean,' Mitch said, sipping the latest beer Chek had bought with Mitch's own money. He pointed at the plans. 'Here, here, here and here – primarily. "H&M", the "Game Zone", that chocolate shop place, and "Cinderella's". I know that's ignoring the two big bastards, but it seems to me that getting the sequence right in these four locations – time and again, remember – is fundamental.'

'You make it sound like a military campaign,' Check said, secretly impressed with his friend's focus and passion.

'A campaign of sorts.'

Mitch's frustration and drive was knowing there had to be a solution to his problem; that there must be a certain combination of rides that actually allowed him to complete the task. There had to be. It was only logical. Thirty three up, thirty three down. Simple.

The next afternoon found him in the mall, not trying out any of the routes he had sketched out thus far (this was no dress rehearsal!), but rather trying to get a sense of how the escalators related to each other. It was all very well examining lines on a piece of paper, but it wasn't the real thing. It was a wet day, and the absence of bright sunlight through the atrium roof made the colour of the escalators more moody and threatening than burnished. He rode the big escalators back-to-back three times, as if in doing so he would gain some advantage over them, dissolve his fear of them. As he went up and down, he caught glimpses of other escalators in other lobbies, camouflaged beyond the shops' neon. In two places, the building arced slightly, sufficient for there to be essentially blind endings to some of the concourses. But now Mitch knew what was round each corner, of course, but the absence of direct line-of-sight still unnerved him a little.

After his final ride down the big escalator pair, he was approached by one of the guards. They were smiling politely.

'Enjoying yourself?'

'I'm sorry?'

'The escalators. I've been watching you for a little while,' smiled the man, 'just wanted to make sure everything was OK.'

He was slightly short, but stocky. His uniform fitted badly in terms of length, but Mitch guessed it had to be the size it was to accommodate his chest. Although he was smiling, his eyes looked cold and unimpressed. Mitch noticed a small scar above his right eye.

'I'm a student', he said. He had rehearsed for this moment. 'Architecture.' He pulled his copy of the floor plans from his rucksack. 'I'm studying mall design as one of my options at the university.'

The guard took the plans and glanced at them before handing them back.

'There are some unique features in this mall,' Mitch went on, trying to sound convincing, 'I was just trying to appreciate them.'

'Such as?'

Mitch look confused.

'Features, such as?' repeated the guard.

'Well, these two escalators for a start,' he returned the plans to his bag. 'Unusual. Innovative. And the hub-and-spoke design.'

The guard looked unsure.

'How there's a central atrium with the other lobbies radiating off it, but without any of them being truly symmetrical.'

'Right.'

There was a pause. Mitch wasn't sure if he had been dismissed or if there was more cross-examination to come. The guard seemed uncertain too.

'Have you finished then?' he finally said. 'With these two?'

'Yes. Yes, thanks. I ought to be getting along anyway. Thanks for your help.'

As he walked vaguely towards the entrance lobby, Mitch wondered why he had made that last remark. The guard had done nothing at all to be helpful, and there was something in the coldness of his eyes which told him that this particular specimen was probably not to be trusted.

6

Rather than leave the mall, Mitch walked away from where the guard stood, taking a couple of sharp turns and even venturing into a shoe shop, until he was satisfied that he was not being followed. Outside "Our Soles, Your Soles", he sat on a bench and checked his floor plans. There were still a couple of things he wanted to see and then he really was done.

He made his way towards the ground floor entrance of "The Cocoa Bar", the chocolate shop he had mentioned to Chek. Mitch had decided that the link between here and "Cinderella's" might be crucial - whichever way he took it - in terms of mitigating the negative impact of the big rides. He had two routes to try out, and, packing the floor plans back in his rucksack, set off for the first one. It appeared simple enough: two up and then one down. There was a degree of mall to traverse in between the escalators, but one of these interludes passed by the toilets - and Mitch was beginning to realise that it was a good thing to know exactly where these were located along any potential route.

As he headed for "Cinderella's", he saw for the first time how the particular confluence of escalators manifested itself just here. Somehow their arrangement appeared different in reality to that on the drawings; in fact, there were three pairs of escalators in closer proximity than he had appreciated. He knew he would have to check his plans again when he got home.

When he reached the end of the escalator he took four or five steps forward and then simply stopped, suddenly transfixed by the window display ahead of him.

Evidently there was a new range of clothing going on display, but the magical thing was that they appeared to be presenting themselves! Three combinations - shirts, jumpers, trousers, skirts - were posing, apparently in mid-air, and at first glance, without any visible means of support. Lounging on the floor (and 'lounging' was the only word Mitch could use) were two completely naked mannequins, each resting on one arm, looking up at the clothes. A third naked Mannequin was leaning against the inside of the window, similarly rapt, and a fourth was sitting on a small stool at the back. This last was positioned in such as way as to be not only looking at the clothes, but somehow directly through them, the glass, and at Mitch himself. It was a stunningly simple effect. And amidst it all, the petite display arranger was administering the final touches to her scene.

'Still enjoying yourself?'

Mitch was so engaged in the window display that he had failed to realise someone was standing alongside him. The voice made him jump.

He turned. It was the Security Guard again.

'Sorry?'

Mitch took the man in. Short, stocky, it appeared to be the same Guard who has so recently accosted him - even the voice sounded identical. Had he been following him all this time?! And then Mitch noticed that this one had a small scar over his left eye. How could they be so similar?

'I've been watching you for a little while,' smiled the man, 'just wanted to make sure everything was OK.'

Before Mitch could reply, there was another shout from nearby.

'Hello, hello! Sorry I'm late! I do hope my Nephew hasn't been causing you any trouble.'

Both Mitch and the Guard turned to see a small, compact older man coming towards them. He had evidently been hurrying.

'Sir?' said the Guard.

'My Nephew', said the man, putting his hand on Mitch's shoulder as soon as he had arrived. 'Not in any trouble, I hope.'

'No, Sir,' admitted the Guard (somewhat reluctantly, thought Mitch), 'not at all.'

'Very good; thank you for your trouble.'

It was a closing statement - accompanied by the offer of a handshake - that gave the Guard no way out. He shook the man's hand, nodded in a meaningful way to Mitch, then walked away.

'I.... Sorry.... Do I know you?' said Mitch once the Guard was out of ear-shot.

The reply was not immediate, as it was now the new arrival's turn to be captivated by the remarkable display.

'Mr Lee,' he said after a short pause, turning to face Mitch. 'I hope you didn't mind; it looked like you needed rescuing.'

Mitch found himself smiling.

'Perhaps I did - just a little,' he agreed.

Mr Lee was drawn again to the display.

'It's really good, isn't in?' suggested Mitch.

For a moment they stood side-by-side looking through the window. From her movements and the adjustments she was making, they could tell that the girl had suspended the clothes from the ceiling using a fine, almost invisible twine of some sort; perhaps fishing line. There were obviously frames inside the clothes to give them depth and definition, but they were so well crafted and disguised as to defy discovery.

The girl stopped what she was doing, picked some scissors up from the display floor, and then looked out at them. Mitch and Mr Lee were oblivious to this - and to her then walking out of the display. A few moments later, she appeared at their side.

'Do you like it?'

Her voice tugged the two men from their reverie.

'It's you,' said Mitch - instantly regretting the lameness of his comment. The girl smiled.

'Wonderfully clever, my Dear,' said Mr Lee, giving her his best smile. 'I'm not sure I have ever seen anything quite like it.'

She blushed, slightly.

'And you?' she said directly to Mitch.

'Me? It's brilliant,' he replied, trying to make up for his opening remark. 'Surreal, but brilliant.'

This time she giggled a title.

'My name,' said the older man, 'is Mr Lee.' He held out his hand which she shook softly, 'Delighted. And this young man is…'

They both looked across.

'Mitch. My name's Mitch.'

'I'm Suzi,' the girl said. She paused. 'This is what I do,' she said, indicating the display. 'I'm glad you like it. I never really know, you see. I get feedback from my manager and the shop staff, but that's about it.'

'Well, if all your displays are this ingenious,' said Mr Lee, 'then you are a very clever young lady, Suzi.'

She blushed again. Mitch shuffled, slightly uncomfortably.

'How about a coffee?' said Mr Lee with sudden enthusiasm. 'Can I buy you both a coffee perhaps? I was just going to have one myself; on my way as it were. Then I saw Mitch looking in need of rescue, and well - here we are.'

'Rescue?' questioned Suzi.

'It's a long story,' said Mitch.

'And one that I'm sure we'd both like to hear,' said Mr Lee with a degree of finality. 'Why don't you pop your scissors back? We'll wait here.'

Five minutes later they were in Starbuck's. Mitch and Suzi were sitting at a table near the entrance while Mr Lee who was waiting at the counter for their drinks.

'Who is he?' Suzi asked.

'No idea,' said Mitch, beginning to feel slightly more relaxed. 'He suddenly appeared from nowhere just as that security guy was about to give me the third degree.'

'What were you doing? I saw you looking in the window. You look harmless, enough. I mean,' she added quickly, 'not like a terrorist or anything!'

'Of course he's not a terrorist, are you Mitch?'

This from Mr Lee who had reached their table just in time to get the last few words of the conversation. He put their tray down and Suzi and Mitch took their drinks.

'No,' Mitch smiled, 'I'm not a terrorist.'

'What are you then,' said Mr Lee, 'if you don't mind us asking? I mean, that guard looked very preoccupied with you.'

'Do they all look like that?' Mitch asked, more to Suzi than Mr Lee.

'Kind of,' she said. 'But then I see them every day - which means in a way I don't see them at all any more.'

'I bet you don't really see the escalators either,' Mitch suggested.

'The escalators?'

'Ah,' said Mr Lee, 'now I think our young friend is really going to tell us what he's up to...!'

Apart from Chek, Mitch had confided in no-one thus far. He had been concerned that doing so would somehow devalue his challenge, or that he would lose control over it. But now, sitting drinking coffee with a strange old man and a young lady who, he had to confess, he found very pretty, he felt relaxed and safe enough to bring them into his enterprise.

Slowly he allowed his tale to unravel, and soon, inevitably drawn into the intricacies and challenges of execution, he became enthusiastic and animated. By the time he had finished explaining, both his companions had almost finished their drinks.

'Cool!' said Suzi. 'That sounds wild! I could never even have thought of doing something like that. Wow! It's just great. Are you going to do it? I mean, do you think you can? When are you going to try? Can...'

'Don't ask,' said Mr Lee, interrupting suddenly. He was not smiling.

'Don't ask what?' said Suzi.

'If you can go with him.'

Suzi blushed, deeply this time. Mitch looked at her. He had not seen that question coming. After all, they had only just met. Even Chek had not ventured to ask that question. He looked at Mr Lee. There was something serious in his eyes that he had not seen before.

'Was that what you were going to ask?' He turned back to Suzi.

She paused before replying.

'It was actually; yes.' She turned to Mr Lee. 'How did you know?'

He was trying to smile again, but it was unconvincing.

'Oh, logic, or luck. Or something like that. I mean, I could see you were enthusiastic; it sounds like an adventure, something unreal if you like. And you my dear,' Mr Lee put his hand on her arm momentarily, 'you have great vision and can see the potential in things. You have a magic touch. Why, your mannequins could even come to life the way you use them.'

There was silence for a short while. Mitch concentrated on his coffee, downing it in three goes. When he placed his empty cup back down on the table he saw Mr Lee looking at him, expecting something - almost as if it were his move.

'I was planning to do it alone,' Mitch said slowly, watching for reactions. 'I have never even considered being accompanied. Maybe that's just me.' He paused, but neither of his companions filled the gap. Suzi's eyes were firmly on his. 'I was going to try it this Sunday. Somehow I didn't know that until now - but somehow, now I do.'

Mr Lee finished his tea and put down his cup.

'I think you can ask him now, my dear,' he said to Suzi. His smile had returned.

'Really?'

He nodded.

'Ok,' she seemed hesitant. 'I mean, well… Can I come with you? On Sunday? I'm free on Sunday. It might be fun. We…we could have something to eat afterwards - dinner or something - if that would be all right. If you wouldn't mind…'

It was the kind of decision that Mitch would never have taken lightly, never mind quickly. It was his idea, his plan, his adventure. If Chek had asked him he would have said no, instantly. But now, there was this pretty girl whom he had just met and who seemed to be effortlessly barging her way into his enterprise with little effort or malice. And leaving him powerless, with nowhere to go.

'Can you be here for ten o-clock. Outside the Wilson Avenue entrance?'

'Anywhere, any time,' she said, her eyes dancing.

Mitch was completely lost.

'That's settled then,' said Mr Lee, rising. 'Glad we've sorted that out. I'll be running along now. Lovely to meet you both.'

'Wait,' said Mitch. 'Just who are you, Mr Lee?'

'Me?!' The older man smiled and rested his hand on Mitch's shoulder. 'I'm just a little old man doing a bit of shopping and having coffee with some new young friends. That's all.'

He nodded to Suzi and started to make his way to the nearby exit.

'And I like to keep my eye on security guards,' he winked at Mitch, 'you never know what trouble they might cause!' And with a short laugh, he was gone.

7

'We sat there for another five minutes or so, and then she left to go back to work.'

There was a vague crackle on the other end of the phone. Reception where Chek lived was not great and often their conversations were punctuated by strangely placed silences and missing words - at least at Mitch's end. He waited briefly.

'....s awesome.' Chek's voice came back. Mitch could tell he was either excited or impressed. Perhaps both. 'And you said she's pretty?!'

'Yes, I did say that', Mitch confirmed, 'though that's not the most important thing, is it?'

'Right,' said Chek, doubtfully. 'If she'd been an old dog I bet you wouldn't have been sitting there drinking coffee with her!'

Mitch knew his friend was right. The fact that Suzi was pretty - as well as clearly creative, intelligent, and so on - did make things easier.

'And I wouldn't have said yes to her going along with me on Sunday, either,' he admitted.

Now there was a real silence. Mitch could tell that it was manufactured and not the fault of the phone company. He imagined Chek going through the gamut of recrimination and accusation - 'why didn't I ask?!', 'what's he taking her for?', and such like - before gathering himself to respond.

'You what?!'

Chek's voice came back slightly quicker than Mitch had expected.

'Umm. She asked if she could come along. You know; on my escalator thing.'

'And you said yes? Just because she's a looker?!'

'No, not just because. It wasn't that at all. We were just talking; I got carried away, I guess. Made it sound like a big adventure - which it isn't, by the way. And she got hooked up, somehow. When she asked, what could I say?'

'Well, how about "no"? How about "sorry, but if I was going to take anyone I'd take my best friend". Something like that, you hor…'

There was a loud crackle and then a pause. Chek must have finished whatever he was saying, so Mitch knew it was his turn again.

'And with Mr Lee there, what could I say? I was in a bit of a corner.'

'In a corner with a boner, you mean!'

'Chek!'

Pause.

'Look, I had no choice… I felt like I had no choice. The way Mr Lee prompted her - there was only one possible answer.'

'Oh yes,' said Chek, scorn and disappointment clear in his voice, 'this new mysterious old man. I mean, like where did he come from?'

'I wish I knew,' said Mitch. Now it was his turn to pause. 'And there's more.'

'What more?' asked Chek, feigning lack of interest.

Mitch looked to the coffee table near where he was sitting. Resting on top was a plain brown cardboard box. It had already been opened.

'Well?'

'When I got back to the apartment, there was a box waiting for me.'

'A box?'

'My name and address on it, all correct. Just waiting for me. From him.'

'Mr Lee?'

'Yep.'

'No shit!'

'Don't ask me how… But there's this note,' Mitch was holding it in his other hand. He started reading. ' "Dear Mitch, just a few things from me that might help you and Suzi on Sunday. Hope you don't mind. Good Luck. Mr Lee." That's what it says.'

' "Just a few things",' Check echoed back. 'Such as?'

'Might be easier if I show you,' Mitch suggested. 'Can you come round later?'

When he had discovered the box, the first thing that had impressed Mitch was the neatness of the script in which his name and address had been written. It was clearly not computer generated, but executed by someone with lots of experience and a very steady hand. Then, once he had opened it, he found the perfection of the packing on which the short note had rested was also remarkable. It was precise, ultra secure; each of the items inside - now loose on the table - had been meticulously encased in brown paper, taped-up well. Every little parcel had been separated from its neighbour by a combination of small foam shapes and little balls of the same brown paper scrunched up to provide a buffer between each component. With one exception, there had been two lots of everything. Mitch could only assume that Mr Lee intended one for him and one for Suzi.

Having finished his conversation with Chek, Mitch went through the inventory again:

- Small torch x2

- Spare torch batteries x2

The mall would we well-lit, filled with shoppers; why would he possibly need a torch? He was only going to be there a few hours at most.

- Small notepad x2

- Pen x2

- Bar of chocolate x2

Then, truly bizarre:

- Small plastic Nerf gun x2

- Foam Nerf gun bullets x12

What on earth would he need a kid's Nerf gun for?! It was an indoor challenge involving riding on escalators. There was no danger there - and even if there were, Nerf guns..?!

- Small compass x2

- Ball of nylon twine x2

- Packet of paper hankies x2

- Packet of skin-coloured plasters x2

- Some marbles x10

- Sunglasses x2 (both with dark blue frames)

The solitary item was a key ring. Attached to the key ring was a small Swiss Army-style pen-knife, two different keys (one small and silver; one larger and brass), and what Mitch could only describe as a 'button'. It was the kind of button that was used for doorbells. He pressed it again and, as before, nothing happened.

The only conclusion Mitch could reach was that Mr Lee was a little soft in the head. After all, consider the evidence. What kind of a man walked up to a Security Guard in the mall and pretended that a young man whom he had never met (young enough to be his grandson!) was his nephew? What kind of man took two complete strangers for coffee, and then deliberately - almost premeditatedly - got involved in their lives? And what kind of a man came up with a stunt like this: a random selection of bits and pieces that seemed relevant to - well, nothing?

Almost in spite of himself however, Mitch found himself dividing his new found booty into two piles. One - the one without the key ring - he then gathered and placed in a small clear plastic bag retrieved from the kitchen. He then took the remainder of the items and put them all into his rucksack, with the plastic bag then on top.

For the next couple of days, when he was not working Mitch was reviewing and revising his plans. Not only did he double check those multiple escalators near "Cinderella's", he also went back over his potential routings, gradually whittling the possible five down to a final two. Now that he had a passenger to consider, he found himself giving additional weight to some aspects of the routing that he had almost ignored before. For example, the distance to be walked along the entire route or the amount of time he estimated each option to take; quicker would be better, surely? Then there was complexity to consider. One or two of his initial itineraries were complex in the extreme, and however pleasing they might appear to him (in terms of symmetry or logic), he found himself rejecting them in favour of the simpler alternatives.

On Saturday evening, he drew up copies of the two routes they were likely to take. He would make his final choice the following morning. He had given Suzi his number, expecting her to call at some point to make sure that the enterprise was still on. Mitch had assumed that she would want to validate that he was still intent on his hair-brained scheme. But no such call was made. He could only assume that either she had total confidence that he would be outside the mall in the morning - or that even if he were there, she would not be.

As he tried to sleep, his head spinning in anticipation of the day to come, he tried to decide which of the two he wanted to be true: Suzi there or Suzi not there. It had, until very recently, always been a solo enterprise. He had considered no-one, made no allowances or concessions; he had worried only about what he thought and wanted. The focus, the outcome, was entirely selfish. From that perspective, he wanted Suzi not to show. He wouldn't wait for her, he had decided on that. If she wasn't there at ten o-clock, he would go through the Wilson Avenue doors alone.

But even as he imagined that, it was a picture that settled uneasily with him. This new notion of having some companionship during the day was actually an appealing one, especially considering who that companion might be. And hadn't she offered him dinner or something afterwards? There was a new dimension - a novel potential - that was not lost on him.

Heads or tails? Eventually, with this coin of his preference still spinning in the air, Mitch must have fallen asleep. When he awoke, the "will she, won't she?" question remained at fifty-fifty, though at some point during the night he felt certain he had actually decided which way he really wanted the coin to land.

8

When the bus dropped Mitch near the Wilson Avenue entrance, a small crowd had already begun to gather waiting for the doors to open. These were housed in the point of an irregular star-shaped construction which rose, three stories high, all glass and stainless steel and tubular framework. At night-time it was illuminated by ingeniously hidden spotlights that, in their hundreds, would subtly morph from red to orange to yellow to green, and on through the spectrum. It was quite a sight - especially at Christmas when the owners went to town with fake trees, sleigh and reindeer.

At each of the other star points - the extremities of the "hub and spoke" design (as Mitch might have pointed out to the guard) - other sets of doors were preparing to harvest their own little cluster of early morning shoppers waiting for ten o'clock. Sunday would, Mitch knew, start quiet, but by lunchtime the mall could be as busy as any Saturday afternoon, especially on holiday weekends. This was not, of course, a holiday weekend, and Mitch was intended to be nearly finished come noon in any event.

As he walked towards the doors, he saw Suzi sitting on the wall of a raised flower bed, framed by shrubs, looking his way. Mitch could see that she had dressed sensibly - which was his first concern out of the way: sweatshirt, jogging bottoms, trainers. Apart from the small shoulder bag she had with her, she might have been pausing for breath before continuing on a run somewhere. His second concern was almost simultaneously dispelled when she gave him a small, discrete wave. She remembered him. If he would have admitted to a third worry, this vanished when he reached her.

She was prettier than he remembered.

'Hi,' she said, when he reached her. 'I didn't want to be late.'

'Great. Just a few more minutes,' he said, checking his watch.

'How long do you think it will take?'

'Couple of hours, maybe. Unless we stop for coffee or something.'

'Cool.'

Mitch put down his rucksack, opened it, and pulled out the clear plastic bag.

'These are for you,' he said, presenting it to Suzi.

'What's in it?' she asked, trying to divine everything through the bag without opening it. 'Looks like some odd stuff...'

'From Mr Lee. The old guy.'

'Him? Why?'

'Beats me,' Mitch confessed. 'When I got back the other day there was this box waiting for me. Two of everything - so I guessed one for you and one for me.'

She moved some of the things around through the plastic of the bag.

'Chocolate I can understand. And maybe plasters if you are being ultra-cautious. But some of it... What are these?!'

'Nerf gun bullets,' Mitch smiled. 'For the Nerf gun.' He pointed to it through the bag. 'I know, I know. Doesn't make any sense to me either.'

She shrugged her shoulders and slipped the bag into her own.

'Where did you get that guy from, by the way? He was nice enough - but a bit weird. Is he your Uncle?'

Mitch was still fiddling in his rucksack. He looked up at her.

'Nothing to do with me. I'd never met him before. No idea who he is. He seemed pretty keen on us though. Harmless.'

'Hopefully.'

'Look,' Mitch held out a few sheets of paper, 'this should be more useful. It's our route. In case we get separated (which we won't), I thought you might as well have a copy.'

He sat down next to her and narrated as she leafed through the sheets.

'First page is the plan. All the steps, in sequence, including where we have to walk between the rides. See the code? Each escalator is numbered one to sixty six; the first extra digit is the floor we start on, the second where we finish. These other sheets contain a printout of the floor plan; five sheets, one for each floor. With the escalators clearly numbered.'

'Very thorough,' she said. 'With detail like this you could give these to just about anybody and they'd be able to find their way through.'

He shrugged.

'I've been giving it a lot of thought...'

Movement nearby made the both look up. The doors were being opened and the people waiting had now begun to edge forwards with a purpose.

Mitch stood up first.

'You sure you still want to do this? I mean, it's a pretty daft idea if you stop to think about it.'

'I don't think it's daft at all,' said Suzi rising. She shouldered her bag, and moved towards the door. 'Come on Columbus.'

'Columbus?' Mitch had caught her up and was walking beside her.

'Why not? He was an explorer wasn't he? Did something no-one else had done. Something like that anyway.'

Immediately inside the Wilson Avenue entrance, as with the other four entrances, were the cash machines, the interactive Mall maps, overhead directions to the nearest toilets, the customer service desk, and the marque stores. Standing unobtrusively here, as elsewhere, one beige uniformed security guard. To the uninitiated, they might have entered the Mall at any one of the five possibilities - but both Mitch and Suzi knew the place well (for different reasons!) and could tell Wilson Avenue entrance apart from all the others.

Ahead of them, the space gradually widened, the first shops appearing on both sides within about fifteen metres. A further thirty metres ahead, a pair of escalators linking them to the first floor. Behind them, hidden from view at this location, a pair to the basement and back.

'Numbers one, two, three and four,' said Mitch, partly to himself as he paused, returning his own route plan to his rucksack. He sensed Suzi observing him. 'Oh, I won't need those for a while. I've rehearsed the first half hour or so over and over in my head.'

'I bet you could probably reel the whole thing off if I asked you too,' she suggested.

'Maybe,' he said, slightly embarrassed that she might be right.

'So,' she said, looking ahead again, 'where do we start? With one of these?'

Mitch nodded.

'We start with number one and finish with number two. It seemed symmetrical somehow,' he said apologetically. 'Then number fifteen - also up - then twenty eight down, eleven and thirty five up. That takes us up to the top floor. All the ones going up I've given odd numbers to; the even ones go down.'

'And after that?'

'After that we walk to number forty six - which is the big one in the central atrium going down from the top floor to the basement.'

'I know the one,' Suzi said, pleased to appear on the same wavelength.

'I wanted to get one of the big ones out of the way early. Then we bounce around between the basement and first for a while, then first and second, second and third. Then it's all the way back to the basement to take the big one up to the top. That finishes off the basement. Then we finish of the top floor, bounce around again between one and two for a bit, then finish the second floor ones. Finally, we have a few left on this level and the first before we finish by coming down number two.'

'What about the ones near "Cinderella's"?' Suzi asked.

'Twenty one and twenty two; forty one and forty two; fifty nine and sixty. We'll go by your place more than once, I'm afraid. Six times, actually.'

She was smiling at him. She squeezed his arm briefly.

'See? I told you that you'd know it all off by heart!'

He blushed.

'Shall we get started then?' She walked forwards, then over her shoulder said, 'I've got a date after this little escapade Columbus, and I don't want to be late!'

Although they started with an undeniable sense of purpose, their pace was leisurely rather than frantic. To any uninformed observer, they looked like a young couple just going about their business. Tourists perhaps. Though if you had watched them you might have noticed how they failed to enter any of the stores, and if they were just window-shopping, they were doing it at some pace. Had you been strolling around on the first floor, you might well have spotted them four times in those first fifteen minutes or so, as they appeared, disappeared, then reappeared just as you were walking along. But the vast majority of people, out that morning for their own purpose and preoccupied with their own thoughts and motivations, wouldn't have seen them at all.

At around ten twenty, Mitch and Suzi could be found on the third floor, leaning against the glass railing, and looking down through the heart of the building and at the four-storey-deep pair of escalators before them.

'You know,' she said, a little quietly, 'in all the time I've worked here, I have never been on either of these two.'

'Really?!'

'And I know people come from all over to do so.'

'There aren't that many escalators this "big" in the world, that's for sure. Great piece of marketing built into the design, if you ask me.'

Without thinking, Mitch had fished into his rucksack and pulled out the bar of chocolate Mr Lee had given him.

'Swiss; nice,' said Suzi as she took the piece offered her. 'Shall we?' she said.

Mitch closed his bag and they walked to the top of forty six. There wasn't a single person on it. This is where it really began. Without realising it, he had taken Suzi's hand and they stepped on to the escalator together.

As they neared the second floor, Mitch looked around, less concerned with the experience of the ride (he had practised enough after all!), and more intent on visualising as much of their route as he could. However, he did notice that there were fewer people around than he had expected. It was a passing thought that failed to register any significance until he felt Suzi squeeze his hand. They were approaching where the escalator intersected the first floor.

'Mitch, look.'

She was pointing ahead of them. They could see the remainder of the escalator stretched out in front of them, but as it was descending, it seemed to be getting darker. As they passed level with the first floor, Mitch noticed that some of the shop lights appeared to have gone out.

'Must be some kind of power cut to the stores' lighting,' he said as positively as he could. 'I mean, this thing's still going.'

'But it's getting…darker.'

Nearing the ground floor, Mitch could see that the basement looked as if it were in total darkness. He looked up behind them. The floors above - the ones they had just been through - were now getting darker too. Suzi had not let go of his hand.

'It must be a power cut; that's all.'

When they reached the bottom, the only visible light came from dim emergency lighting in the ceilings and walkways - a kind of soft, diffused blue light. Too weak to throw any shadows. All the shops appeared to be in darkness. They walked forward a few paces then stopped.

'Mitch,' said Suzi in a whisper, 'where are the people?'

Simultaneously, they went into their bags and pulled out Mr Lee's torches, but before they could switch them on, they heard slow, rhythmical footsteps coming towards them. Mitch recognised the sound. He should have shouted out; he should have cried for help. Instead of that however, one word escaped from his lips; escaped in urgent, hushed tones.

'Hide!'

9

Crouching in the tight triangular space beneath number forty six, they saw the pale trousers and dark shoes of the guard walking around the base of the escalators. He was not more than three meters away. His pace was slow, measured. It was the pace of a person who was looking around intently, checking. Mitch felt this was an important distinction. The steps carried on for a few seconds and then stopped.

'I think he's the other side of the escalators; at the bottom,' Mitch whispered.

After their sudden dash to their dark hiding place, Suzi had taken his hand again.

'What do we do now?' Her voice was low and urgent, but there was no hint of panic in it.

'Well, the good news is that he isn't looking for us.'

'How do you know?'

'Because if he was he would have switched his torch on - and he'd be checking all possible hiding places. So he's not searching. I'm sure of that.'

'But what do we do now?' she asked. 'I mean, what will he do if he finds us? We can't go back the way we came. And why did we hide anyway? He might have been able to help us out.'

'I don't know,' Mitch had none of the answers. Suzi's guess would have been as good as his own - probably better. 'Look, something weird's going on. Maybe it is just a power cut, I don't know. But all the other people seemed to disappear awfully quickly.'

'Maybe they found a guard to let them out,' she suggested.

'Maybe. But I've met two of these guys already - and I don't want to have to trust them. I'd rather find my own way out.'

'And how do we do that - in this dark?'

'We've got these,' Mitch tapped his torch, 'and they don't know we're here. If we're careful we should be able to get back up to one of the entrances.' He paused. 'Look. The next escalator is just along the way there, as the passage turns a little. We'll be hidden from his view by this big one for most of the way, and if we're quiet and only turn on our torches when it's safe...'

He allowed his sentence to trail off. It was all he could think of.

'Where's the next escalator?' Suzi asked slowly.

'What do you mean, the "next" one?'

'On our plan. Where should we be going next?'

If he had known that she could have seen him clearly, Mitch would have given her a quizzical look. He just replied in a flat whisper instead, a slight questioning in his voice.

'Fifty nine, up to the ground floor. We can see one of the exits from there. Originally we would have gone along to eight. Then nineteen, sixty, three... Why?'

'Because I think we should carry on,' she said, slowly.

'Carry on?!' Mitch struggled to keep his voice down.

'Because maybe you only get one chance to do this. Because - I don't know - maybe this is all part of the test. Maybe it will be fun. What's the problem anyway? If we get caught, we can say we got lost in the dark. That's reasonable enough. They'll just throw us out anyway...'

Mitch heard the excitement and conviction growing in her voice as she spoke. He wasn't convinced, but what choice did they have? He didn't want to give himself up to the guards - and maybe when they got back up to the ground floor, they might make a run for it. Number three was near where they had come in after all.

'Ok,' he said slowly. 'When you're ready. And quietly; slowly.'

They edged out from their cramped space, Mitch first checking quickly either side that they could not be seen. By the time they were standing upright, he was convinced that the guard was still there, but obscured. Now it was a blessing that they were both in trainers as they were able to move almost silently. By moving close to the shops on the right, they were able to get round the small kink in the mall's floor plan and out of sight of the central atrium. A little way ahead, two further escalators rose.

'That's good,' said Mitch, attempting to comfort both himself and Suzi. There was no sign of anyone else around. 'Fifty nine's the one on the left. Takes us up near the Mellon Street exit.'

The dim glow from the emergency lighting was just about enough for them to find their way, especially as their eyes had become adjusted to the dark. The shops looked eerie, with just random spots of light coming from things like computer monitors, or the occasional display.

'Weird,' said Suzi, 'it's like they're haunted or something. And if it was a power cut, wouldn't all the power be out?' She pointed to a small neon sign in a shoe shop that was still illuminated. It said "Try them for size!".

'Let's hope the escalators are still working,' said Mitch, though it was soon evident from the low hum they could hear as they approached that at least fifty nine and sixty were still working. 'And let's hope - when we get to the top - that there's no-one there waiting for us.'

Suzi squeezed his hand; he could just about tell she was smiling.

Stepping on fifty nine, they rose slowly upwards, and it was soon evident that the ground floor was as much in darkness as the basement. Once at the top, they took a couple of steps and stopped. Ahead of them, partly obscured by two escalators linking to the first floor, Mitch could just make out the doors that opened out onto Mellon Street. He could also make out a two metallic legs of a chair that had been positioned to face them - and the back of the person sitting there.

'That's Mellon Street out,' he whispered to Suzi.

'No problem,' said Suzi. 'The big problem is what happens when we go back down the next one...'

Mitch looked at her. She was clearly determined to carry on as long as possible.

'Well let's get to the atrium first.'

As before, they hugged one side of the shops for a short while until the central atrium opened out before them. Mitch tugged her hand to get Suzi to stop, and they carefully looked around. This was the area where they would be most exposed, potentially visible not only from each of the five legs of the mall, but from the floor above too. Number eight - their next target - was right in front of them.

'When we get to the bottom, if the guard hasn't moved, will he be able to see us?' Suzi asked.

'You're sure you want to do this?' Mitch replied with his own question. There was a very large part of him that wanted to loudly declare their presence and get the hell out - but he needed Suzi to be the catalyst for that. In a strange way, although it was his plan originally, in these new circumstances she seemed to be the one in control.

'Will he see us? Suzi repeated, ignoring his question. They were standing about eight metres from the top of their next ride.

'If he hasn't moved, yes.'

'So,' said Suzi - Mitch could see her smiling again, 'we'll just have to make him move.'

She dropped onto her haunches and opened her bag. After a moment, she closed it and stood again. She had one of Mr Lee's marbles in her hand.

'When we get to the bottom, do we need to go left or right?'

'Right. A quick dash out of the other side of the atrium,' Mitch indicated with his hand, 'and then to nineteen.'

'OK. So, half way down - or as soon as we can - we need to throw this to the left. Hopefully it will make enough of a noise to get that guard away from the centre, and give us a chance to make a run for it.'

'Maybe,' said Mitch, a little doubtfully. The plan seemed a little theatrical to him. 'But what if he's not the only one down there?'

'How many do they need?' she countered. ' Apart from the emergency exits - which will be alarmed anyway - wouldn't you assume for the basement you needed just one person in the centre?'

Mitch couldn't doubt her logic, although he was struggling with some of the bigger questions: who? why? and so on.

'Come on,' she said, leading him forwards, 'nothing to lose!'

They crouched down as soon as they were on the escalator, Suzi keeping her head just about the handrail, marble at the ready. As they slipped beneath the floor that separated the two levels, the guard became immediately visible. Without hesitating, Suzi stood and launched the marble away to the left.

When it landed, the sound it made was incredible. Not only was the marble hitting marble, but against a background of zero noise - and with the echo that followed, as well as the multiple bounces thereafter - it was like a machine gun going off.

The guard leapt to his feet, and immediately moved down the Wilson Avenue leg in search of the noise.

'Wow!,' whispered Mitch as they reached the bottom.

Suzi was off, running towards number nineteen. She was faster than Mitch had expected, and he only caught her as she gained the next escalator.

'Quick!' he said, pulling her onto the moving steps. 'Down!'

The sound of the marble had been so loud that it had not only drawn the basement guard towards it, but the ones who had been patrolling both the Wilson Avenue and Fern Avenue entrances had also responded - and the latter was heading down number twenty at exactly that same moment.

Mitch held his breath, waiting for the guard to shout, anticipating their discovery. But no shout came. Instead they reached the ground floor safely.

Now ahead of them were the doors to Fern Avenue - and the empty chair just vacated by the security guard. They both looked towards the door. Bizarrely, it appeared to be as dark outside as it was inside.

'Should I try them?' Mitch asked.

'You can,' said Suzi, 'if you're very quick. They'll be locked though - and the guard will be back up soon.'

Mitch sprinted to the doors and tried them, gently. They were all shut, refusing to move. All he could see in them was his reflection - and the reflection of Suzi as she started to move back towards the atrium.

'Sixty, right?' she said as he joined her. 'Mustn't forget the Mellon Street guard.'

As it turned out, that guard was also no longer on his chair.

'Mr Lee's marbles must have greater powers than we thought!' said Suzi, jokingly as she jumped on number ten, Mitch right behind her. 'Basement time again!'

'As we get off, there's a loo right there,' said Mitch. 'Maybe we should just take a moment to confirm what the hell we're doing.'

'Sure thing, Columbus,' said Suzi.

'And I need a leak.'

10

They arrived in the basement in darkness again. After a quick check towards the base of the atrium, they dashed into the small alcove that led to the toilets. As Mitch turned to the right, Suzi grabbed his arm.

'Not the gents,' she whispered. 'We need to stick together. And if that guard's about, then he's going to use the men's, isn't he?'

Mitch smiled as he followed Suzi into the ladies'. It was a mirror image of the gents; there were no urinals in this mall.

'It's exactly the same!' he said.

'You do surprise me,' said Suzi, mockingly. Then, as she entered a cubicle, 'Remember, don't flush!'

A few minutes later they were standing side-by-side washing their hands.

'What next?'

'You want to carry on?' She didn't reply. 'Then we should do seven, then twenty, but those are tricky.'

'Why?'

'Because we have to go to the centre which is where seven is, and if that guard's back there… And then when we come back down twenty, we'll have to go across the atrium to get to nine. Same problem again.'

'We've got the marbles,' Suzi suggested as she dried her hands on paper towels. 'That should work again.'

'It might.'

'Well, they can't ignore it, can they? I mean, they've got to investigate when something makes that much noise. What other choice is there?'

Suzi pulled the chocolate from her bag and broke off a piece for Mitch.

'Ready?' she asked. He nodded.

Opening the door, they immediately noticed that it seemed a little brighter outside. Cautiously pausing in the frame of the alcove to check for any guards, Mitch immediately saw the source of this new light. Indeed, given everywhere was in darkness, it was impossible to miss it. Across the way, a gadget shop - "Toys 4 Boys" - was fully illuminated, and its doors clearly open.

'What?!'

'Maybe they're starting to get the power back on,' suggested Suzi.

'To just one shop?' Mitch sounded incredulous. 'Should we take a look?'

'Is it empty?'

'I can't see anyone in there,' he said, then started walking quickly towards the store. 'Come on; maybe we can find out what's been going on.'

They paused once they had crossed the threshold. On the shelves, row after row of electronic gadgets, gimmicks and toys, many shining brightly where the ceiling spotlights were trained on them. Suspended from the ceiling, a battery-powered aeroplane flew in a lazy circle. In the far corner, on a raised table with a perspex surround, a number of self-righting fighting robots were engaged in mortal combat. After the darkness of the emergency lightly, the variety and brashness of these new colours were striking.

Mitch looked at Suzi; they were both smiling in a bemused, "I don't understand" kind of way.

'Looking for something?'

The voice made them freeze. There was nothing particularly remarkable about the voice itself - other than the fact that it was there at all. Their smiles suddenly vanished, they looked towards the cash desk. A small, elderly lady was looking at them hopefully. She seemed astonishingly out of place for such a shop; Mitch could imagine her behind the cheese counter of an artisanal delicatessen, or working in a charity shop perhaps, but not in "Toys 4 Boys".

'Sorry?' It was Suzi who spoke next.

'I wondered if you were looking for anything in particular,' the woman expanded. Then, after a short pause, 'Or if you aren't, to let you know that I might be.'

'Looking for something?' Mitch checked. 'You should be selling, not buying.'

'Two sides of the same coin,' she said semi-cryptically. 'Anyway, I'm more interested in trading right now. I can't get into the till.'

There was a short, forced pause.

'I've got these seven sided dice,' she suggested, 'or some magic pens - invisible ink and all. You need sunglasses to see what's written. They're very clever.'

Mitch thought of Mr Lee's gifts.

'We've got sunglasses.'

'Perfect!' She smiled. 'Have you got anything to trade?'

'Not really,' said Suzi. She tried to remember what Mitch had given her. 'Some string of sorts; a notepad; a compass...'

'No?!' The lady emerged from behind the counter and walked towards them. 'Really?! I need a compass or two. Can you see any in here? At all?'

Mitch automatically scanned the shelves quickly.

'Look,' she held out two pens, one red, one blue. 'You could have these - one each - if you had two compasses… Can I see?'

Suzi removed the compass from her bag and handed it over in exchange for one of the pens. The woman's small fingers took it gently but greedily. She turned on the spot slowly, watching the compass needle moving. Suzi had written something on a piece of paper the woman had given her. Mitch donned his sunglasses. Sure enough, Suzi had written her name - but it was only visible with the glasses on. He noticed how she dotted her 'i' with a small cross, rather than a dot.

'You have another?' the woman asked.

'You can have mine,' said Mitch. He was suddenly in a hurry to get out of the store.

Within a few seconds, the two compasses had been handed over and Mitch and Suzi had deposited their new pens into their respective bags. They looked at each other, and then back to the counter - but now the woman was nowhere to be seen. Before either of them could say anything, they were simultaneously aware of something else that was different.

Turning towards the door, they were hit by a flood of light and noise: the mall now appeared to be fully lit. Not only that, but there were people walking up and down outside; and as Mitch and Suzi stood in the doorway, they saw people going in and out of the other shops, all of which now seemed to be fully functioning.

'Wow!', said Mitch, 'what happened here?!'

'Looks like they fixed the power cut, then,' Suzi suggested. 'And maybe we don't have to worry about guards and marbles any more!'

She gave Mitch's hand a squeeze.

As soon as they stepped out into the throng they realised just how many people there suddenly were in the mall, Mitch was bumped from behind and instinctively made sure he had Suzi's hand.

'Crickey! Where did this lot come from?! It's manic.'

There seemed to be two general flows, one in each direction, a little like a motorway. This didn't stop people cutting across as they dived from one side to the other to make it into - or out of - a shop. Above the general hubbub, occasional shouts and apologies could clearly be heard.

'Stay close,' said Mitch.

They followed the flow along to the atrium where, almost without needing to make any decision on direction, the crowd served them onto seven. The both looked upwards as soon as they were on the escalator: above them, as far as they could see, the mall was bright and colourful. But this turned out not to be the most extraordinary thing. If they had thought it was busy in the basement, the ground floor was astonishing.

Suzi let out a small yelp as they made it off the escalator when someone trod on her foot. Mitch tried to put his arm around her, but even this was difficult.

'This way', he said, indicating the leg that led towards Fern Avenue. Down on twenty.'

But there was panic in his voice as he felt himself being torn away from Suzi by the crowd. At one point he was actually able to lift his feet from the ground and still be propelled forwards. And the sound was deafening.

'If we get split up,' he shouted, 'make for Starbucks; I'll meet you there.'

Then, as soon as he had spoken, he felt Suzi being ripped away from him by the irresistible tide of people. He could see her just two or three metres away from him. They were both still heading in the same direction, which was good - but gradually the distance grew, and as he seemed to be successfully making for his desired destination - number twenty - Suzi's stream of humanity was taking her towards twenty three. Before he knew it, he saw her being propelled upwards towards the first floor just as he began his descent on twenty.

'See you at Starbucks!' he shouted again.

She tried to wave. It looked as if she was smiling, but if it was a smile, it was an incredibly forced one. As Mitch felt his heart sink, he suddenly noticed that just in front of and behind Suzi were two figures in beige uniforms - and they were both looking his way. Then he was in the basement.

11

By the time Mitch reached the basement just a few moments later, it appeared that the incredible crush they had just witnessed was over. There were fewer people around - to what he assumed was a more 'normal' volume - and there was space to move around in. This was just as well even though running was not on his agenda, right now, with a desire to get to Starbuck's as quickly as possible to meet Suzi there, running was exactly what he was doing.

He was across the atrium and stepping onto nine in less than a minute. His burst had caused a few people to look his way somewhat questioningly, but most importantly, he seemed to have not been noticed by any of the guards. As he waited to reach the ground floor again, he wondered about the two he had seen flanking Suzi as she had risen out of sight. Surely that was just coincidence; how could they possibly have been able to manipulate themselves into such precise positions given how crazy the crowds had been?

When he stepped off nine on the ground floor, the picture again emerged of a normal volume of people, a normal volume of noise. Perhaps the crush had just been the result of a sudden influx caused by people who, waiting outside, at all the entrances, had simultaneously charged back into the mall as soon as the power had been restored and the doors opened again. It was the only explanation.

But now he faced a new dilemma. Starbuck's was on the second floor, just across from "Cinderella's". If he stuck with his original plan he wouldn't get there for a little while yet as he still had a few more trips to the basement to resolve. The quickest way there was to jump straight on to twenty one - a dual-floor escalator that joined the ground floor with the second, bypassing the first. If he took this one he would be in Starbuck's in less than a minute - and certainly ahead of Suzi. But it would mean compromising his plan. He would have to replan his route on the fly. He didn't doubt that he could rearrange the sequence of things, but there was a small element of risk…

Moments later he was riding twenty one, all the while looking around the ground floor - and then the first as he traversed it - for any sign of Suzi. A girl whom he had not known less than a week ago was now uppermost in his thoughts. He was concerned for her; that she was all right. He wanted to see her again, and very quickly. Where had all that come from?!

Starbuck's was quiet. There were just a couple of tables occupied, otherwise it was empty. The patrons already there ignored him when he entered and went and sat straight down as close to the exit as possible, from where he held an almost unbroken view from the end of that particular wing to the atrium. He remembered sitting here before and being able to see three pairs of escalators, but now it appeared that he could also just about see those in the central foyer too; so five pairs in total.

How he missed seeing the two mugs of coffee being placed on the table in front of him he had no idea. One minute he was scanning fifty nine and sixty, the next he was drawn by the smell of hot latte, and it was only then that he glanced down. He looked back into the cafe, but there was no indication who had placed the drinks there.

Outside, people walked by, milled in shop doorways or admired the window displays. Just the other side of forty one and two, he suddenly noticed Suzi's stunning display as if for the first time and caught his breath. It was still fantastic, though it appeared that, between now and a few days ago, she had moved some of the mannequins a little; he was sure they were not in the same places as before.

'How's it going?' said a voice nearby.

Mitch looked up.

'Mr Lee!'

'Where's your friend?'

'What are you doing here?!'

'She hasn't got lost has she? Or given up?'

Mitch knew one of them had to answer a question at some point.

'I'm waiting for her actually.'

'I thought you might be,' said Mr Lee, indicating the two coffees and suggesting that he had in fact purchased them.

'And we haven't given up. Not at all. We just ran into a few… difficulties.'

Mr Lee just smiled, betraying nothing.

'Actually, how long have you been here?' Mitch asked; surely he would have experienced the blackout or the crowds?

'Here in Starbuck's?'

'No, in the mall.'

'Oh, not long,' Mr Lee answered a little indecisively. 'Just came in really. Happened to see you here as I was passing, and I thought... You know.'

'That's kind, thanks.'

There was a pause. Mitch went back to examining the crowds. He was conscious of Mr Lee, having now sat down, just watching him.

'Oh and thanks for those things you sent me. Very - useful...'

'I thought they might be,' Mr Lee laughed. 'Yes, indeed.'

There was another pause.

'So what are you going to do now?'

Mitch looked at him. The old man had picked up one of the mugs of coffee and was drinking it himself.

'I mean, if the young lady - Suzi, wasn't it? - If Suzi doesn't show up? How long are you going to wait for her?'

Until this moment, Mitch realised that he hadn't even considered that possibility. He had assumed she would show up here, and soon. That's what he believed they had agreed between his shout and her little wave. There was also a third question to answer.

He pulled his copy of the floor plans from his bag.

'Actually, I need to look at these first,' he explained. 'We got a little side-tracked, and I need to get us back on course. We were forced - I was forced to take a different route. Got to re-plan a little bit. I'm sure Suzi will be here before I'm done, and then we can get cracking again.'

Mr Lee said nothing for a moment.

'Of course, that's the real question.'

'What is?' asked Mitch.

'You were wondering what you would do if she didn't show up by the time you had finished your little planning exercise. Do you sit and have another coffee? Do you assume that she's given up for some reason - and if so, do you carry on or postpone until another day. Or…'

'There's an "or"?' queried Mitch, impressed that Mr Lee had been able to read his mind. Maybe it was just obvious what he would have been thinking.

Mr Lee finished his coffee and put the mug down.

'Or do you try and find her?' He let the suggestion hang for a moment. 'I mean, if you assume that she hasn't given up, and that she wanted to rendezvous with you here, well - something must have stopped her. So maybe she needs finding. If that's the case, then what does that do to your replanned route?'

His mind flitting briefly back to the image of the two guards on the escalator, Mitch knew that Mr Lee was absolutely right. And in knowing that, his next sequence of actions were clear.

'I'll re-chart the route. If she's not back by then, I'll get another coffee. And if she's not here after that, then I'll go looking for her. And I'll make sure my new plan covers as much ground as possible to get me through as much of the mall as possible; it will give me the best chance of finding her, won't it?'

Mr Lee stood up.

'Well, must be getting along. Couple of things to do myself as it happens. Good luck, again. I'm sure it will all work out.'

And with a wave, he was gone, almost instantly invisible in the crowd.

Fifteen minutes later Mitch had a second coffee in front of him. The floor plans, lightly re-annotated, lay in front of him on the table. He had been able to get so far, but no further. He found it was difficult to concentrate, and planning how to get around the remaining fifty two escalators seemed a bit of a pointless task just at that moment. He would be a traitor to just carry on and pretend nothing happened, without knowing what had happened to Suzi or where she was.

He suddenly remembered his phone. He had no idea if she had brought hers with her, but it seemed like a safe bet. Mitch called up his contacts, found "s". After a second or two her was ringing. He waited, but there was no answer. She didn't even have voicemail turned on. Well, at least she would know that he had tried to call.

He looked at the plans again. He had mapped out the next fifteen or so jumps. By taking as many of the dual floor escalators as possible, Mitch knew he could cover the maximum amount of ground - and when he traversed a floor, he would have the opportunity to see if he could catch a glimpse of her.

Standing, he began to put his things back into his bag again. Across the aisle, the mannequins in "Cinderella's" looked as if they had moved again, but it was undoubtedly just him not paying attention. There were still three by the window, two further inside, and the one against the far wall staring straight out - and even here in Starbuck's, he felt as if it were looking directly at him.

12

Mitch left Starbuck's attempting to muster as much determination as he could. It was around eleven o'clock; he had been in the mall for around an hour and so much seemed to have happened in that time, so much changed. Even his own outlook was going through some kind of metamorphosis, and it was something he seemed to have no control over. He had gone from a well rehearsed, planned and mapped out view of the world (or at least a few hours of it!) into a haphazard, chaotic scenario which, even now, he knew he was just pretending he could corral.

He walked back to the atrium, paused to scan the crowds, then left and immediately down, through the first floor, to the ground on sixty six. There was nothing untoward in what he saw. People continued to go about their business as they should be; children either ran around or cried for food; husbands trailed their wives, some laden like beasts of burden. There was a steady and somehow rhythmical flow as if normality had returned.

On the ground floor again he paused in the atrium, his eyes searching for something that would trigger a change in his circumstance, the change he was looking for. There was nothing. Not far way, he could see one of the Security Guards talking to a couple who appeared to be seeking directions. Even the guard was smiling.

Turning again, he saw both his next leg - fifty five back up to the second - and the Wilson Avenue doors in front of him. The latter represented an immediate, physical and real opportunity to grab his old life back; to wipe out the last couple of hours and eradicate the whole notion of his challenge, and thus revert to what he was used to and comfortable with. To go back to his old self.

Yet, as he stepped into the escalator and headed upwards again, he was certain that the old Mitch was gone, at least part of him dying as he hid in the basement under forty six holding Suzi's hand. Then again - this as he scoured the first floor as he passed through it - there was a better, more positive interpretation; not that something had died, but that something had been born.

When he reached the top of fifty five, the second floor looked exactly as he had left it just a few minutes previously. In fact, the resemblance was so striking, he had to stop to look around.

Mitch had the strangest sense that someone had taken a 3D photograph of the scene he had just left and that he had been transported right back into the middle of it.

'Can I help you, sir?'

Something was different.

It was not one of the two short, scarred guards he had previously encountered, but a guard nonetheless. This one, however, was a woman.

'You seem to be lost,' she suggested, 'going up and down to the same place. Are you looking for something? Perhaps I can help.'

Mitch found himself relieved that she appeared to be normal and genuinely trying to assist.

'No, I'm not lost,' he tried to smile, 'but I think my friend might be. I'm just trying to find her.'

'I see,' said the guard. There was something familiar about her that Mitch couldn't quite put his finger on. 'Where are you going to look next?'

'Thir…' Mitch was going to quote the number of the escalator - his number - but immediately realised that this would have been meaningless to the guard. 'Third floor,' he suggested, pointing to an escalator nearby.

'I see,' said the guard. 'Well, good luck; I hope you find your friend. She might just be shopping, of course. You know what us women are like!'

The guard chuckled, more to herself than to Mitch, then turned and walked into the atrium. Mitch, after another quick look around, walked the few metres to thirty seven and then headed upwards.

The ambiance on the third floor was slightly different to the other floors in the mall. In part this was owing to the two "Food

Courts" that were located at the end of the Wilson Avenue and Mellon Street wings. Fast food restaurants, take-aways and pizza outlets vied with each out for custom with an explosion of music and brightly lit seating areas and counters. It was also different because the noise people made when they were sitting down eating - just talking to each other - was different to when they were in amongst the shops; the change in focus led to a change in the timbre of the sound. Here it was more lively, chatty; children were able to run amuck with a greater degree of freedom than elsewhere - there was even a small play area to encourage just that.

Thirty seven emerged at the edge of the Wilson Avenue food court. Mitch gave a cursory glance over the tables and people located there. He would not have expected to see Suzi there - after all, they had arranged to meet at Starbuck's - and not surprisingly he could not see her. As he walked towards the atrium he suddenly wondered if she might be down there now, just a floor below him, waiting. But that, he knew, was an argument that led nowhere other than him being rooted to a Starbuck's chair and never moving.

He walked past fifty just to look over the rail and down through the centre of the mall. Forty six was right in front of him; forty six with its long traverse down into the basement - a basement which, he could clearly see, was still well-lit. The flow of people up and down seemed now a constant, as it should be, and as it always was. The last hour felt more and more like an anomaly. Even so, Suzi was missing, and that was his first priority.

As he turned back towards fifty, he noticed an unobtrusive glass door set in the wall between two shops and the entrance to another set of toilets. Above it was a slightly faded sign that read "Lost and Found". It seemed worth a try.

Beyond the door was a short counter, and beyond the counter were two doors, one off to each side. Behind the counter were two members of staff dressed in the same style of uniform as the security guards, except that one of them wore blue and the other green.

'Hello, Sir; lost something?' said Blue - somewhat hopefully Mitch felt.

'Or - even better - found something?!' Green prompted; a remark that immediately drew a scowl from Blue.

'If so, this is where you need to be, Sir: "Lost and Found".'

'Though why they don't call it "Found and Lost" I don't know,' said Green, a little huffily. 'That would be the more positive way round - wouldn't it sir?'

'Actually,' Mitch began, and they both leant forward slightly, 'I've lost something.'

Green's demeanour sagged a little and Mitch tried to offer a "sorry" signal in a shrug of his shoulders.

'Excellent!' said Blue, then corrected himself: 'I mean, oh dear; sorry to hear that... What is it you've lost, Sir? Umbrella? We've go hundreds of those. Bag of shopping? Ditto. Coat? You wouldn't believe how many coats we've seen in here...'

'All coats that have been found!' Green chimed in, trying not to be left out entirely.

'But we keep them on the "Lost" side, rather than the "Found" side because, well, we like to be customer-focussed. After all, the person who comes in here looking for their coat doesn't say "I'm looking for a coat that may have been found", do they? They say, "I'm looking for a coat I have lost" - so it makes more sense for me to hold on to it. You see?"

'No,' said Mitch, answering Blue's original question, 'actually, I've lost my friend.'

There was a short silence. Blue and Green exchanged glances.

'I see,' said Blue, more solemn now. Indicating the door behind him on his side of the counter, he continued, 'Perhaps you had better come this way.'

Mitch moved behind the counter and followed Blue through the door. There was a short corridor (it's walls also painted blue, Mitch assumed just to make sure you knew which side you were on) and then another door at the end. Blue pushed it open and ushered Mitch in.

There was a long row of chairs on each side of a room that was surprisingly extensive. Eight or so of these were occupied by people who all turned and looked at him hopefully. There were three men, a woman, two teenagers - who seemed more interested in each other than anything else! - and two children. All were sitting patiently. Mitch wondered how long they had been there. Indeed, he wanted to ask them, but as soon as they saw him, the brief flicker of hope he had seen in their eyes was extinguished; it seemed wrong to make it worse, after all, some of them might have been in there for a while. One of the men had a considerable growth of stubble on his chin. Most significantly, however, none of them was Suzi.

'Afraid not,' said Mitch, turning to Blue.

'Hmmm. Well, you could wait, Sir, and pretend to be lost, then your friend might come here and find you…'

Blue's voice was a little too enthusiastic for Mitch's liking. He wondered how many of the people here had fallen for that one. Maybe the stubbled man.

'Thanks - but no.'

'Are you sure, Sir?' said Blue, partly blocking Mitch's exit from the room.

'Certain,' said Mitch, not standing on ceremony to get back to the corridor and then to the entrance counter.

'No good?' asked Green unnecessarily.

'No.'

'Well,' he suggested, 'we could always say that we "found" you, and you could wait on my side…'

Mitch couldn't believe what he was hearing. He nodded towards the door on Green's side: 'Do you have anyone through there now?'

Green hung his head slightly.

'No sir.'

'Do you have anything at all on your side?'

This time the reply was just a shake of the head.

'Thought not,' said Mitch, harshly. And with that, he turned and went back outside. As he left, he could hear the recriminations and arguments starting between Blue and Green.

13

Walking the few feet to the top of fifty, Mitch took a few deep breaths to try and calm down. He hadn't expected any success from his impromptu visit to "Lost & Found", but he had been upset by what he had discovered there. It was crazy to imagine that Suzi would just sit and wait in there for him; she wasn't that kind of girl. From what he knew of her already, Mitch felt more and more sure that she would have wanted to try and help him find her - if indeed she was lost in some way.

As he travelled down through the second to the first floor he found himself preoccupied with that notion - and one that was growing on him by the moment. 'But how would she leave me a message?' he asked himself, 'And where?'

The answer hit him just as he stepped off the escalator. He came to a sudden halt with the shock of it - so sudden, in fact, that a large woman in a fur coat bumped into the back of him, forcing him to apologise. Of course! The magic pens!

Mitch reached into his rucksack and retrieved the red sunglasses. He knew he would look a little suspicious wearing these in the mall - especially as they were truly garish and so very easy to spot. He also withdrew his magic pen and drew a small mark on the back of his hand. Then, donning the glasses, he checked that he could see it. There it was! He then also looked around. The mall was not surprisingly duller, with the bright neon a little dimmer - not that that was a bad thing! But he could see well enough. If anyone asked he could say that he had sensitive eyes or something.

He put the pen back in his bag. Now the next question was where would Suzi have left the message. His first thought was for her to have written something on one of the interactive mall maps - or perhaps at Starbucks, on a menu or something. But then Mitch realised the difficulty of doing so: if she were being accompanied somewhere by the two security guards, then they would hardly let her take time out to leave him a message.

There was one obvious answer! Mitch jumped on the nearby sixty four - which miraculously he had recently replanned to take next anyway - and headed down to the basement. The only place Suzi could possibly be alone to leave him a message would be in the ladies toilet, and the obvious one to use would be the one they had both already shared. But when he had seen her last, she had been on her way up to the first floor; might she have persuaded the guards to let her go back down to the basement? Might they have wanted to take her there anyway? Perhaps their trip up to the first had been some kind of ruse; how could he be sure that was their final destination?

There were too many questions, and too many unknowns. A message left in that basement ladies' lavatory was the only option Mitch had right now.

Anyone noticing the young man soon sitting on a bench near the entrance to one of the basement conveniences would have almost certainly made the usual assumption; namely that they were waiting for a friend - female, almost certainly - to emerge from the toilet there. But - luckily, Mitch thought - there seemed to be fewer people around at the moment to notice him; perhaps it was owing to it being lunchtime, and consequently there would have been a degree of migration to the food courts on the third floor.

Mitch was waiting, but he was essentially waiting for himself. He needed to make a decision. As he saw it, he had three options to check the ladies' loo. The first was to just walk in: not that appealing a prospect. The second was to try and disguise himself as a woman somehow and try that way. This was something he was giving serious consideration to. The woman in the fur coat he had bumped into a little while previously had given him the idea. If he found himself a big coat - and a hat, probably - then this might make the resemblance passable; but there were clearly some issues here, no hat and coat for a start. And he was built like a man; too tall for a normal woman.

The third choice was to ask someone to go and check for him. He wondered about the woman in "Toys 4 Boys" just behind him, but he had glanced through the store's window and been unable to see her. Indeed, there appeared to be a man serving there now. He wanted a fourth option.

The appearance of one of the mall Cleaners forced his hand. He had been sitting counting women in and out of the toilet to see if he could judge when it would be empty, when the Cleaner arrived. Her sudden presence coincided with Mitch's belief that the ladies loo was currently empty, and the cleaner taking their trolley in there and then placing the "Closed: Cleaning In

Progress" sign outside seemed to confirm as much. Mitch knew that within moments, any message that Suzi might have left him could be destroyed.

As he stood up, still unsure as to his next move, the Cleaner emerged. Between the two doors for the Ladies' and Gents' was a third door; evidently some kind of cupboard. The Cleaner paused before it, unlocked it, and then went in. Mitch didn't hesitate. He darted forwards, feigned to go into the Gents' then dived to the left. Inside it was deserted. Where would there be any message?! He looked around the walls wildly and then to the mirror. There, clearly visible, he read: "HMV. Sx". The small cross after the "S" was exactly the same as Suzi used to dot her "i"s, so it could only be a message for him. He quickly peered over the top of his sunglasses to confirm nothing could be seen without them, then dashed out again. As the Cleaner emerged from their cupboard they would have seen a young man moving away from the Gents' in some haste and probably thought nothing of it.

Mitch now needed to get up to the second floor. HMV was in the central part of the mall. He walked back to the base of the atrium and then across to fifty seven, which would take him straight up to the first floor; from there, thirty nine in the centre itself would deposit him just outside the music store. Although he wanted to get there as fast as possible, he restrained himself and, rather than running, tried to walk as slowly and normally as possible. He had stopped looking for Suzi in any of the shops as he passed them, and as he walked through the ground floor on his way up to the first, he hardly glanced at the crowds.

If Suzi was in or around HMV, then why - and how had she got there? He could only assume that she wasn't there of her own free will. And if that was the case, then she must have found a way to get back down to the basement to leave him the message before she went up to the second floor, either voluntarily or forcibly.

The mall seemed only moderately busy just now, though Mitch knew that after lunch there was usually another rush and that it would fill up a little. Consequently HMV had few shoppers in it; there were a number of people browsing the CDs, but most were looking at DVDs or were in the games section. Mitch paused near the "top 40" section just inside the door and wondered what to do next. He checked all the faces he could see, but Suzi's was not among them. If she was still here then she would be out of sight somewhere. Beyond the cash desk and at a couple of other points towards the rear corners of the store, there were nondescript doors beyond public access. He could hardly just try those out given there were probably four or five staff on duty, and one security guard he had passed on his way in.

Having got here, he was uncertain what he should do next. Was he supposed to just wait? That would arise suspicion after a while for sure. Or perhaps Suzi had left him another clue here - but if so, where? This wasn't like the toilets where there were only one or two options to leave messages; here there were thousands and thousands of individual items, the wall spaces were covered in posters and display cabinets. There was nowhere obvious. Slowly he walked further into the store, pretending to browse. In the centre of it was a huge display of CDs, perhaps three metres tall, made up of a range of titles that were on offer in a special promotion. It was a massive pyramid of music.

Mitch paused and looked down at the rows of CDs in front of him. He had arrived at "R to S". And then something caught his eye. A small section of CDs from "Siouxsie and the Banshees". The name triggered a thought: if she was going to leave a message, then perhaps her name was the clue? Mitch looked further along. There were a few Suzi's there: Carr, Grant, Lane,

McNeil, Quatro... Although he didn't know what he was looking for, he began to flick through the CDs; where would she leave a message, if here at all?

His fingers found a Suzi Quatro CD called "In the spotlight". If you were searching for something, wouldn't a spotlight help? The CD was the only one placed in the rack back to front. Mitch lifted it out and turned it around in his hand. The cover was largely plain - and written on it, with the pen from "Toys 4 Boys" - were the words:

Create a distraction! S x

14

For a moment Mitch just looked at the CD, his heart thumping. Then, as calmly as he could he replaced it and tried to give the appearance that he was still browsing. If Suzi needed him to create a distraction, then she was probably still here, though he could not be certain. If she was, then her plea for a distraction would have been a genuine one. What could he do? If possible, he would have to think of something that didn't put himself at any risk.

Looking around the store, his eyes were drawn again to the unmissable tall pyramid of CDs. He knew if that fell down all hell might break loose. He walked around to the other side of the CD bench, closer to the structure. Given that he could see right through it, it appeared to be free-standing. But he couldn't just push it over, or kick it. That might be distraction enough, but he doubted he would make it out of the shop! And then he had an idea.

Bending down ostensibly to re-tie the laces on his sneakers, he pulled Mr Lee's piece of twine from out of his rucksack. Then, as carefully as he could, he treaded it into the bottom of the pyramid, behind three of the lowest stacks of CDs and then out again. Carefully he tied the string into a loop at that point and then stood up. His current position was partially hidden from the cash desk and, on checking, the security guard by the door seemed more interested in looking outside rather than back into the shop.

He edged along the CD display, slowly feeding out the twine as he did so. It was about two metres long - sufficient length for him to get to the end of the "R to S" rack and back a little round the other side. Crucially, he was also nearer the door. Again he paused. If he had been noticed, then someone would have accosted him by now, but no-one approached him. He felt the string. It was taut. Given that he now had a display rack between him and the pyramid, he would not be an obvious suspect when it came down - but he needed someone to be closer than him. Apparently taking an interest in Roxy Music's oeuvre, he waited.

Soon, a woman and her young son moved away from the games section at the rear of the shop, evidently on their way out. Mitch waited until they were about a metre from the tower and then yanked the string hard. It tightened then instantly gave way as the blocks of CDs around which it had been fixed were pulled out of position. The rest seemed to happen in slow motion.

At first one portion of the pyramid seemed to wobble, and then the whole tower simply imploded. CD after CD - hundreds of them - came crashing down. The noise was astonishing! Helpfully the woman who was now closest to the structure screamed with fright. There were other shouts. Staff from behind the cash desk came rushing out; the security guard from being the door came rushing in. For a few seconds there was pandemonium.

Mitch, for a moment trying to look like a startled shopper, waited for a couple of seconds, then dropped the twine and made for the door. In the melee others did too. Outside, the noise of the collapse had drawn people towards the store too, so it was easy for Mitch to slip into the crowd. Here he paused and looked back. The security guard and one member of staff were comforting the woman who was now sitting on the ground; her young son was laughing. Other people were pointing towards the chaos; some of those who had been drawn in from outside were taking photos with their phones. And then Mitch noticed that two of the inner doors - one behind the cash desk and one in the far right-hand corner - were now open.

At that moment he felt a tug on his arm and turned. Suzi was standing next to him, smiling. Without thinking, Mitch instinctively gave her a hug - and then instantly surprised himself by feeling her body pressed against his.

'Come on!' She said after a short pause, easing herself away from him but taking his hand as she did so.

Mitch waited until they were away from the HMV.

'Where are we going?'

'Starbuck's', she said, 'I'm hungry - and I need a coffee!'

A few minutes later, they were sitting at the same table Mitch and Mr Lee had occupied around an hour previously. They could see HMV across the atrium. The crowd had just about dispersed and things were returning to normal. They had hardly spoken since they had left there.

'That's better!' said Suzi, taking a bite from an almond croissant.

'So what happened to you, after we were separated?'

'Did you look for me?' she asked.

'Of course I did!' Mitch replied, not sure if she was asking seriously. 'I did find your message after all.'

'You did! I wasn't sure if you would...'

'So what happened? Did those guards force you onto that escalator?'

She was chewing on the croissant, so there was a slight pause. Mitch sipped his coffee.

'No. Once I got to the top of twenty three I knew that you were in the basement, so I tried to get to you as quickly as possible. So I walked across the centre to the double one from the first downwards...'

'Fifty eight,' Mitch prompted.

'Yes, fifty eight. I thought I might catch you there before you tried to go up to the first to find me. And if I missed you in the basement, then I was going to make my way back up here. That's what you tried to suggest to me as we were separated, wasn't it? I couldn't really hear you in that crowd.'

'Yes,' said Mitch, 'that's what I had in mind.'

'Well, when I got to the basement, I intended to look around for you quickly first. But that's when the guards got me. Apparently they had been watching us - one of the them recognised you from a few days ago, he said. They were convinced that we were up to no good. They were worried we were terrorists of something, I suppose. Anyway, they told me they were going to take me upstairs to ask me some questions and mentioned that they had an interview room out the back of the HMV store. I had to think fast! So I decided on trying to leave you a message. I feigned needing the loo, persuaded them to let me go to the Ladies', then wrote my message. Who would have thought those stupid pens would come in handy?! Anyway, after that they took me up to HMV - using forty one and sixty five,' she had her floor plan open in front of her now. 'I tried to persuade them that we were harmless. I told them what we were trying to do; that it was just a game. They let me wander round the store for a while

while they discussed things - which was when I left you that second message. Then they took me back into their little room.'

'Are you OK?'

She squeezed his hand.

'Fine. They didn't give me anything to drink or eat or anything, but I'm OK. Were you worried?'

'Of course I was worried! Especially after all the weird stuff that's been going on. Even Mr Lee turned up!'

'Mr Lee?!'

Mitch related his side of the story from their separation to being reunited just a few minutes previously.

'So you have a revised plan then - to carry on, I mean?' She sounded worried.

'I do. And if we consider it a joint plan, then we can include the ones you travelled on as done; tick them off.' Mitch sensed concern. 'Why?'

Suzi used drinking some of her coffee as a break in the conversation as she weighed up what to say. Mitch waited.

'They said that they want us to stop.'

'They want us to stop?'

'The guards, yes. And not just the guards.'

'Who else?'

'They said...' she hesitated, 'I don't know how to explain it... but they said that the mall wanted us to stop.'

'The mall?!'

'I know! Like it was some person, with its own feelings and desires.'

'That's crazy!'

'It is, isn't it?' She tried to sound reassured. 'But some weird things have been happening, haven't they? The guards said that the power failure was the mall's way of trying to stop us.'

Mitch laughed - but stopped as soon as she saw Suzi was not joining in.

'Their concern is that, once we've finished, people will find out. It will become news. And then others will come here not to shop, or browse, or eat - but to try and beat your record, to do it faster, or in a different way. They think there's a danger that the mall will stop being a mall and become some kind of "theme park". That people will stop coming here to shop even!'

'But isn't that silly? Paranoid? Do you think they're right?' Mitch asked.

'I don't; not really.' Suzi said, a little slowly. 'I can understand why they would be concerned, but this isn't a big thing, is it? I mean, we're not going to ring the newspapers of anything afterwards are we?'

'I thought we were just going to have dinner together,' Mitch suggested. Suzi leant forward and kissed him lightly on the cheek.

'What do you want to do?' she asked. It was a question delivered entirely without bias or weight; it betrayed no preference one way or another.

Mitch thought about the options. There were only two after all.

'I'd like to try and carry on. To finish. You?'

'Even though they know about us? Even though they will be on the lookout for us?'

'Even though the mall will be trying to stop us too?' Mitch suggested.

Suzi laughed.

'And?' Mitch prompted.

'I think I would like to carry on too…now that we've started. But I don't see how we can. As soon as they find us still here, still going up and down, they'll throw us out…'

'Unless we change tactics somehow,' Mitch suggested.

15

It was an easy thing to say - "change tactics" - but what did that mean? Whichever way Suzi looked at it, she said, they still had to go up and down another thirty or so escalators - and they could hardly do that without being seen.

'But there must be options,' suggested Mitch, 'things we could do.'

'Such as?'

'We could leave now - and then come back some other time. Maybe even days later. Pick up where we left off.'

'But they would still see us, wouldn't they? I'm sure they would remember us.'

'Or we could pretend that we weren't carrying on?'

'Pretend?'

'So maybe actually do some shopping; take time out; buy some things. That would give us a reason to go from floor to floor wouldn't it? And if we were shopping - actually buying things - then how could they throw us out?!'

'That's true,' said Suzi, 'and having an excuse to buy things would be great! But it could be really expensive; we'd have to buy things in lots of stores to convince them to leave us alone.'

'At least the mall wouldn't be trying to stop us!' Mitch laughed.

'What else?'

'How about wearing a disguise? We could buy some different clothes, wear hats, a false beard - that might work for a while.'

'And it might make us look even more suspicious!' Suzi suggested with a laugh.

'We could finish the rest of the escalators off separately; that might do it. If we weren't together and the whole thing took much less time…'

Suzi shook her head.

'I don't like that option,' she said. 'It feels risky - and I don't want to be alone in here again.'

Mitch looked out at the people moving between stores. Now lunchtime was pretty much over there seemed to be more people around: the afternoon shift. He was beginning to despair; to imagine that their only option was actually to abandon the attempt altogether.

'The only other option is to become invisible.' Mitch looked at Suzi. She didn't respond. He carried on. 'And the only way to do that? Maybe when the mall is closed and dark. When only the emergency lights are on.'

'Playing hide-and-seek with the guards?!' Suzi looked alarmed.

'We've done it already. We know what that feels like. We could take a break - maybe go to the cinema on the top floor - and then….well, hide.'

'You're not serious?'

'It's an option,' said Mitch, unconvinced. 'More risky - especially if we got caught.'

'Aren't there cameras and things?'

'Oh I wouldn't worry about the cameras.' Suddenly there was a different voice.

'Mr Lee!'

'Hello again,' he smiled, 'I'd just finished my shopping and I saw you there. Heard you talking as I came over.' He laughed lightly. 'Something of a conundrum you face it seems.' He came round to their table. 'May I join you?'

'Of course,' said Suzi, making room for him.

'What were you saying about the cameras?' Mitch reminded him.

'Those? Well, I'm told that they're not switched on all the time, only when the mall is actually open. They're there to catch shoplifters. Once the mall is closed, they're linked to the main entrances and alarms, and only come back on if someone tries to break in. So if you were still in here after dark, well they wouldn't be on.'

There was a short pause. Suzi looked between Mitch and Mr Lee.

'You can't be serious?!

Mr Lee laughed and Mitch shook his head.

'I think not,' said the elder man, 'but you would imagine that there must be some kind of solution to your problem. Don't they say that every problem has a solution?'

'Do they?' Mitch asked, unconvinced.

'Why don't I get us another coffee? Then we can see if we can work something out.'

He stood up and left the table. Mitch and Suzi looked after him.

'He's a funny one,' said Suzi.

Mitch returned her gaze.

'He does seem to keep turning up, doesn't he?'

And then they were both suddenly laughing. Mitch relayed again the story of their escape from HMV, focussing on the reaction of the poor woman who had suffered most with the shock of the whole thing. Somehow released from the tension of the debate, they soon found themselves laughing so hard that tears started to roll down their cheeks. It felt like a tremendous sense of relief to Mitch, as if somehow a pressure value had been released. He felt - well - normal.

'Where would you like to go for dinner?' Suzi asked, changing tack.

'Dinner? You mean that you're still prepared to entertain me, even though I'm a complete failure and never finish anything I start?!'

'I wouldn't say you were a complete failure just yet,' said Suzi, smiling, 'and you never know, there might be some things you are capable of seeing through.'

Mitch said nothing, just looking at her. Chek would be very, very jealous; that much was certain.

'Where's that coffee?' he said, turning to look back towards the counter. 'I'll see if the old boy needs some help.'

He found Mr Lee emerging from behind the counter, looking worried.

'What's wrong?' Mitch asked.

Mr Lee scratched his head.

'There's no-one here. The staff have vanished!' He walked out to join Mitch and then stopped. 'Look.'

Mitch followed where Mr Lee was indicating. Starbucks was entirely empty - with the exception of Suzi who was now looking towards them, still smiling, but with a quizzical expression on her face. Before Mitch could say anything, Mr Lee placed his hand on his arm.

'Outside,' he said.

Beyond where Suzi sat, the mall was still brightly lit, the elevator music still sounding from hidden speakers, the neon in shop displays still purring. But there were no people. They hurried back to Suzi who was now standing, responding to their evident concern.

'What is it?' she asked.

'Turn around and look,' said Mitch. As she did so, he asked, 'Where are all the people?'

It was a rhetorical question. He walked out of the coffee shop and a little way into the mall. He looked across the central atrium to HMV. The escalators were still running, but there was no-one on them. Indeed, there were no people anywhere. Suzi and Mr Lee joined him. Slowly they gazed around the what they could see of the second floor. It was empty.

'What the hell's going on?'

'Was there an alarm?' suggested Suzi. 'Did we miss something? Maybe there was a fire drill or something? But I didn't hear any bells. Did you hear anything?'

'Nothing, my dear,' said Mr Lee.

Mitch felt a little comforted by the fact that he was with them, and that this new strange experience was going to be shared by someone other than just he and Suzi.

There was a pause when none of them seem prepared to speak. They continued to look around, almost as if they expected people to suddenly appear from the stores shouting "Surprise!", as if it were some great game that everyone except the three of them were playing. But there were no people - and no shouting.

'What now?' said Suzi, 'Maybe we should try and get out - just in case.'

'In case of what?' Mitch wondered.

'Or…'

They both looked at Mr Lee. He was staring at the long escalators in the central area.

'Or this might just solve your conundrum, don't you think? It's bright in here, no crowds, no security guards probably… You could just finish off your challenge.'

'Finish it?!' Mitch was stunned at the notion. Secretly he had already given up. Now there was suddenly a new option on the table again.

'You could pretend you were on your way out, if it made you feel any better - but why not? If there's no-one here, who's going to know? Who's going to stop you?'

Suzi wanted to say "the Mall", but couldn't bring herself to do so. Partly because it felt like a silly thing to say - and party because she wasn't sure it would have been that much of a joke.

'Why don't we take twenty two back down to the ground floor and see how things are down there,' Mitch suggested. 'Then we can decide. What do you think Suzi?'

She nodded, and took his hand. Mitch could tell she wasn't convinced.

'We can't stay here,' he said, ostensibly to Mr Lee, but primarily for Suzi's benefit.

'You are undoubtedly correct,' said Mr Lee, nodding. 'Why don't we do what you suggest?'

Slowly they walked the few metres to twenty two, still looking incredulously around as they did so. Before it disappeared out of sight, Mitch caught a glimpse of "Cinderella's", and once again he had the strangest sense that someone had changed the display in Suzi's absence.

It was the same scene as they descended through the first floor: the lights were on, but there was no-one home. Impulsively, Mitch tried a shout; the sound he made was absorbed by the mall apart from the slightest of echoes that came back to them.

'You wouldn't have heard that if there were people in here somewhere,' Mr Lee suggested from a couple of steps behind them.

They reached the ground floor and then walked into the centre of the atrium. Looking up, they could see the upper three floors all illuminated, and leaning against the centre rail, staring down into the basement; the same appearance there. Slowly they turned, looking down each of the five arms of the mall in turn. In three of the wings their view to the entrance doors was almost entirely unbroken; in every instance, not a soul could be seen.

'What's the time?' Mitch asked.

Suzi checked her watch.

'Nearly two,' she said.

'Really?' said Mitch, pointing towards the external doors that led back to Wilson Avenue. 'It looks later than that outside. A bit too dark for two o'clock.'

'That's interesting,' said Mr Lee, his voice even and unemotional, 'I have nearly six.'

'Six?!' Suzi looked at her watch again to make sure she hadn't misread it.

'You two wait here,' said Mitch, 'I'm just going to check the doors.'

Before they could protest, he left them and jogged quickly down the Wilson Avenue wing. He knew that he would be in full view all the way and that if they needed him - or vice versa - it should be easy to get back together. Suzi and Mr Lee watched him run to the doors, pause there for a few moments, and then begin his run back towards them. He had run away from them down the left-hand side of the aisle, past fifty five and fifty six, three and four, and one and two. On his way back, Mitch chose the other side, which meant that for a few moments he would be out of sight as he passed behind the latter two pairs of escalators.

As she watched, Suzi knew that he would only be out of sight for perhaps two seconds at most.

'Here he comes,' she said to Mr Lee, beginning to walk forwards.

And then he was hidden. Suzi's eyes focussed on the space from which Mitch would reappear; she almost filled in the void he would occupy with a mental image of him in readiness. Two seconds passed, then three. She stopped walking. Then five seconds; ten. The void remained.

'Mitch!!' she shouted.

16

Face down, lying on the escalator and travelling downwards, Mitch was stunned to find himself prone and in such a position. He was uncertain what had tripped him up. Perhaps he had jogged a little too close to a waste bin, or a bench, or the mall map. One minute he had been heading back towards the centre of the mall, the next he was flying briefly through the air to land, sprawling face-down on the silver steps. In the background he heard Suzi's scream.

By the time he found his feet again, he had already disappeared beneath the ground floor and the basement stretched out before him. 'Stupid idiot!' he scolded. But he knew it would be simple enough to take another escalator back up to rejoin Suzi and Mr Lee, so he focused on the layout before him. As above, it was still brightly lit - and empty. Down here, the emptiness seemed a little more total, with the hum of the machinery providing a monotone accompaniment to the mall music still falling from the variously concealed speakers.

Mitch knew that, given he had inadvertently travelled down number four, then if chose - and was prepared to break his rules - he could simply turn around and go back up three. Although unplanned and out of sequence, at least that would be another two ticked off. Maybe Mr Lee was correct; maybe they could finish what they had started. As he stepped onto the solid faux-marble floor, Mitch was reminded that now there was no such thing as "out of sequence": he didn't have a plan any more; everything was currently just a little ad hoc.

Doubling back to the base of three, confident and relaxed, Mitch stopped dead. The escalator in front of him was also travelling downwards! But how could this be? This was three; three was an odd number; all odd numbered ones went upwards! He stood at the bottom and looked up. Not only was it going in the wrong direction, it was moving so fast that it would have simply been impossible for him to jump on and run up it against the flow to get to the ground floor; he would never have made it.

He turned and looked towards the pair behind him. The same story there: both travelling downwards, both incredibly fast. And the noise they were making, spinning at these ridiculous speeds, was suddenly very loud.

Mitch tried shouting upwards, but even as he did so, he knew there was no way that Suzi or Mr Lee would be able to hear him. He tried to make out any sound from above, but there was nothing he could distinguish; even the omnipresent piped music was swamped. And in the same way that three's travelling so fast prevented him from trying to run up it, he also knew that it would have been far too dangerous for anyone to try and jump on it to come down.

He would have to find another way.

Behind him the sixty one/sixty two pair rose in double aspect up to the first floor. He walked towards them, but even before he got there Mitch knew what he would find: speed. They too were hurtling, their steps flying at a ferocious rate, and both downwards. He spun round and began jogging towards the centre. Sixty three and sixty four were next. It was the same story there. His jog became more of a run as he left the Wilson Avenue leg and tried the next one. Here, fifty seven and forty one - both of which he had already ridden upwards - had been reversed, and again were too fast to even contemplate. In the next arm, and the ones for Mellon Street and Fern Avenue above, all the escalators were just racing uncontrollably - and all downwards.

Mitch, having covered the entire basement at pace, returned to the atrium, paused and looked up. He tried shouting again, but it was no use. He had hoped that Suzi or Mr Lee would be looking over the balcony to try and see him, but there was no sign of them. Indeed, there was no-one around. All the stores were open and well-lit; in "Toys 4 Boys" he noticed, as he jogged past it, gadgets and gizmos spinning and whirring - but there was no-one there to supervise them.

That left the stairs as his only option. Even though opening a door to gain access to them would set off the emergency alarm, he had no choice. And perhaps they needed the alarm to be set off; for the first time, Mitch felt, somewhat obscurely, that they needed to be "rescued". But it was as he looked about to find the nearest emergency escape, that he noticed number forty five. It was not going downwards. More than that, it was going upwards at the speed it was meant to be. Mitch walked over to the bottom of it and looked up. It rose high through the centre of the mall, carving its way right up to the top floor. That wasn't where he needed to go, but suddenly it was his only option. Mitch realised that, if he took the stairs, it would be as if he were resigning; the whole thing would be over, his effort wasted. He was also suddenly aware that, even if he did manage to get out through the stair well, what about Suzi? Where was she now? What would she and Mr Lee be doing? Clearly they had not tried the emergency escape route themselves, otherwise the alarms would have gone off. He would have heard them, even above the current din. Could he abandon them?

He put his rucksack down in front of him and removed the key ring. At the base of each escalator was a small embedded box which contained the controls used by the maintenance men. He didn't know why he hadn't thought of it before, but he had two keys, weren't they worth trying? Mitch tired them in turn, but neither fitted. 'Not for here then,' he said to himself. Then he tried the button also attached to the key ring. Again nothing. He straightened up and looked back at forty five. If it suddenly accelerated whilst he was on it…if it started to run just as fast as all the others - upwards or downwards - then he would be in trouble. For no reason he could think of, he removed the notepad he had in his bag and placed it - pen attached - onto a step of the escalator and watched it move slowly upwards.

After a few moments - perhaps somewhere after the first floor - it became indistinct, and then invisible. Mitch waited, timing roughly when it would have been thrown off the escalator on the third floor. There was no change in the rhythm or speed of the steps, no sign that anything had interrupted their path; it seemed to have reached its destination successfully. He zipped up his bag and shouldered it once again. He tried one last shout, paused long enough to hear that there was no reply, and then stepped onto forty five.

Slowly - slower than ever, it seemed! - he rose upwards. Standing in the centre of the step, he held on to both handrails simultaneously, something he had never done before. The prospect of suddenly being hurtled at a ferocious speed - in either direction - was very real. Mitch had never felt scared of riding an escalator - at least not since he had been a very small child - but those subliminal fears were not far away as he watched the ground floor appear around him.

Looking out for Suzi and Mr Lee pushed those fears momentarily to the back of his mind. He had felt sure he would see them still somewhere in the atrium, but there was no-one there. He tried calling out again, but it was a half-hearted attempt to get their attention; in part because of the cacophony of noise, and in part because something told him that they would not be there. As he passed through them, the scenes on the ground floor, and then on the first, were identical: shops open, lights on, no people, the whirring of escalators out of control. Seeing no-one, and being resigned not to be able to see his friends, the noise - and the fear that noise engendered - returned to him again. And then, in the suddenness of an instant, the fraction of a moment between states, he was thrown forwards as simultaneously the escalator stopped and the mall was plunged in darkness.

From somewhere indeterminate he heard Suzi scream.

'Suzi!' he shouted in return, his voice vibrating with the fierce pumping of his heart.

As if in response, he saw a dim light appear. A torch. 'Suzi has found her torch' he said to himself. He tried to orientate himself and his relationship with it, but it was harder than he imagined it would be. The dim glow was ahead of him somewhere, but was it above or below? It came from either the first or second floor, but establishing the horizontal seemed strangely impossible. Mitch removed his bag from his shoulder intending to find his own torch, when suddenly he was jolted backwards, needing to grab the handrail as the escalator started moving again. All around him, power was restored; lights came back on with a flicker of neon, escalators began to move again. But the sound was different, normal. The mall music had stopped, but the power interruption seemed to have reset everything else. There was no wild whirring, no screaming of flying metallic steps, and as he passed through the second floor, he could make out from nearby escalators that each pair was behaving itself once again.

Looking ahead, as he rose and drew level with the third floor, he saw the notebook lying just a few inches from the end of forty six. It was open.

17

Stepping off the escalator, Mitch paused to look around. Brightness, quiet. As he bent to retrieve the notepad that was lying open in front of him, he immediately saw it had been written in. How was that possible? The pen was neatly clipped down its spine. Was that how it had been when he had sent it on its journey? He couldn't remember, but it must have been so. But writing?!

He picked up the book. It was open about a third of the way in. Three words, written in large, neat, nondescript capital letters presented themselves to him: "Load the gun". What did that mean? He flicked backwards and forwards through a few pages to see if he could see anything else, but the rest was blank. Where had this come from? But surely it couldn't be a mystery? Mitch assumed that the words must have been previously written in the pad by Mr Lee - after all, the notepad and pen had been a gift from him. It was the only possible explanation.

Mitch looked at the words again - "Load the gun" - and weighed the book in his hand. It was a bizarre thing to write, those three words alone in the middle of a notepad without anything else; no context whatsoever. "Load the gun". It had a sense not only of instruction, but of warning about it - which, in the middle of a deserted shopping mall, seemed faintly absurd.

He crouched down and rested his rucksack on the floor in front of him, then unzipped it to put the pad back inside. As he did so he noticed one of Mr Lee's other gifts - the plastic Nerf gun - and then heard a new sound somewhere ahead of him. Mitch looked up, scanning the area around him. He could see nothing out of the ordinary; there was no-one there. But then again, the sound. A kind of slow, scraping noise, like someone rubbing something together; it was the sound of friction. It was not a metallic sound; there was nothing sharp or reverberative about it. It was more a shuffle. Mitch thought about someone shuffling a pack of cards incredibly slowly, card at a time. The absence of volume, the rhythmical nature of it - now definite and distinct - carried a threat nonetheless.

"Load the gun." Mr Lee had been uncannily right about everything else he had given Mitch - where would they be without his marbles?! - so he withdrew the Nerf gun and the pack of bullets, and loaded six of them. He felt a complete idiot. And then he realised the shuffling sound had a grown a little louder.

Some way ahead of him, in the Mellon Street arm food court, he saw a figure moving, slowly. Its motions were slightly ungainly and laboured; there was a stiffness in the way it almost limped in his direction. The shuffling sound; the way the feet were being dragged along the ground. Mitch froze momentarily. Although apparently well-dressed, there was something not quite right about the way its clothes hung on the body.

And then he realised that it was too far away for him to be able to hear the sound made by its feet. With trepidation, he glanced around, still crouching over his bag. From his left, his peripheral vision located a second figure heading in his direction. This one - also well dressed - was heading his way, its movements almost identical. And then a third echo, from behind him. Mitch chose not to look over his shoulder, knowing what he would see. But he was not looking at people heading towards him. These stiff, awkward shapes with their perfect figures and blank looks were more menacing than anything he had ever seen; more threatening than the guards. They were mannequins. Mannequins from the stores; well-dressed, inflexible, barely mobile.

Rising from his crouching position, rucksack in one hand and Nerf gun still in the other, Mitch leapt forward to his right. The third figure, however, was closer than he had imagined, and as he straightened up to run - he was going to head towards sixty and down to the second floor - he suddenly found the third mannequin (this one in tennis attire) just a few feet from him, its arms raised. Instinctively he lifted his own arm and pulled the trigger on his gun. The first pellet flew wide of the mark, but the second one caught the mannequin square in the chest. It halted, as if hit by a live round, and then toppled backwards.

Mitch paused for the briefest of moments before a scream from somewhere below him forced him back into action. Leaping over the prostrate and now motionless plastic figure that had fallen in front of him, he ran to sixty without a backward look and leap onto the escalator, running down the first few steps before he stopped. Immediately emerging ahead of him was the small section of mall that housed "Cinderella's" and Starbucks. Momentarily he wondered whether Suzi and Mr Lee might be waiting for him in the latter, their common rendezvous point it seemed, but the scream he had heard suggested otherwise.

Wondering what his next move should be as he stepped off the escalator, he turned back towards the centre of the mall but then froze. Ahead of him the window of "Cinderella's" was dark; a blind had been pulled down to prevent anyone seeing inside. It was the kind of thing display workers did to protect prying eyes as they changed the window dressing. For some reason Mitch fell sure that this was probably something Suzi would refrain from; he also felt sure that in this particular instance, whatever was going on inside her store had nothing to do with her. The blind was dark grey, bland and completely impenetrable.

As he paused, Mitch heard from somewhere ahead of him the shuffling sound again. He had to move quickly towards the atrium and away from the dead-end behind him. He had options right there for going back up to the third floor or down to the first, but knew he had to at least check if he could see Suzi where he was. Running past forty one and forty two, then twenty one and twenty two, he made it to the edge of the atrium. Ahead of him, guarding the two central pairs of escalators were three mannequins, now all looking his way.

Mitch decided that he would go down again.

'Suzi?!' he cried out, to see if there was any immediate response - but the only reaction was the sound of additional shuffling as, ahead and to the right a further figure appeared from the Mellon Street arm.

If these Nerf bullets worked, he knew he would need more of them - and that meant "Toys 4 Boys" in the basement. With the goal of getting more ammunition now his priority, Mitch ran round to his left. He knew if he could take sixteen down to the first floor, then he would be right by sixty two, and that would take him all the way down. He would be the wrong side for the toy shop, but it was probably the fastest way down from where he was.

Getting to sixteen was easy; a short sprint was all it took, and even though the mannequins had been heading towards him, out-running them was simple. He gathered his breath as he rode downwards, tightening the straps on his backpack as he did so - and tightening the grip on his gun.

He shouted out for Suzi as he got off sixteen. Again no response. A quick check over his shoulder revealed two more mannequins in the atrium and one much closer, near sixty four. Moving quickly, he stepped on to the dual height sixty two, wondering what he would see as he moved through the ground floor. Not only were there mannequins in the atrium, but as he traversed the Wilson Avenue leg of the building, he could see more there too. One or two were emerging from the clothes stores as if they had been awoken from a slumber and called to reveille.

Close to the two-floor sixty one/two pair he was now riding downwards, was another similar pair; they had already taken sixty four down to the basement from the first floor. Mitch knew he could have chosen to take that one again this time, but not only had there been a mannequin close by the entrance to sixty four on the first floor, there was still something in him - instinctive, subconscious - that was driving him to refrain from duplicating rides.

Whether his decision had been entirely conscious he couldn't say. Keeping clear of the mannequin however, seemed the sensible thing to do. Their lack of mobility was one source of comfort to Mitch - he knew they were slow, and he assumed they were constrained by an inability to traverse vertically. Tangentially he thought of Daleks. But then just as he recalled that in the end they had found a way to conquer stairs, so he saw something that caught his breath. The mannequin that had been at the top of sixty four had managed to shuffle onto the escalator and was now tracking him downwards. Not only that, but it would be the first immediate obstacle between him and "Toys 4 Boys".

18

As he neared the bottom of sixty two, Mitch knew that in terms of elevation he was about two or three metres ahead of the mannequin riding downwards in parallel to him. That was perhaps no more than a four to six second difference; certainly not enough to be able to sprint past sixty four before the dummy got off. He crouched down to see if there were any other nasty surprises awaiting him, but could see none. He just needed a plan to get past sixty four.

He knew he could come out firing with his Nerf gun, but he also knew that it was only accurate close up, and it took too long to reload. There was a big risk there - especially as he had no idea what might happen to him if he was actually caught. Suzi's scream came back to him. Had she been caught? If so, what did that mean, exactly? He needed another plan.

When he got to the basement he stepped away from the escalator far enough to be able to see beyond the one/two pair and to where his pursuer would emerge. He was confident that he should be able to sprint the other side of that closer pair, once he knew which side the mannequin would take - assuming it would come after him. As he bent down and waited, he noticed another metal box at the base of the escalator he had just travelled. It was similar to the one in which he had previously tried My Lee's key; similar, but not identical. It was worth a try. Taking a gamble on the few seconds he might lose, he fished the key from his pocket and tried the lock. This time it turned! A small flap dropped open to reveal a red button. Without hesitation, Mitch pushed it.

The first thing he noticed was the handrail in front of him slowing, then the escalator stopped. The background hum began to dissipate quickly, and then there came the sound of a crash nearby that echoed across the mall. He stood up. Ahead, he could make out the legs of a mannequin, twitching as it lay prone on the ground. He must have stopped all the escalators on this floor, and the jolt had thrown his pursuer off sixty four!

Checking his gun was still loaded, he edged forwards, now hugging one side of the shops to ensure he got as quick a view of the prone figure as possible. From somewhere ahead he could hear the faint sounds of movement, but right now it was one thing at a time.

The mannequin, which appeared to have come from one of the more up-market shops on the ground floor, was lying on its back in front of him. Its arms and legs moving in a slow, absurd, robotic motion that was getting it nowhere. It simply wasn't flexible or dextrous enough to be able to right itself. Mitch, suddenly aware that he was still crouching, stood up to his full height, now less than two metres from the figure. He could simply walk past it and on to the atrium, then across towards "Toys 4 Boys". But he could hear the movement ahead of him getting slightly louder; he was not clear yet.

Slowly he raised his gun and aimed it at the chest of the prone figure. The mannequin slowed its movements a little as if aware of his presence and what he was about to do. It didn't feel right, even if this was a faceless lump of plastic - but he had to know for sure if the Nerf gun was to be his saviour. He pulled the trigger.

The bright green foam pellet shot downwards, hit the dummy and then bounced away. The mannequin stopped moving. If it had possessed eyes, Mitch felt sure he would have seen them close or glaze over. He knew he needed more bullets - and maybe a more powerful gun. Walking over to where the pellet had bounced, he picked it up and reloaded, then looked ahead towards the atrium.

Once he had managed to complete his mission here, then he would need to come back to sixty one or sixty three to head back up; both of these went to the first floor. Escalator three to the ground was his only other option now, all the others heading upwards he had already taken - and he was saving number three for this final ride. Or, as they were now all stationery, perhaps his final climb.

Mitch, staying close to the shop fronts on the right, edged forwards to get a view ahead. There were two mannequins shuffling around in the centre of the atrium, but without any apparent aim. He was sure he could hear other sounds nearby, but was unable to exactly define their source. He pulled four more bullets from his rucksack and stuffed them into his jacket pocket; that would make them be easier to get at.

He crept forwards a few more feet - and then, suddenly, all hell broke loose.

With a smooth whoosh that sounded like a volcanic eruption in the quiet of the mall, the shop doors he had just reached slid open, their sensor triggered by his movement. Mitch started at the sound, turning just in time to see two mannequins suddenly upon him through the doors. That had been where the shuffling sound had been coming from! Taken by surprise and slightly off balance, he staggered slightly and then started to fall - a movement that luckily allowed him to avoid the agricultural sweep of an arm from the dummy first through the door. As he fell backwards, he raised his gun and fired.

It was a poor shot from that range, but the glancing blow he managed to achieve was enough to stop his assailant. It had only been sufficient to immobilise it and it didn't fall. As Mitch reloaded, prone on the ground, the second mannequin pushed past the first and began to lean forwards. Getting his sense of equilibrium back, Mitch waited that extra second to assure his aim, then fired. The bullet hit home, square on the chest. The dummy fell instantly, and in doing so, knocked the other over onto its front.

As Mitch gathered himself and started to rise, he was aware of more noises. The two from the central atrium were now heading his way, homing in on the melee. They were of such a distance apart that running around them simply wasn't going to be an option; they were slow enough, of course, but they would have time to respond to whichever direction Mitch took. He would have to fight it out.

Checking his pocket, he pulled out one of the three remaining bullets and reloaded. He would take out the one on the right first, then retreat a few metres to give himself time to prepare for the second. Establishing a crouching position, he waited again. It seemed to Mitch that having the mannequins reach downwards as the best tactic as this meant they were essentially unstable, and most likely any kind of contact - even a glancing blow - might be enough to topple them.

The one closing in on him was dressed in a thick parka jacket, waterproof trousers and walking boots. The boots made its shuffling sound more sinister than those that had been barefoot. When it was about two metres away, Mitch raised his arm, aimed and waited. As soon as the dummy started to lean, he fired. A hit! But, perhaps because of the coat, it was less effective this time. The mannequin paused, almost as if it were getting its breath. Mitch fumbled to reload. This time he aimed lower, to the thigh where the parka wasn't protecting the body. Again the dummy leant; again Mitch fired. This time the impact on the leg sent the mannequin crashing down.

But this had taken too long! The fourth figure was almost upon him. Mitch shuffled backwards, his hands shaking as his primed the Nerf gun one more time. This figure was also dressed in outdoor wear, but of a sporting variety; not only that, but it was wielding a golf club. As it closed in, it managed to raise it's arm a little; the intent was clear.

Mitch waited as long as he could. The club was on the way down when he fired. The Nerf gun kicked, and without waiting to check the result, Mitch rolled away to his left then stumbled upwards. As he rose, the sound of the golf club and then the dummy hitting the floor echoed around him. Standing, he looked back. Now four dummies, in various attire, now lay prone on the ground. Mitch could feel his heart pounding; his breath was coming in short, sharp bursts. He tried to ignore the sound of the blood pumping through his veins, and listened.

All was quiet.

Managing to retrieve two of the bullets, Mitch reloaded with one of them and put the other in his pocket. Then, slowly, he began to walk forwards. The atrium was empty. He glanced down each leg of the mall in turn, but it appeared the basement was now clear. Above him he could make out the feint hum of the escalators running on the floors overhead, and the tell-tale sound of movement. He knew he would need that bigger gun.

He broke into a jog and ran across the atrium and to "Toys 4 Boys". It was open and empty. Once inside, he quickly scanned the shelves and located a small pile of Nerf equipment - guns and bullets - along the far wall. He selected two of the larger models, both multi-loaders with rapid fire. Quickly he ripped the boxes open, then loaded each in turn. Although it was a little too big to fit, he placed one of the rifles in his backpack, its butt sticking out the top. He then opened several boxes of bullets and tipped those into his rucksack, keeping a few in his pocket. Once he had shouldered his bag again, he picked up the second rifle. Maybe he had fifty or sixty shots available now, if not more.

As he walked towards the exit of the store, he was conscious that, had he been caught on camera, he would no defence against stealing or looting - but these were desperate times and he had no choice. He tugged his wallet out of his pocket and left a few notes on the counter. It was a gesture at best, but it eased his conscience. Grabbing the gun again, he headed back towards his next upward route. He had to find Suzi and Mr Lee.

19

If he had, even momentarily, felt like he could relax for a least a few minutes - knowing he had 'secured' the basement - then this sensation left Mitch within just a few metres of leaving "Toys 4 Boys". The escalators were running again.

Instinctively he checked his pocket for the key. It was still there. Hugging the walls again - this time mindful of passing stores that might have contained mannequins - he made his way slowly towards the atrium. All was still; apart from the sounds that floated down from the floors above, he could hear no shuffling, he could see nothing moving. Still unable to shake off his attachment to his original goal, Mitch knew that, whilst the mannequins were about, it made sense to try and travel on the escalators at the ends of each mall arm. This logic was based on the assumption that they currently appeared to congregate in the centre to get the best field of view, and that while this was their tactic, getting the 'dead end' escalators out of the way made sense. If they started to spread out and wait in each leg of the building, then taking the rides at the extremities of the mall would be like walking into a trap.

That meant sixty one now, up to the first.

Mitch, senses alert, walked towards the Wilson Avenue section as quietly as he could, trying to remain as much out of sight of any dummy that might be looking down into the basement from above. Successfully traversing the atrium, when he came to the foot of sixty four - the scene of his last shoot-out - he stopped. There will still mannequins on the floor, immobile; this was good. But the fact that there were only three and not four - that was bad. The first mannequin in that battle, the one that had surprised him from the store and that he had only grazed, was missing. Evidently it being knocked over by another dummy had not been enough to render it out of the game. But what was worse, was the fact that it not being there also meant that it had been able to crawl away or get up on its own; probably both.

How was that possible? First there had been the mannequin that had been able to wield the golf club, and now this. How long would Mitch's little plastic Nerf bullets be a good enough defence?

At the foot of sixty one he paused and looked up. He could see precious little at the top, essentially just the ceiling above it and the store direction sign that hung down from it. He knew, if necessary, he could always run back down it against the direction of travel; that wasn't the issue. But once on it, Mitch would want - almost be compelled - to step off the other end. He ensured his rucksack straps were tight enough, checked his rifle again, then stepped forwards.

Passing through the ground floor, the scene was pretty much as before with a couple of dummies near the central escalators where he still had a few to ride. He could see one or two others moving around nearby, and was fairly certain he caught a glimpse of at least one more inside H&M. None were looking his way, so he refrained from drawing attention to himself.

When he came to the end of this ride, he knew that, if he kept to his plan of eliminating the extreme pairs whilst still searching for Suzi, then his next options were down to the ground floor or up to the second. Given there appeared to be at least five of his adversaries on the ground floor, he decided to go up again. On that basis - and wishing to avoid "Cinderella's" for the moment - he decided on twenty seven up. This was in the Fern Avenue extension that would, in theory at least, give him the chance to hug just one wall as he made his way across the atrium. It would also give him a view down both Mellon Street and Cross Street arms in his search for Suzi.

From a rescue mission perspective, it wasn't an ideal plan. If the assumption that she was either hiding or being held somewhere, then this was likely to be inside a store; and the only way to resolve that particular challenge was to go store-to-store. With the mannequins on the lose, right now that was a prospect he was not keen on. Indeed, from almost any perspective his plan was flimsy at best. Keep looking, but without taking risks and without getting caught. And - although he didn't really acknowledge this - hope for something to happen that would make things normal again.

Stepping off sixty two, Mitch wondered if his unspoken wish might have been coming true. Immediately ahead of him, one mannequin lay prone and immobile on the ground, with two more a little way ahead. As he walked past them, he saw five Nerf gun bullets scattered on the floor. Mr Lee's other gun! So he wasn't the only one putting up a fight! Sticking to his plan, he continued round the left hand set of shop fronts, through the central area - which on this floor was deserted - and then round towards twenty seven. In both Mellon and Cross Street legs, all seemed quiet; he could neither see or hear anything threatening. Perhaps the first floor was the one safe area he had.

And then a dreadful thought struck him. Mitch didn't know why it hadn't occurred to him before; it should have done as soon as he was surprised by the mannequin jumping him through the shop doors. He has wasn't fighting half a dozen of these things on each floor; that was stupid! Once you included all the dummies in all the shops - especially the clothes shops - there might be hundreds of them, all 'waking up' somehow. What chance did he have with a few plastic pellets?! The only was to give himself a chance of finding Suzi was to reduce their numbers; make it so that his Nerf gun was good enough. But how could he do that?

He crouched down at the base of twenty seven and opened his rucksack. Was there anything there that might help? He could only disable them with the gun, but what if he could stop them getting out in the first place? He paused and looked at the shop doors around them. They were uniform, that was good; if he could find a way of keeping them closed, then the dummies would be trapped inside, and being able to jam one set of doors closed might just work for them all.

The ball of twine wouldn't be strong enough, that was certain. Apart from that, what did he have? He had found a use for one of the keys on the escalators, so that was out of the question. The Swiss Army Knife wouldn't be any good, either. He had one other key, and the big red button. Mitch wondered about the colour. Red meant stop, didn't it? He walked over to the nearest set of doors and pressed the button. Nothing. "Of course, nothing!", he admonished himself. He scanned the door. High up in one corner was a small key hole. Mitch pulled out the other key and tried it. The fit was lose; it wouldn't turn. As he fumbled with the key, he dropped the button. When it hit the floor, the doors suddenly hummed silently closed!

Mitch looked down at the button then up at the key, still sitting in the hole. "Maybe…" he said to himself. He retrieved the key and the button and went to the next door. He placed the key in the door lock, left it there, then pressed the button. Again the door hummed closed! Mitch removed the key and jumped around in front of the door to see if his movement would trigger the motion sensor and opened the door. It did not. Now he had another option; now he could tip the odds more in his favour! He could secure a floor by eliminating any mannequins that were already out, and then lock all the doors to the stores where others might be resident.

He quickly shouldered his rucksack, then, rifle in one hand, key and button in the other, Mitch began to run around the perimeter of the first floor. His approach was simple: he paused by each store front, glanced inside to see if he could see any mannequins - or any likelihood of there being any - then fixed the door shut. Where he was confident the store was a safe one, he left the doors open; he might just need somewhere to hide later! The benefit of this approach was that it also allowed him to search for Suzi at the same time; knowing he was going to lock the doors allowed him a quiet call of "Suzi!" inside the store before he did so.

The process took time; a lot of time. Once he was surprised by two mannequins appearing from a jewellery and accessories store, but the rifle had proved its worth, and the encounter helped him to understand its accuracy and effective range. Remembering to retrieve the spent bullets, he carried on around the mall. Some thirty minutes later he was back where he started, ready to go up twenty seven to the second floor. It had taken him longer than he had expected, and Mitch wondered if he could really afford the time. But what choice did he have? He had heard no further screaming from Suzi and nothing else to suggest danger or peril elsewhere. Perhaps they were safely in hiding somewhere. As he stepped on the escalator, it was the best he could hope for.

20

Mitch had already decided that he would try and fully secure the second floor last. He was worried about the blanked-out windows of "Cinderella's" and what that might mean. It could be that Suzi was hiding in there - or that she was being held there. In many ways it seemed the focal point. There was a part of him that wanted to burst in - in true Shining Knight mode! - rescue the damsel, and then ride away. Perhaps, as well as being instinctively the thing to do, on some level it might also have been the right thing to do. But Mitch was worried about escape. He wanted - as soon as he had freed Suzi - to get the hell out of the Mall, and that meant two things were prerequisite: securing all the floors, and - ideally - having ridden virtually all of the escalators in doing so. He didn't want to have to fight his way out.

This ambition, allied with his new-found ability to lock the stores, allowed him to formulate a plan. Now that the first floor was safe, he could use it as his hub; he could get to all the other floors from there. Mitch also knew that it had been relatively easy to secure all the stores on the first floor, because the majority of the mannequins had already been taken care of; on the other floors, this was not the case. Even the basement - although apparently bereft of active dummies - still had all the store doors unlocked, so that wasn't yet without peril.

On the short journey up twenty seven to the second floor, he ran through his plan - and prepared himself for some shooting. He would skirt the northern side of the mall, closing all the relevant doors as he did so, and make his way across to thirty three, up to the third floor. Then the same exercise in reverse, taking thirty back down to the second. From there he would close all the doors on the Wilson Avenue leg, then take fifty six down to the ground floor. Once there, he would try and tackle as many of the shop doors as he possibly could before deciding on his next jump.

As soon as he was off twenty seven, having ascertained that there were no dummies in sight, Mitch started on the doors near where he was. He established the rhythm of 'call for Suzi, enter key, press button' very quickly - with a quick check for hostiles before and after each execution - managing to get each cycle down to around fifteen to twenty seconds. Having shut all the relevant doors at the end of his current arm, he made his way out towards the centre.

He managed to close one set of doors in the central area (the stop next to HMV) before he was spotted. Three mannequins that had been standing in the middle space, came towards him as one. Mitch crouched down and lifted his rifle. Although they seemed to be moving slightly more fluently and slightly quicker than before, they were still no match for the Nerf rifle which spat it's plastic bullets with some pace and accuracy. It took two hits on each of the mannequins to down them, and the sound of the guns firing and then its targets falling, echoed loudly around the mall. At least Suzi would know he was still there and still fighting. Mitch collected the spent bullets that were immediately accessible and made his way towards thirty three, store by store.

As he closed in on the final sets of doors on the north wall, he could see two more dummies making their way towards him. Mitch decided to leave these for later, finished the last two shops, and stepped onto thirty three to take him upwards. He had made progress, but there was so much left to do.

Jumping off on the third floor, he immediately dropped to his knees to check how things looked. It seemed quiet enough, with just a single dummy away near the central area. The escalator had deposited him in the middle of the Food Court and close to a baker's outlet. He grabbed some croissants and cakes, and put these into his rucksack before he moved on.

As it was the Food Court, there were actually few shops to close between where he was and number thirty. The dummy he had seen, plus another that appeared from one of the southern arms, were easily disposed off, and within ten minutes he was riding down to the second floor again. There was a small reception committee awaiting him. Two mannequins, instead of remaining in the central part of the mall, had ventured closer to HMV and thus very near to where he emerged. Perhaps they had begun to work out what he was trying to do; Mitch couldn't be sure.

He had only been able to take three steps off the escalator before his rifle was raised again. One of these two was carrying a briefcase and actually managed to throw it limply in his direction before he despatched it. Collecting up what bullets he could, Mitch reloaded and check his ammunition. He was still Ok for now.

As quickly as he could, he worked his way around the western side of the mall, into the Wilson Avenue leg, and then round to fifty six. As this was almost back out into the atrium part again, there were a few store to cover this time, and half of them potential homes to the mannequins. Indeed, just as he closed one set of doors, two dummies dressed smartly in men's pin-stripe suits with white shirts and floral ties suddenly appeared the other side of the glass. Their attempts to leave the shop was the first real test Mitch had of the efficacy of his plan. They were unable to get out.

As he got to fifty six, another appeared from one of the stores further round and headed towards him. Mitch decided to test the range of the rifle. He waited until the dummy was around five metres away, then fired. He missed. A metre closer and he hit his target, but with little effect. It wasn't until the dummy was two to three metres away that the bullets had any effect, and then it took two more to bring it down. Again Mitch scavenged the spent bullets, then headed downwards.

Mitch scanned the ground floor from over the sides of the escalator as he descended. He could see the familiar shapes of his adversaries near the centre, but ahead of him - between the base of fifty six and the Wilson Avenue exit doors (which he knew would be locked) - the coast was clear. He needed to refine his plan, he knew that; and needed a little time to do so. Consequently, he jumped off the escalator and jogged as silently as he could towards the big glass doors, always keeping at least one of the three sets of escalators in that area between him and the atrium. When he got near the doors, he made his way behind one of the large interactive maps, sitting on the floor with his back against the display. He couldn't see what was going on in the atrium for there and would need to rely on his sense of sound as his warning system.

He unpacked one of the croissants he had scavenged and, for the first time in a long while, his floor-plan of the Mall. His basic premise of securing the doors and the floors in a systematic way was still a sound one, but Mitch was keen to think ahead to the moment when he and Suzi emerged from "Cinderella's" (he was certain that was where she was) and needed to make their exit.

After a couple of minutes, he had it mapped out. Assuming he had managed to secure all the floors and doors with the exception of the few around "Cinderella's" and the second floor Cross Street leg, then he would approach Suzi's store by coming up on forty one from the first floor; that was the closest and gave him the most effective element of surprise. Once he had rescued her, there would still be the two remaining un-ridden escalators near "Cinderella's" to complete. They would go up to the third on fifty nine, then round to thirty six and back down. Then forty two (the last one by "Cinderella's") down to the first; immediately by that was fourteen down to the ground floor, and right next to that was ten into the basement. That would leave a short walk across to number three which would take them up to where he was now in the Wilson Avenue arm, and then out!

Mitch looked through the large doors. It seemed like a nice afternoon outside, but he could see no-one about. He had given up being surprised. An echo from somewhere else in the Mall brought him back to his task. Now all he had to do was to plot his route from now to number forty one, allowing him to close all the remaining store doors on the way and taking in all the unused escalators. He calculated that there were twenty six of those - he was already over half-way through!

It took him five minutes and another croissant to complete the plan. There were some tricky transitions to be made, especially where the central escalators were involved, so he tried to leave those as long as possible. He checked the rifle by his side and ensured that it was fully loaded; then he removed all the loose bullets from his rucksack and placed those in his pockets. The rifle in his bag was still fully charged. At some point he knew he might need to make a detour in the Basement for "Toys 4 Boys" and more ammunition, though he recalled another toy store somewhere on the Third that might just have what he needed. The key and big red button were also to-hand - he had found a way of attaching them securely to one of the toggles on his bag so that he wouldn't lose them. He was ready.

As he prepared himself, he heard the tell-tale sound of plastic on marble getting closer. It was now or never!

21

For the next two hours, Mitch fought his way around the mall. He was like a man on a mission; an action figure from a low-budget B-Movie. Progress was steady, rather than rapid. Most of the time he was able to complete the closure of sections of shops with little difficulty. Dummies came at him most often in pairs, and for the most part, his pausing to take them down was all that was needed. Anyone listening to events in the Mall - and more than once or twice Mitch thought of Suzi - would have heard a constant pattern of running, doors whooshing, the rat-a-tat of the Nerf gun, and the collapsing of mannequins on to the ground.

He had begun to sweat within the first few minutes, the impact of his exertions somehow multiplied by his knowledge of how long he was likely to be in combat and the importance of what he was trying to do. Once he had started, he knew there was no pause to be had. It was almost as if his adversaries had acknowledged his declaration of war and were themselves on high alert. They seemed to be increasingly ready for him at every turn; each time he stepped of an escalator, they were closer than before, better prepared, almost ready to ambush.

The first rifle proved trusty for the first ninety minutes or so, and then jammed permanently just as he was passing a bag and luggage store. That led to him taking cover in the store while he retrieved the second gun from his bag. Three mannequins followed him inside, and for a short while he was trapped, and had to fight his way out as they tried - with increasing prowess - to throw briefcases and bags at him.

Mitch was right about the ammunition. As he made his way round the mall, his opportunities to harvest spent cartridges lessened, and his supply began to dwindle. He needed to take that detour back to "Toys 4 Boys", or to raid the toy section of a department store - with the subsequent fire-fight to get out afterwards.

On one level progress was slow. Although he was closing doors and the body count was rising, it was not until he had been working hard for well over an hour that he secured his second level - after that, the other floors (except the second) followed relatively quickly.

Apart from the bag shop and the department store, he had only been in serious trouble once. Two mannequins had been approaching him from behind as he tried to close the doors of a ladies underwear outlet. He should have eliminated those two before progressing, but felt he had time enough. As he placed the key in the lock, one of the female mannequins in the shop display - that had been totally stationery - suddenly sprang to life and made him jump. The shock led to the key falling from the lock.

The next moment, Mitch was on his knees, firing rapidly and wildly upwards at three dummies all crowding in on him. He felled them - just - with the now inert female dummy actually falling on top of him before he pushed it away.

As he walked towards forty one, preparing himself for his final assault, he tried to relax a little. He took time to lean over the railings in the atrium to look up and down the mall. Everywhere - around him on the first floor, and elsewhere - there were fallen mannequins. Often they were in little groups of twos or threes. He also knew - though this he was reluctant to acknowledge! - that they had become more flexible and dextrous; that their movements were more fluent; that they had been increasingly able to throw things at him; and that they were now better able to anticipate and intercept him. Towards the end, it had started to take more than two bullets to fell each one of them.

Mitch sat at the base of forty one and looked up. "Cinderella's" awaited him. There had been no further screams from Suzi and he had not discovered her as he worked the rest of the mall, so he could only assume she was in there. He checked his supply of ammunition. He still had around thirty bullets, which was good; but he guessed that he had used many, many more. Part of him wondered if he shouldn't spend time going around all the floors to collect spent bullets, but he was tired now and just wanted to get things finished and get away. Would thirty be enough for one store? Mitch remembered the six mannequins from Suzi's last display. If they were all still there, that was five each. He quickly scavenged the area closest to him and found another dozen or so; they could be useful. Whatever happened, his shooting would need to be accurate.

Half way up the escalator, two female figures appeared at the top. Given he had - he hoped! - closed all egress from the relevant stores, they would have to have come from "Cinderella's". Each of them was carrying a large suitcase, something Mitch was sure Suzi would have used previously in one of her displays. He had shot on the move before, so the precedent had been set, although not whilst travelling upwards like this.

Mitch fired off one round from about half way to check the range. The bullet dropped harmlessly away, partly deflected by a subtle draft generated in the space between the floors. He knew now that it would be hard to fell these two, and that he would have to wait until he was very close. As he crouched a little to prepare himself, one of the dummies suddenly threw their suitcase towards him. The combination of gravity and the steps of the escalator, sent the case bouncing towards him in a wildly unpredictable way. Squeezing to one side in an attempt to let it pass, Mitch was diverted from his preparations for shooting - and he was still hit a glancing blow by the case. Then, without any time to prepare, the second one suddenly appeared and caught him high on the shoulder, the corner of the case jabbing into his flesh. It hurt.

Already shaken and unsteady, he suddenly found that he was within just a few feet of the mannequins. He had no time to set or prepare himself, he pulled the rifle towards the horizontal and simply let fly. He finished firing just as he gained the second floor, and just as the second dummy fell to the ground. The rifle was empty, and many of the bullets he had just spent had bounced away over the railings and on to the floor below. Mitch was suddenly grateful for those extra few pellets he had collected.

He jumped off the escalator and turned towards Starbuck's, outside of which he sat down, leaning against their shop front and reloaded his gun.

'That was impressive.'

A voice, sudden and unexpected, made him leap out of his skin. Mitch spun round. Peering over the edge of the Starbucks' boundary was Mr Lee.

'Yes, indeed; you certainly finished those two off!'

'Mr Lee! What are you doing here?!'

'Hiding, my dear boy - obviously. I heard you coming, of course; you've been making so much noise! It was just a matter of time. I thought my little guns might be useful, though I wasn't sure why. Glad to see you managed to 'upgrade".'

'Yes, great. Thanks.' Mitch looked over the little wall; the coffee shop was clearly empty. 'Where's Suzi?'

Mr Lee nodded across the aisle, and Mitch followed his eyes to the greyed out shop front of "Cinderella's".

'In there,' he said, his voice now flat. 'You heard her scream I suppose?'

'Yes. What happened?' - and then, more broadly - 'What is happening?'

'I really wish I knew,' Mr Lee replied, his response lacking any urgency or excitement. 'First the lights go out, then I find you two still in here; then the people disappear (or was it the other way around?) - we got confused about the time, remember? My watch must have been wrong. Then the escalators go haywire, just about the same time as the shop dummies suddenly started walking about...'

'You've been here the whole time?'

'If you mean most of the day, then I suppose I have - though I've clearly lost track of time given all the excitement and confusion.'

Mitch tried to think back.

'What happened after I got separated from you?'

'You went to check the doors, didn't you?' said Mr Lee, recalling slowly. 'We saw you going down to the basement, and you were lying on the escalator…'

'I fell,' Mitch explained.

'Oh, I see. Anyway, after that suddenly all the escalators were going really quickly; there was no way we could come down and join you. So we wandered around on the ground floor; Suzi was running around trying to get a sight of you, to see where you might appear. After that the escalators went back to normal. Suzi insisted we try another floor, so we went up to the second; why there I don't know. That was when the lights went out the second time. She and I got separated - I think while I was searching for my torch.'

'So it was your light!'

'Yes. Did you see it?'

'I did, but I had no idea where it was coming from.'

Mr Lee shook his head.

'That was when I heard Suzi scream. I assume you heard it too?'

'Of course.'

'I tried to find her - first by the light of my torch and then afterwards when the lights came on - but then the mannequins appeared.'

'They didn't come after you?'

'I suppose I was lucky,' he said, 'I had been in some shop or other looking for Suzi when I saw them. Because I was in a shop, I had plenty of cover. I was able to just wait. I couldn't go far of course, because there seemed to be always one or two of them around. But then you helped.'

'Me?'

'Yes.' Mr Lee chuckled. 'When you started running around, shooting at them, well, they became distracted. They started trying to get you; leaving their post, if you like. I was able to make my way here in relative safety - especially once you'd armed yourself with your bigger gun.'

'Did you see me, when I was locking the doors?'

'I did,' Mr Lee nodded and smiled, 'and if I may say so, a brilliant strategy.'

'Why didn't you let me know where you were? You could have called out.'

'Indeed, Mitch; but remember, the dummies didn't know I was here. It was the only advantage I had, and I didn't know if it might come in handy. Anyway you've found me now.'

He placed his hand on Mitch's shoulder. There was a brief silence. Suddenly his hand went tense.

'Yes, of course you must - and quickly!'

'What?' Mitch was confused.

'Your question.'

'But I didn't ask one.'

'Oh,' said Mr Lee. 'Well, I think you were going to. You were going to ask if you should go into "Cinderella's" - and I'm afraid the answer is yes - and that you need to go now!'

Mitch stood up.

'Will I need my bag?' He asked the question somehow assuming that Mr Lee would know the answer.

'If you think the rifle is enough, leave it with me.'

He paused then shouldered the bag.

'You never know. I might have to throw at something if I run out of bullets!'

22

It took just a dozen paces or so to cross to the entrance of "Cinderella's". Through the open door all Mitch could make out in the gloom were the vague shapes of the clothing rails. He stepped forwards until he was sufficiently advanced to be able to see behind the grey shade that had been dropped in the window. Suzi's old display had been completely destroyed, with elements of it in disarray and scattered across the floor. All the mannequins were gone. If Mitch's assumption about the original number was correct, there would be three somewhere in the shop.

He edged further forwards, crouching down behind the first rail of clothes he came to, and then listened, trying all the while to ignore the beating of his heart and the blood pulsing through his veins. There was nothing. He waited, unsure of his next move. The store was relatively narrow, but he expected that it was one of those that extended back a deceptively long way. He knew at the far end there would be at least one door leading to the storeroom and office. As in HMV, that was probably where Suzi was being held.

Then he heard the first sounds; hangers scraping slightly on a rail. Something was moving - and it was nearby. Mitch gingerly tried to part some of the clothes immediately in front of him to see if he could see beyond them, but it was to no avail. He knew it was likely that he would have to make a decisive move; he would need to stand up, reveal himself, and in all probability, start firing. As soon as he did that, it would be a sudden death shoot-out; he would have no other option.

And then he remembered the nylon twine. As quietly as he could, he eased the bag off his shoulders and rummaged inside it. He pulled out the ball of twine and Mr Lee's original Nerf gun for insurance. He also pulled out the Swiss Army Knife - the only other practical item he had yet to use. Leaving the bag tucked under the clothes rail, he attached one end of the nylon to its upright nearest him. Across a small corridor, perhaps no more than four feet away, was the next rail - and the ideal location for a trip wire. First he had to get over there - and then lure his enemy towards him.

Of course! They had done something similar before! He dived back into the bag and pulled out the four remaining marbles. He took a deep breath then, with as much force as he could muster, fired the marble hard underneath his clothes rail towards the back of the shop. In the stillness, the sound it made as it ricocheted off something metallic was considerable. The scraping of the hangers stopped, only to be replaced by the inevitable shuffling. Without waiting, Mitch dived across the space to the second rail, twine in hand. He waited for a few moments, listening; then he fixed the other end of the twine, cutting it free from the ball with the knife. It was stretched taut about six inches off the ground.

Now the second marble. This time he threw it behind him and into the window display. It clattered off something then rapped hard against the glass pane; the sound echoed briefly. Again shuffling. Mitch hoped it was just one dummy; that was all it sounded like. The noise got closer and closer, then, within just a few inches of him, a naked plastic foot appeared. As it hit the twine, the rail started to give, Mitch pushed it the other way and the mannequin, even given its limited speed, was suddenly off balance and falling forwards. It crashed down alongside him. Mitch, raised the little Nerf gun and from point blank range fired into the back of the mannequin's head. It was motionless.

Even though the pistol was much smaller than the rifle, and even though he had fired at close range, the sound was still enough to trigger more movement within the store. Mitch listened and waited. It sounded like the other two mannequins were now heading his way. Knowing he would need the rifle, he lay the smaller gun on the floor and moved the larger into a suitable firing position. Again his choice was limited, and additionally he was pretty sure that the trip wire routine wouldn't work a second time.

He heard the clumsy steps getting closer, then they stopped. He couldn't see the dummies yet, but sense and experience told him they were just a few feet away. Then the rattling of clothes hangers began, immediately followed by a sweater suddenly appearing over the top of his hiding place. Then another, this time it brushed his hand as it came down. They were trying to distract him - and it was working!

Rapidly now, more clothes - mainly sweaters, but with an occasional pair of jeans - were showering down around him. Not only were some of them landing on him, they were keeping him from being able to hold his gun steady. He tried moving slightly away from the central end of the rail and towards the wall, but it made no difference, the clothes kept following him. Then, taking him by surprise, the rail started to move. They were trying to push it on top of him.

Out of options, Mitch sprung onto his feet. There were indeed two mannequins, each holding some clothing recently lifted from the next rail down. With some dexterity, they managed to throw these towards him and quickly made to grab the next item. He couldn't afford to wait. Levelling the rifle at them, he opened fire in a rapid spread pattern. Many of the bullets were deflected by the garb his adversaries were carrying, and as they were comprehensively clothed themselves, shots that hit extremities were now ineffective through shirt, jumper and jacket.

Mitch raised his sights and aimed for their heads. Two hits in quick succession caused one of the dummies to fall sideways and behind the original rail that had been Mitch's outpost. As the last one leant forwards towards him, a combination of one direct hit on the forehead and the trip wire was sufficient to unbalance it and send it to the ground, its impact softened by landing on the pile of clothes now strewn on the floor. Mitch waited for any further sign of life before gathering what bullets he could find within reach.

As he loaded, he looked down the store towards the back. He could indeed make out two doors at the far end; both were closed. Although there was no sign of any other mannequin, Mitch still held the rifle level and ready as he stepped out from the debris of clothes and over all three spent bodies. There was now only one further thing on his mind; to open those doors and release Suzi.

Walking slowly towards the end of the shop, Mitch manoeuvred around the various rails and displays that had been laid out in such a way as to prevent people making a bee-line for what they wanted. It was a standard retail tactic, Suzi had explained, to force people to take the most circuitous route, past the greatest volume of merchandise, to get them to spend the largest amount of money. In a way, his current progress regulated, Mitch was glad of the minor hindrance; it was preventing him from rushing headlong towards his goal and potentially arriving there somehow imbalanced. Steady progress was good.

He paused by the counter a few metres from the end of the store and listened. He could hear nothing out of the ordinary: the air conditioning hummed overhead; outside, the vague purr of the escalators kept up their accompaniment. There was no music in the store, and - he now realised - no music outside either. He glanced over his shoulder, half-expecting to see Mr Lee suddenly there behind him, but he was alone.

Between the tills on the counter were clothes tags, hangers, carrier bags, all strewn in a haphazard fashion, as if they had been hurriedly tipped out of whatever had been holding them. One of the scanners lay on its side, projecting dancing red laser lines onto the wall. From beneath a pile of carrier bags, something metal glinted a reflection of the scanner's beam. Mitch retrieved it. It was a staple gun. Probably something Suzi used when she was constructing her displays; it would be ideal for fixing material or posters to the backdrops. Mitch was still weighing the heavy object in his hand when a sound forced him to look up.

In the back of the shop, one of the doors was swinging open.

23

Suzi was sitting behind a desk, her head bowed. From the way she was slumped, it looked like she was asleep. Mitch could tell she was now wearing different clothes to those in which she had started the day; he was sure the sweater she had on was one that "Cinderella's" was selling. He knew that she could not be alone in the room - how else would the door have opened? - And this prevented Mitch from throwing caution to the wind and simply rushing forwards. He resumed his forward movement slowly, conscious that at any moment someone might appear from that room, or that the second door would swing open.

Keeping close to the counter side of store, Mitch's perspective on the room gradually changed, and he began to see a second person also behind the desk. It was a woman. He had no idea who she was, but she was similarly dressed. As he brushed past a rack of t-shirts, his rifle caught a small sign displaying prices and sent it to the floor. It clicked three times as it bounced; not a huge noise, but loud enough for the woman to look up from where she was sitting. Mitch stopped. She was heavily made up, her face made to look as much as possible like that of a mannequin. Without needing the evidence, he knew Suzi would be the same.

There was a noise from within the room and she looked back down at the desk. Whoever else was in there was still in control, that much was clear. Mitch was about three yards from the door when he heard the voice.

'Why don't you join the party?'

At this both Suzi and the woman looked towards him. There was a sudden crack as something was rapped against the desk and the two immediately averted their gaze.

'I'm sure we can find something for you to wear too,' said the voice, its tone slimy. 'My friends will be here soon; you can't have hurt them all.'

Mitch, now motionless, could only assume that the "friends" being referred to were the mannequins.

'They're all…', he searched for the words, 'out of action I'm afraid…'

There was a hollow laugh from within the room.

'I doubt that very much! I have hundred of friends here; hundreds.'

Involuntarily, Mitch looked back over his should to check that the store wasn't full of dummies who had managed to creep up on him silently, but it was still empty. When he turned back, there was a man standing in the doorway.

Although he too was made up to look like a mannequin, Mitch could clearly see that his features were mobile and human. A strange smile sat on his painted lips, and his eyelids flickered as he blinked. He too seemed to be dressed in closes from the store, although the combination of a man in predominately female clothing made him seem all the more eerie.

'Who are you? What are you doing?'

'Me?! That's rich! No-one ever notices me, or asks about me. I'm the invisible one; the one who gets bossed about, told what to do. I'm the one whose talent gets overlooked; who's job gets taken by that young bitch in there because "people" think she's got talent.' At this the woman at the desk glanced up. As he was now in the doorway, the man couldn't see her move. 'My name is Derek. I used to work here, but now I run the place. No! More than that! Now my friends and I run the entire Mall! I'm in charge now!'

He laughed a strange, strangled, inflexible kind of laugh, as if he was suddenly having trouble controlling himself.

'I don't think so, I'm afraid,' said Mitch, stalling for time as he tried to work out what his next move should be. 'All your friends are either lying on the floor somewhere unable to move, or they're locked inside their stores unable to get out.'

'You're lying,' Derek said.

Mitch moved to one side to ensure that Derek had a full view towards the front of the shop.

'Look; down there. Three of them buried under that pile of clothes. Two more outside at the top of the escalator.'

Derek took one step forwards. There was something awkward about his movement now, and his face seemed to be contorted slightly. Mitch wondered if he was having some kind of seizure.

'So let them go. They've done nothing to you.'

'Nothing! Nothing!' Derek was really struggling now. 'Order me around; take my job. Nothing? They have taken my life away from me.'

As he spoke those words, Derek's eyes began to glaze over, to change. He stood more stiffly upright. At first Mitch thought this was a display of pride or emotion, but quickly he saw what was happening. Derek was changing; he was being transformed into a mannequin! He was becoming exactly what he was dressed up to be!

His next step forwards proved it; a halting, scuffing kind of step, his joints stiffened. In his hand he held a staple gun - similar to the one from the counter - and slowly he raised it and pointed it towards Mitch. He tried to say something, but all that reached Mitch was a vague, muffled sound. Then a second step forwards. Derek's aim was clear.

Mitch froze. Even though he had his rifle ready and loaded, he found himself unable to move. This was a man now coming towards him, not a dummy. He had just spoken with him, had a conversation of sorts; how could he possibly shoot him, even with a plastic pellet? What would happen to Derek the man if he did so?!

Derek took another step, then another. He was just a few feet away now. The staple gun was almost at the height where he could fire it. If one of the staples hit Mitch from close range it could do some real damage. Yet still Mitch was unable to move.

Then suddenly - and almost simultaneously - a scream from the back room; Suzi screaming; her voice jolting Mitch from his paralysis. And from over his left shoulder, the tell-tale rap-rap of a Nerf pistol firing. Then the metallic twang of the staple gun and a sharp pain suddenly in Mitch's arm. Through eyes watering with the sudden pain, Mitch saw two pellets hit Derek in quick succession; saw Derek stop and totter. Twisting to look behind him, Mr Lee stood, eyes cold and focussed, raising the gun again. Bam! One more bright bullet flew past Mitch, hitting its target. Derek fell to the ground, immobile.

While Suzi and Jasmine got changed in the privacy of the office, Mitch and Mr Lee started to tidy up. First they took all the mannequins - Derek included - into the store room next to the office; then they gathered up all the clothes that had been scattered near the front of the shop, and carried those through to the storeroom too. As they emerged from their final load, the door to the office opened again and Jasmine and Suzi stepped out. Suzi immediately ran over to Mitch and kissed him. There were tears in her eyes.

'Thank you,' she whispered into his shoulder.

Mitch put his arms round her and hugged her tightly.

'And thank you', he heard Jasmine saying to Mr Lee as he snuggled into Suzi's hair.

Mr Lee laughed.

'Oh, it was nothing really, my Dear,' he said - Mitch could hear him blushing, 'we just happened to be in the right place at the right time. And my young friend here should take all the credit; he was the real hero.'

Suzi released him as Jasmine's arm went to Mitch's shoulder. Mitch winced.

'Oh, but you're hurt!' said the Manageress, looking down to where some blood had seeped through his clothing. 'Come back in here, I have some plasters. We'll get you sorted.'

Suzi led Mitch into the office behind Jasmine who was already rummaging through some drawers in search of the first aid kit. He removed his jacket and rolled up his sleeve. There were two small puncture wounds where the stable had penetrated the cloth; it was nothing serious.

'How did you know where to find us?' Jasmine asked as she applied a long thin plaster.

'Partly a process of elimination,' said Mitch. 'I mean, I'd tried just about everywhere else. And knowing this was where Suzi worked, in a way it was logical.'

Suzi squeezed his free hand.

'You could have got away,' Jasmine suggested, 'freed yourself and then called the police or something.'

'The doors seemed to be locked. And I didn't want to have to wait to find Suzi - not after I heard her scream.'

'Well, we seem to be fine now - and thanks to you and your friend.'

Just then they heard an additional voice. It came from inside the shop.

'Excuse me.'

All four turned to see a woman standing at the counter, with some clothes in her arms.

'Can I pay please?'

'Of course!' Jasmine, smiling at Mitch and Mr Lee one final time, negotiated her way past them and out into the shop.

'What...?'

It was as if nothing had happened. There were two other people browsing the rails. Mitch could hear music again, and through the open door, saw people moving outside in the mall. He glanced at Suzi and then Mr Lee. It was the latter who spoke next.

'Shall we get a coffee?'

Five minutes later they were sitting, once again, in Starbucks, steaming cups of coffee in front of them. It was busy.

'I was lucky to find this table,' chuckled Mr Lee as they joined him.

Mitch's head was spinning. For a few moments they sat in silence, then the inevitable question.

'What the hell just happened? I mean, it looks so normal! Where have all the mannequins gone; there were dozens, all over the place. and Nerf gun bullets everywhere. Its as if none of what we've just experienced happened.'

'But it did happen,' Suzi said. She lifted her sweater to show some marks on her wrist. 'This is where I was tied to a chair. If none if it happened, how did I get these marks? And what about your arm?'

'I don't know,' Mitch said in a quiet, confused voice. 'I just don't know.'

'What happened to you after you left us to check the doors?' Suzi asked; and Mitch related the intervening two hours pretty much as he had done to Mr Lee, the latter adding a little colour to the description from his perspective once or twice. Suzi then explained how she had been separated from them, and how she had been absconded into "Cinderella's".

'Someone hit me,' she said. 'Just as I screamed, someone hit me. I suppose it must have been Derek. The next thing I remember I was tied to a chair in the office alongside Jasmine. I could hear all sorts of strange noises from outside - I guess that was you on your crusade - but I couldn't move. And Derek made it perfectly clear that we shouldn't shout out. I just had to have faith that someone would show up to rescue me. That you would show up and rescue me.'

Mr Lee, who had been quietly drinking his coffee, stood up at this point, shopping bags in his hands. Mitch looked at them, dumbfounded.

'These?' said Mr Lee, following his gaze. 'I left them here when I followed you into "Cinderella's". For safe keeping. And now I can finish my shopping and go home.'

'But doesn't it worry you, what happened? Don't you think its totally bizarre?'

The older man looked at Mitch.

'Of course - but then lots of things in life are a little strange and difficult to explain, aren't they? You could spend a lifetime trying to work things out instead of just getting on with it I suppose. And yes, you do need to finish what you started.'

'Sorry?' Suzi admitted her confusion.

'I think,' said Mitch, smiling, 'that Mr Lee has just answered a question that was going round in my head - again.'

'What's that?'

'Should I finish the escalator rides?'

Mitch explained to Suzi how he had gone about his locking down of the Mall - and what that meant in terms of the number of unridden escalators.

'So there are just a few left. A handful. We should just do those, quickly, and then leave. Unless,' Mitch noticed Suzi's hesitation; almost a shiver, 'you just want to go now.'

'Would you do that?' she asked, 'for me? Even though you're so close?'

'No question.'

'Then we need to finish the ones that are left. Isn't that right Mr Lee?'

But Mr Lee was no longer there. He had slipped away without them noticing. Mitch laughed softly.

'Just like him. Either there or not there, just when you need him somehow. And all that stuff he gave me! We needed just about all of it.'

'Except the plasters,' Suzi suggested.

'But I did get my wound, so I can use them,' Mitch suggested. 'And we do need the tissues even now.'

'Why's that?'

'Because you're crying...'

After leaving Starbucks, they walked the short distance to fifty nine and then rode the last seven escalators as Mitch had planned. Everywhere the Mall was busy, all the shops were open. It was the normal scene of people milling and browsing, children running and shouting, music playing; neon hummed in the shop windows, and all the doors were open. Even "Cinderella's" window display was back to normal somehow, just as Suzi had left it.

As they rode up three, the large doors onto Wilson Avenue were wide open. It was bright and sunny outside, and there was a constant flow of people in and out. Mitch had no idea what the time was, and couldn't be bothered to check. Just before they stepped out of the Mall, he stopped and pulled Suzi towards him to kiss her. It seemed a fitting way to end.

'Wow!'

A sudden shout in their direction as they stepped outside. From the wall nearby - the same wall where Suzi had been waiting for Mitch - a figure bounced down and came smiling towards them. It was Chek.

'You guys! He shouted, enthusiastically. 'Man, that was fast!'

'Fast?' Mitch questioned.

Chek smiled at Suzi.

'Hi. You must be Suzi. Nice to meet you.'

'Fast?' said Mitch again as Suzi and Chek shook hands.

'Yeah. I know you said you wanted to try and do it in two hours. I thought I'd come down and see how you were getting on. Just got here in fact.'

'And? Fast?'

Check showed Mitch his watch.

'One hour fifty two!' he said, 'that was really quick - assuming you did them all.'

Mitch paused, then glanced at Suzi.

'If you are asking me, did I ride all the escalators, once only, and within the rules that we set down for the challenge -'

'I am,' Chek confirmed.

'Then the answer is "yes", I did.'

'No problems?'

Suzi laughed and whispered in Mitch's ear.

'Problems?' Mitch echoed. 'Nothing you'd be interested in. Had to do a bit or re-planning on the fly once or twice, but it was plain sailing really.'

'Stunning!'

Suzi tugged his arm.

'Well, now that's over, I think it must be lunchtime - and I've got a date! Let's eat. Come on Columbus!'

THE END

Basement Floor

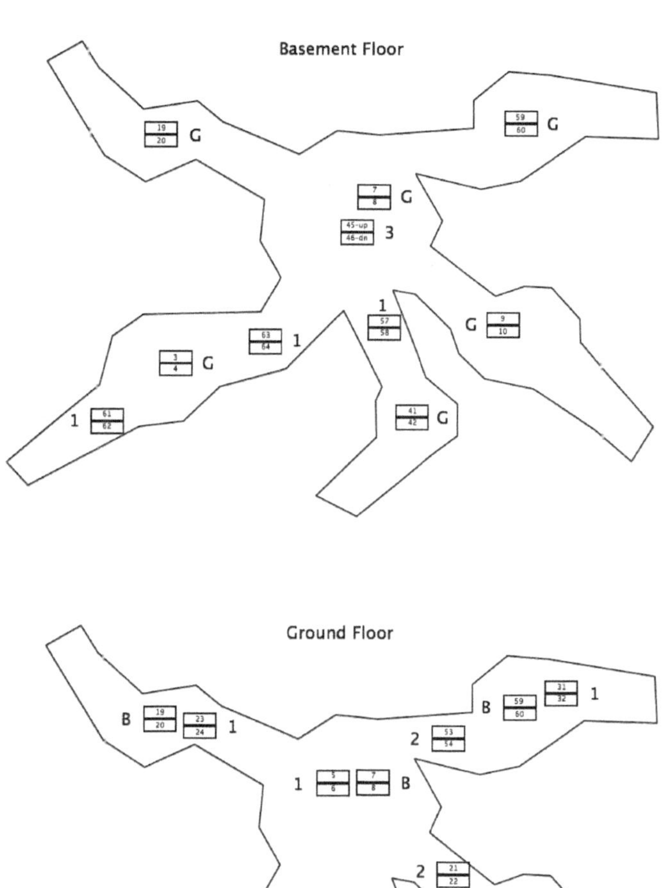

Ground Floor

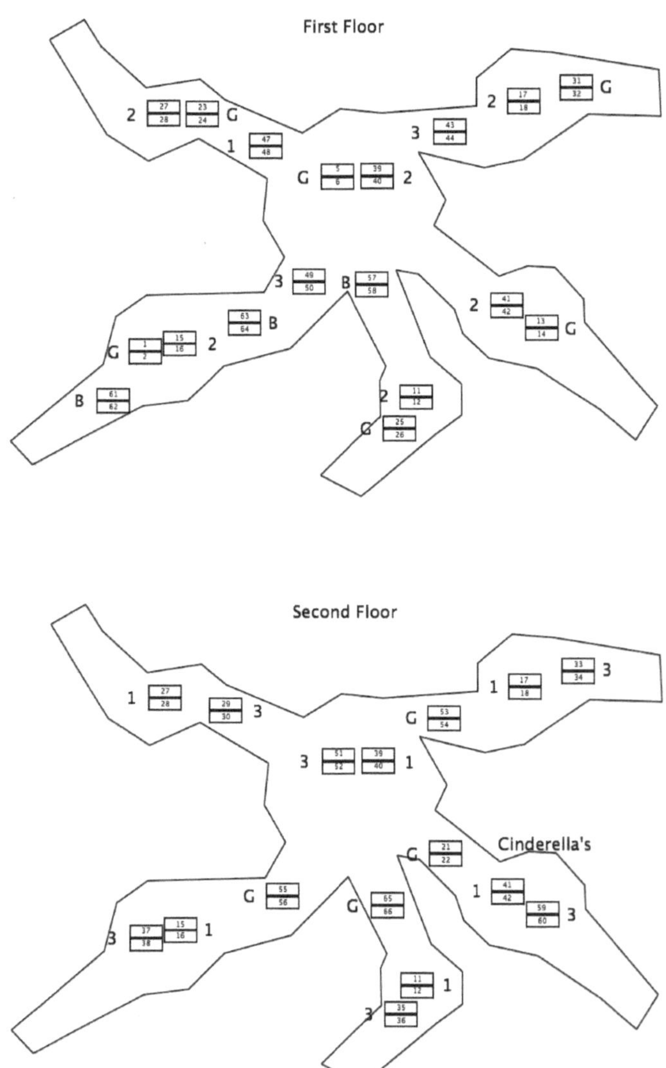

First Floor
Second Floor
Cinderella's

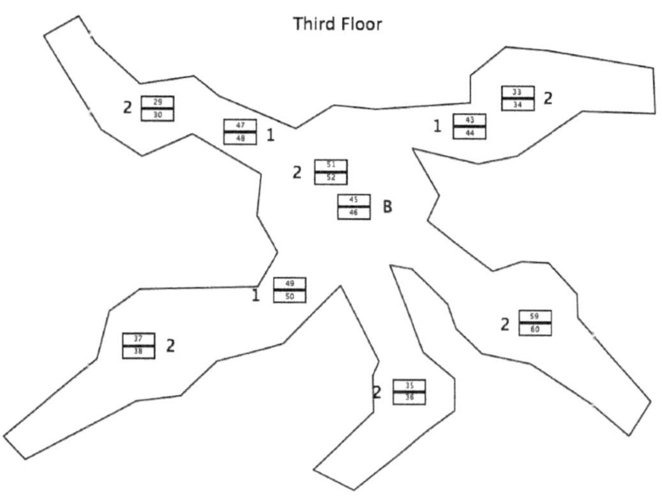
2
29
30
33
34
2
47
48
1
1
43
44
2
51
52
45
46
B
1
49
50
37
38
2
35
36
2
59
60
2